SCORING WITH HIM

BOOK ONE IN THE MEN OF SUMMER SERIES

LAUREN BLAKELY

LAUREN BLAKELY BOOKS

Copyright © 2021 by Lauren Blakely

Cover Design by Helen Williams.

All rights reserved. Without limiting the rights under copyright reserved above, no part of this publication may be reproduced, stored in or introduced into a retrieval system, or transmitted, in any form, or by any means (electronic, mechanical, photocopying, recording, or otherwise) without the prior written permission of both the copyright owner and the above publisher of this book. This contemporary romance is a work of fiction. Names, characters, places, brands, media, and incidents are either the product of the author's imagination or are used fictitiously. The author acknowledges the trademarked status and trademark owners of various products referenced in this work of fiction, which have been used without permission. The publication/use of these trademarks is not authorized, associated with, or sponsored by the trademark owners. This book is licensed for your personal use only. This book may not be re-sold or given away to other people. If you would like to share this book with another person, please purchase an additional copy for each person you share it with, especially if you enjoy sexy romance novels with alpha males. If you are reading this book and did not purchase it, or it was not purchased for your use only, then you should return it and purchase your own copy. Thank you for respecting the author's work.

ALSO BY LAUREN BLAKELY

Big Rock Series
Big Rock
Mister O
Well Hung
Full Package
Joy Ride
Hard Wood

Rules of Love Series
The Rules of Friends with Benefits (A Prequel Novella)
The Virgin Rule Book
The Virgin Game Plan
The Virgin Replay
The Virgin Scorecard

Men of Summer Series
Scoring With Him
Winning With Him

The Guys Who Got Away Series
Dear Sexy Ex-Boyfriend
The What If Guy
Thanks for Last Night
The Dream Guy Next Door

The Gift Series

The Engagement Gift
The Virgin Gift
The Decadent Gift

The Extravagant Series
One Night Only
One Exquisite Touch
My One-Week Husband

MM Standalone Novels
A Guy Walks Into My Bar
One Time Only

The Heartbreakers Series
Once Upon a Real Good Time
Once Upon a Sure Thing
Once Upon a Wild Fling

Boyfriend Material
Asking For a Friend
Sex and Other Shiny Objects
One Night Stand-In

Lucky In Love Series
Best Laid Plans
The Feel Good Factor
Nobody Does It Better
Unzipped

Always Satisfied Series
Satisfaction Guaranteed

Instant Gratification
Overnight Service
Never Have I Ever
PS It's Always Been You
Special Delivery

The Sexy Suit Series
Lucky Suit
Birthday Suit

From Paris With Love
Wanderlust
Part-Time Lover

One Love Series
The Sexy One
The Only One
The Hot One
The Knocked Up Plan
Come As You Are

Sports Romance
Most Valuable Playboy
Most Likely to Score

Standalones
Stud Finder
The V Card
The Real Deal
Unbreak My Heart
The Break-Up Album

The Caught Up in Love Series

The Pretending Plot (previously called *Pretending He's Mine*)

The Dating Proposal

The Second Chance Plan (previously called *Caught Up In Us*)

The Private Rehearsal (previously called *Playing With Her Heart*)

Seductive Nights Series

Night After Night

After This Night

One More Night

A Wildly Seductive Night

ABOUT

Falling for the rookie wasn't part of the plan.

As a pro athlete, I have one unbreakable rule when it comes to men — Don't date another baseball player.

Good thing I haven't been tempted once in four years in the majors.

Until the day a rising star walks into my locker room. Outgoing, affable, and sexy-as-sin, Grant has confidence and talent for miles. He seems to get me too, maybe because we each have our fair share of secrets and scars — ones we'll both fight to protect.

But, I've got far too much trouble in my past to want to bring any into my present.

All the more reason to resist the kind of dirty deeds his lips and eyes promise.

Even after I plant a scorching, hot kiss on the rookie one night after a game.

Even after he sends me the world's sexiest selfie.

But when Grant reveals his biggest secret, I'm so damn ready to rip up the rulebook.

Turns out he's a virgin and he wants me to help him get around all the bases.

The only rule? Don't fall in love with him as we go.

SCORING WITH HIM

By Lauren Blakely

Want to be the first to learn of sales, new releases, preorders and special freebies? Sign up for my VIP mailing list here!

DEDICATION

This story is dedicated to both the women who helped shape the story—Helen, Jen, and Kim, and most of all to Kayti, who attained Goddess status in our plotting. And to the men who helped make sure it was authentic—Jay, Trent, and most of all, Jon. Thank you for helping build the foundation of this love story with me. I am endlessly grateful for all your support and insight. Also, thank you to Dan Levy, creator of Schitt's Creek, for the way he crafted his TV show. He has said that his show would not include any storylines about homophobia, but rather love and tolerance. Likewise, The Men of Summer series exists in a world of pro sports that has been imagined as largely free of homophobia - a world where queer and straight athletes exist and play the sport with the same opportunities for success, sponsorship, acceptance, and of course, love, as anyone else. While this fictional world is not a utopia, the sports universe in this series and in the locker rooms was deliberately constructed with acceptance and equality. I hope you enjoy their world. Love is love.

PROLOGUE

Five Years Ago
At the Start of Rookie Year

Grant

If I were the kind of guy who made five-year plans, mine would include winning a World Series, playing in an All-Star game, and having my pick when it comes to endorsement deals.

Just putting that out there, universe. I'll check back in when I'm twenty-seven and see what comes true. K, thanks.

And to do that, I need a killer first season.

I have to go into spring training and play hard every day.

Baseball is my one and only dream. This sport saw me through the toughest years. Hard times are in the rearview mirror at long last, and good riddance to those days I'd like to forget.

Hell, if I play my cards right, the opportunities for my career are endless.

That's not cocky.

That's just true.

Fine, maybe it's a little bit cocky, but facts are facts, and these are mine. I'm twenty-two. I earned a degree in history from a good college, I racked up one bonkers season in minor league baseball, and thanks to going in the first round of the draft, I'm making bank as I get ready to head to Arizona for spring training. My goal there? Lock up the starting catcher slot. Lock it up so damn tight that the coach can't picture anyone else but me behind the plate for the team.

Pretty sure I don't have time for extracurricular activities. And that's okay. I don't need to be a hookup maestro. Besides, I bet the quest to be a player after hours is a recipe for disaster on the diamond.

So yeah, I suppose *that's* my five-year plan. Don't look back. Move the hell forward. Leave it all on the field.

Which means—*don't be distracted by men*.

That shouldn't be a problem for me.

I've learned to live, breathe, and eat the sport, and romance has taken a back seat. There will be time for men later in my twenties.

Not at my first spring training.

Not during my rookie year.

And definitely not with a man on my team anytime soon.

No matter how charming, sexy, smart, or easygoing a certain guy is. No matter how hot the attraction burns between us. And no matter how close I want to get to him.

And this turns out to be the biggest problem in my brand-new career. Not hitting a wicked fastball. Not scrambling for a wild pitch.

Nope, the problem is my shortstop.

Declan Steele.

From his easy confidence, to his deadpan wit, to the way he guides me through the complicated world of pro ball, I'm hooked on the man from the second I meet him.

Add in his movie star face and a carved body that makes me want to throw him against the wall and kiss the breath out of him—or hell, let him shove me against the door. I don't care—and I'm not sure I stand a chance at my five-year plan.

Let alone a one-month plan.

Already I'm behind in the count, and if I'm not careful, I'm going to strike out on my first chance to make it in the pros.

But with Declan, I'm not sure I can be careful.

Or if I want to. Because he just might be everything I didn't know I needed.

PROLOGUE

The Same Time

Declan

A good thing about being a Major League baseball player is that dates aren't hard to come by.

The pickings are plentiful, and I've enjoyed the offerings that have come my way over the last few years.

The off-season is *me time*, and I've used the winters to turn up the heat, to wine and dine to my heart's—and dick's—content.

Both organs have been quite happy, *thank you very much*.

My stomach too. There was that fling with the chef at a three-starred Michelin restaurant in Napa. Let me tell you, seared scallops are even better when a man makes them just for you in his fantastic wine-country home overlooking a vineyard. I then showed him how much I appreciated his skills in the kitchen by showing off mine in the bedroom.

Pretty sure I earned more than three stars with the things I did.

The year after, I played globe-trotter alongside a rich-as-sin internet executive with a private jet, and we hardly ever wanted that Gulfstream to land.

Then there was *that* TV star. You know, the guy in the Wall Street show who wears the fuck out of tailored suits.

I date here and there on my own time and dime. There's no hiding, and I'm definitely not in the closet, so I'm sure pics of me out with guys surface now and then in gossip rags or where-the-fuck-ever.

Don't know, since I don't read them or follow them.

But I do make it my mission to keep my romantic escapades off *my* social media. They don't belong there.

No matter who I date, I'm not going to post selfies of us the morning after at some too-cool-for-school sidewalk café eating avocado toast and sipping soy chai lattes.

First, I don't drink soy chai lattes.

Second, I'm a private guy.

Finally.

I've wanted that more than almost anything—beautiful, blissful, calm. For the longest time, I craved privacy more than breath.

No one gets to know me, what makes me tick,

or what twists my heart unless I *choose* to share that information.

Too many people knew too many things about my family when I was growing up. My life is different now, and I live it on my terms.

This approach has served me well for the last four years in the Major Leagues.

Well, for the most part.

My penchant for serial monogamy doesn't always end well.

But it *always* ends, and that's a damn good thing because, come February, when the calendar flips to the most glorious time of the year—the return of baseball—my focus narrows to one thing and one thing only.

The unconditional love of my life.

The sport that got me through my worst years.

Come baseball season, I put dating, men, and romance behind me, and no matter what, I always followed one ironclad rule.

Don't date a baseball player.

At all. And it goes without saying, don't screw one on your own team.

There aren't *that* many options on pro sports rosters anyway.

So, I figure it'll be easy this year to renew my vows for solo love after a hellacious winter when everything went south with that certain TV star.

I'll be so goddamn single-minded with baseball I'll be a racehorse with blinders. One-Track Steele will be my new nickname because I'm all about the game and only the game.

That strategy works until one hotshot rookie walks into my locker room.

The rising star.

The man you want behind the plate.

The guy with a smile for days, a laugh that wins over anyone, and blue eyes that see everything.

Including me.

Well, doesn't that just make a hard situation even harder?

I'm iron.

I won't bend.

I won't give in.

I *will* resist.

Until the night he tells me his greatest secret . . .

1

DECLAN

Shortly before spring training

As good as new.

That's how Benji describes my sleek i-8 when I arrive to pick up the BMW on a Saturday morning at his body shop in San Rafael, just past the Golden Gate Bridge.

"Check it out, Declan. You can't even tell that the butterfly door was smashed," he says, sweeping an arm out to show off his handiwork.

I wince at the reminder of how terrible those beautiful doors looked a few weeks ago and how much it's cost to fix them.

I'm not talking about money.

I'm talking about the ugly scene in front of my home in Pacific Heights when I saw what my ex had done to this hot tamale of a sports car.

"You, sir, are a master at covering up all the

mistakes of my past," I say, pointing to the man in coveralls.

Benji laughs. "We've all been there," he says, then opens the gorgeous car door. There's not a single nick in the paint, much less a gargantuan crack down the middle.

"Let's hope none of us go there again. Promise you'll never date a jerk who thinks knocking back a bottle of merlot and taking your new car out for a joy ride is a good idea." The words are bitter, but nothing compared to the acrid memory of the damage the TV star had done that night.

Not just to the car.

To my trust.

Benji holds up a fist for knocking. "I'll do my best to avoid it. But I have dated jerks. Happens to all of us. So don't be so hard on yourself."

But that's what I do.

If I don't stay disciplined, if I'm not obsessed with doing my best . . . I'll do my worst.

I thank Benji and pay him, adding a fat tip, then I slide into the black beauty and pat the dash.

"Missed you, babe," I say, even though I'm not a car person.

It wasn't the car I missed while it was under the knife with Benji.

It was the control.

As I turn the engine on and cruise onto the highway, that sense of order starts to return. It floats through the air in the vehicle, wafts around like a new cologne. *Scent of Sensibility.*

I laugh at that, but sensibility is precisely what I need, along with discipline and order.

With the car fixed and the relationship

kiboshed, I'm getting my life in order. I despise messes like this—Nathan getting loaded while I was recording a radio spot in a studio on this side of the bay, then grabbing my keys and speeding across the Golden Gate Bridge in this baby. I hated how his Ari Gold-esque agent showed up to triage the debacle and spin it into something less damning for his A-list client than getting drunk on merlot and wrecking his boyfriend's car.

Oh, I mean, ahem, getting a ride home from Ari's *assistant* who was totally sober when they took out the hapless hydrant. Which didn't even make sense.

After the tow truck arrived, I said good riddance, but Nathan showed up at my place after midnight, swore he wouldn't do it again, and made a public scene on the front steps until his agent arrived (again) and carted him off to a "spa" for a month-long rest.

As for me, I erased Nathan's number from my phone.

Clean break is the best way to go.

My jaw clenches as I rewind past that night to too many nights when I was younger, too many lies from people I trusted. But as I hit the bridge, the Pacific Ocean spreading out to the west, the bay to the east, I leave those lies behind—those from men, those from family.

Once I reach the city, I cruise over to Russian Hill, snag a sweet spot on the street, and meet my mom and her husband for lunch at one of our favorite cafés.

Inside, I drop a kiss to Mom's cheek—we have the same dark brown hair and the same color eyes

—then hug Tyler and ruffle his sleek black hair. The dude has locks like a K-Pop star in his fifties. "Ty, I know Mom likes you for you, but it's hard to believe the hair didn't factor into her saying I do."

Mom brings her finger to her lips. "Shhh. He doesn't know I married him for his hair," she whispers. "Don't tell anyone."

"I get it. There's nothing like a full head of hair on a man," I say.

Tyler flicks his hair around like a shampoo model. "If you've got it, flaunt it."

I love that these two are so into each other eight years after tying the knot. My mom deserves it after the shit she went through with my dad.

Scanning the table, I spot a glass of water with my name on it, and I lift it and toast, "I'll drink to the two of you and the start of baseball."

"Let's all drink to that," she says, and both of them raise their glasses.

Just a few more days till Arizona, and that means it's nearly time for blinders.

Family, friends, and baseball.

I'm seeing family now, and then tomorrow I'll head to New York to visit some friends before spring training begins.

That is all I need.

That is all I want.

* * *

Things I've learned about good friends: they will always take you out after a breakup.

Things I've learned about breakups: pool makes everything better, and it's a necessity since most dates don't work out. Most men don't amount to much. And it's a good thing too. Balancing a man and this life would be hard.

I circle the table, then line up the shot at The Lucky Spot in Chelsea, where I play the game with my buddy Fitz and his sister.

"Bet you miss," he rumbles as I pull back the cue, the red ball in my crosshairs.

"Yeah, because my eye-hand coordination is soooo bad," I drawl as I take aim at the white ball, hit it, then send the red ball into the corner pocket. I gloat at the pro hockey star, squaring my shoulders. "Take that, player of a less popular sport."

"Ouch," he says, wiggling his fingers like I've scared him. "Also, that was a lucky break."

Emma laughs, leaning against the corner of the table, nursing the tail end of a margarita. "James, you do realize this is the third game in a row where Declan has destroyed you?" She's the only person who calls James Fitzgerald by his first name. Everyone else, present company included, shortens his last name.

Fitz scoffs, shrugging off his sister's most accurate scorekeeping. "I won the first game."

"The first game *last* night," I point out.

Emma holds up a palm to high-five me, and I smack back. I return my laser sights to the table, moving around it to send the purple ball, then the orange one, to their homes before I miss with the green.

"Damn," I mutter.

"Have you considered that maybe I let you win the other games because I felt sorry for you on account of your douche of an ex?" Fitz asks as he strikes the cue ball square in the center, knocking it against a striped ball that spins straight into a corner pocket.

"You are so damn competitive that even if you felt sorry for me, you don't have it in you to *let* someone win," I say.

He growls. "Dammit. You're right."

I pat my chest. "Ergo, I won fair and square."

Fitz raises his right arm and points to the side of the table. "A hundred bucks says I hit the blue stripes into the center pocket."

"What are you, Babe Ruth calling your shot? Five hundred bucks says I crush you in this game."

"How about both of you sit in the corner in time-out for beating your chests like boys?" Emma asks with a laugh. "It's just a game. Who cares?"

I freeze in horrified disbelief. *"Just a game?"*

Fitz blinks, staring at her like she's speaking math. *"Who cares?"*

I point at her, steel in my gaze. "Nothing is *just* a game. Games are life. Games are everything."

Fitz nods solemnly, stabs a finger against his sternum. "And *we* care. We care completely. Allow me to demonstrate how much."

But he misses his shot, and I proceed to destroy him, and fifteen minutes later, I collect $500, thank you very much.

I set my cue in the holder on the wall. "Too bad you're not better, Fitz. I'd have expected you to win a few since you play a game with a stick." I take a beat. "But then again, I play with sticks *and* balls."

Fitz scrubs a hand across his jaw, lifts his beer

from the edge of the table, takes a drink, then says drily, "I'm pretty sure I do that too."

"Guys." Emma shoulders her purse, shaking her head. "Is it possible to spend one game of pool with you two without some dirty innuendo?"

I look at Fitz, screw up my lips in consideration, then shake my head. "It's not possible, I'm afraid."

"Ems, just cover your ears if you don't like it," Fitz says.

Truth is, though, she doesn't care.

She's used to us—and to me. Back in college, where I met her, I helped her in math, and she helped me in poetry, of all things.

But I needed it. Hell, did I ever.

She's how I met Fitz, too, when she took me to one of his hockey games shortly after I was drafted. Nothing ever happened between her brother and me, and that's a good thing. I like having him in my life—friends are constant; men come and go.

"So, did you pretend all night that the eight ball was Nathan? Is that why you were so zoned in?" Emma asks, draping an arm around me as we make our way out of The Lucky Spot.

"I'm over him. He's yesterday's news," I say. "I deleted his number."

"But has he contacted *you*?" Fitz asks, pinning me with a stare.

"Nope. Just the way I like it."

"Nobody does clean breaks like you do," Emma says.

She's not wrong. It's my special skill, and

Nathan is the latest red-hot reminder that relationships belong on the back burner.

Now, more than ever—this is a critical time in my career.

I'm twenty-six, entering my fifth year with the San Francisco Cougars. The money is good, the sponsorships are great, the perks are awesome, and I treat my body like a temple, so it treats me the same way.

"Besides," I add, "I'm not looking for a relationship, let alone a fling or even a hookup. I'm heading into spring training with zero distractions, just like I do every year. This season will be no different."

Fitz chuckles—a knowing, self-deprecating sort of laugh. He went into training camp a season or so ago with the same mentality. "Famous last words."

I toss him a smirk. "Famous for *you*. You broke your pact, but you're the exception."

He flashes the platinum band his husband gave him several months ago. "Breaking it did work out pretty well."

"Ignore my brother. He's a big love showoff," Emma chimes in, then links her arm through mine. "But you're tough as nails, Declan. You'll go to Arizona with Nathan behind you and the game ahead of you."

"Exactly," I say. "I'm not looking to meet anyone, but it doesn't matter because I won't do anything. I won't give in to temptation."

* * *

A few days later, I arrive in Arizona, refreshed, renewed, and determined.

Then I meet Grant Blackwood.

After the one day spent with him, I'm pretty sure he's about to become the biggest temptation of my life.

2

GRANT

A week before spring training

I've wanted *this* since I turned six. Knew when I would do it too. When I'd walk through the door of this tattoo shop, strip off my shirt, and flop down in the dentist-style chair, skin on display, ready to be marked.

The one thing that has changed over the years is what *kind* of ink I'd want when this moment arrived.

At six or seven, I imagined a ball or a glove, but later, those seemed too childish.

When I was a teen, I thought I'd get a saying. One of those great baseball adages from Yogi Berra about how it's not over till it's over.

Eventually, I realized *this* ink needed to be something bigger.

A tattoo to mark the dream I've been chasing

since I was a kid, and what I hope is the start of the rest of my life.

I'm even at a shop in the town where I grew up. Seems fitting.

The electric-blue-haired, lip-ringed tattoo artist tugs on latex gloves, snaps them, and shoots me a *now-or-never* look. "Ready?" Echo asks.

"I'm always ready," I say.

That's how I've learned to live my life. Lord knows I was blindsided too many times when I was younger. I learned too many things I didn't want to know about people I loved. People I trusted.

I toss my navy-blue T-shirt to my best friend, Reese, who catches it one-handed then clutches it to her chest. "Should I act like one of your adoring fans? Try to steal your shirt? Ask for an autograph?"

I laugh. "They're free for you, babe."

She hugs the shirt tight. "I'm so lucky."

"Course you are," I say with a wink. Then I shrug. "And I don't have *that* many adoring fans."

"Emphasis on *yet*," Reese says.

"Did I say *yet*?"

"No, but I heard the *yet*," she says.

The tattoo artist laughs as she rubs alcohol on my right pec. "Gotta say—I heard it too."

"Fine, fine. If you ladies insist, I'll try it again." I clear my throat. "I don't have that many adoring fans. *Yet*."

"But you will so very soon," Reese says as she sinks into the chair facing me in Echo's work area.

"How long have you two known each other?" Echo asks as she reaches for a razor, quickly adding she's going to shave the location for the ink.

"Since I was eight. She was six," I say, tossing a glance at Reese, her blonde hair curling over her shoulders, her face as familiar as my sister's. "We grew up on the same block, across the street from each other."

"Our grandmothers are besties," Reese adds. "They played competitive Scrabble together as teammates, and on nights when I would fall asleep in his room at their house, we'd hear them arguing over whether *'ew'* is a word."

"It's definitely a word," Echo says as she works the blade across my chest. Delicate vines and tiny flowers twine along the porcelain skin on her right arm. "And that's adorable. The grandmas and the sleepovers. And that you've known each other forever."

Reese's blue eyes twinkle in my direction. We've been down this road many times, people always trying to figure out if we're childhood sweethearts.

But Echo doesn't ask the usual next question —*are you two together?* She just tosses the razor into the trash, grabs the stencil paper, and transfers it to my chest. The design is a simple arrow; my style is minimalist when it comes to my ink. No swirly lions or elaborate skulls for this guy.

"What's the story with this arrow?" Echo asks, sounding genuinely curious.

I'm happy to share the meaning behind this ink —my words to live by. "Reaching your goals. Finding your way. And keeping your momentum."

"Finding your way is a good message. A good

reminder." As Echo preps the needles and ink, her eyes stray to my other tats—the mountain design, the compass, and the bands around my biceps that look like water.

"Nice art. When did you get your first?" she asks, and I'm glad she's not prying open the *why* of each one.

Echo seems to sense it's best to tread carefully. Smart woman. Ink is usually personal, but I drop a nugget I bet she'll dig. "My grandpa brought me here for my first one when I was eighteen. He wanted to make sure I went to a good shop with a good rep," I say.

Her smile deepens. "Let me guess—Grandpa's got some ink too?"

"He does." I keep going, staying ahead in the story. "I like to mark the big events in my life. That's kind of my thing. When I hit a milestone, I like to celebrate with a tattoo. Or a piercing."

In some ways, I am an open book. People ask me questions, and I answer them.

A lot of times, I offer info.

I don't see the point in being all secretive and shit about who you are. It takes you long enough to figure it out sometimes, but once you do, there's no reason to hide it.

"Once you've figured it out" being the operative phrase.

"What about this one?" she says, pointing to the stainless-steel barbell on my left pec. "What's that for?"

I glance down at the piercing that runs through my left nipple. I definitely want to get ahead of *this* story.

Sometimes it's easy to say.

Sometimes it takes serious cojones.

It depends on who you're telling, and you never know with people.

"Ah, this thing?" I say, "Got that when I knew for sure I liked guys."

I wait for the momentary surprise, the quick rearrangement of her expression. Everybody's got some sort of reaction. But this woman with the chill attitude? She just laughs then leans a little closer. "What do you know? I've got one too, on my left boob. Feels great when a guy touches it, right?"

I crack up. "I highly recommend it."

Echo glances at my friend and shoots her a smile. "I had a hunch you two were just friends."

Reese, who shares a name with the famous actress she looks like, twists her hair into a ponytail, smiling too. "He's my best friend."

I wink at Reese. "You're mine, woman." Then I turn to Echo. Since she didn't assume we're together, I have a chance to satisfy my curiosity. "What gave away that there's nothing more between us?"

The tattoo artist gives me a smile. "You look at her like she's your sister, not your lover."

"Fair enough," I say as Echo dips the needle into ink and gets to work.

Of course I don't look at Reese that way. But what *would* it be like to look at someone like he was my lover rather than a hookup?

I've no clue. No clue at all.

As Echo colors in the stencil, she chats more about my ink, asking the what, why, and when. I give her some answers, but I don't dive into the nitty-gritty of everything the tattoos mean to me.

There *is* more to them.

There's more to almost anything in life. But I've learned that you need to pick and choose who you share your shit with.

I don't mean the shit I'm *easily* open about now—I play baseball, I love board games and thrillers, I dig dudes, I will stand by my friends come hell or high water, and if you make bank and you don't give a ton of it away, you're a dick and not the good kind.

I'm talking about the darker truths.

The things that lie deeper beneath the skin.

That's why I'm open about some things and closed about others. Some pieces of yourself you wear on your body, and others you bury so goddamn far inside you that you're not sure anyone will ever see them.

"But the arrow is my favorite," I say, glancing down at the one she's doing.

She smiles as she works, her gaze never straying from my chest. "I'm flattered, but it's not even done."

"Almost though, and I already know it'll be the one I like best," I say.

"Why's that?"

This is easy to share, part of the open book of me. Because nothing is hidden with baseball; everything is on the field.

"I promised myself this ink back when I was six."

I'm stoked to be getting this milestone marker. I got the news from my agent the other day that the San Francisco Cougars were calling me up from Triple-A and sending me to spring training with the chance of making the majors.

"I haven't met a lot of clients who planned to be tattooed when they were six," Echo says.

"The first time I hit a homer in Little League when I was seven, I told my whole family I was going to get a tat when I had an opportunity to land a slot in the majors," I say, shifting my gaze to Reese.

My best friend lifts her phone, angles it toward me, and snaps a picture. "And look at you now."

Echo smiles, bright and wide. "Nice! When do you start?"

"Next week. Pitchers and catchers report first, and I'm a catcher. I'm heading to Phoenix. First time at spring training."

"Then this arrow is even more perfect. Goals, focus, forward momentum. What's your name so I can watch you become famous?"

Reese answers like a ballpark announcer, warbling the lineup. "And now, batting fourth, and hailing from the great state of California, with a .327 batting average in Triple-A, is Grant 'Knows He's Hot Shit' Blackwood."

I crack up. "Tell us what you really think, Reese."

Reese shrugs. "Actually, I think you're hot shit too. So, I suppose it works."

Echo laughs as she finishes, putting down the needle on her work stand. "I will look out for that and maybe tell my brother to watch." She gives me the instructions for tattoo aftercare, then sets her hand on my arm. "River lives in the Phoenix area if you're looking for a *friend* during spring training. He runs a bar—The Lazy Hammock in Scottsdale. Don't worry—it's not a baseball bar."

She whips out her phone and shows me a picture of a guy standing at the sign for a trailhead. He has a full sleeve of ink, a trim beard, and kind eyes. He's white, like her, but his skin is more tanned, closer to mine. Bet he enjoys the outdoors like I do.

"Cool shot," I say.

She's not showing me his picture for feedback on the framing of the pic. She wants to know if I want to meet him, and sure, he's good-looking, objectively.

Would I feel a spark in person?

Maybe.

Maybe not.

But I won't know because that's not what spring training is about.

I'm hunting for a diplomatic answer when Reese slides over, peering at the pic then chiming in with a laugh. "I swear, Grant. You can pick up cute men anywhere. You don't even have to be in the same state."

The tattoo artist simply shrugs and locks eyes with Reese. "Right? It's just kind of how it goes with the hotties, right? All you want to do is set them up."

"And they don't need it," Reese says, shaking her head. "Hot queer guys need no help finding other hot queer guys."

I'd beg to differ, but I'm not going to let on in front of Echo.

Besides, Reese knows the truth. And I should

keep up appearances—that I put my money where my rainbow mouth is.

I grab my shirt, pull it on, then say, "Thanks, Echo. I appreciate the offer, and I'm sure your brother is a cool dude. But I think I'm going to lock it up during spring training."

"His loss," she says with a smile.

I pay for the tattoo, head out of Ink Lore, and wander down the street with my best friend.

She arches an eyebrow, giving me a questioning stare. "Lock it up? Are you really?"

"I am, indeed. Is that a surprise? *Lock it up* is my middle name."

She taps her chest. "Yeah, I have the same one."

I drape an arm around Reese, squeeze her shoulder. "You and me. We're cut from the same cloth. Besides, I'm pretty damn sure spring training isn't the place."

She frowns. "The men of Phoenix will be so sad. Especially River. He looked cute from the pic."

"Doesn't matter," I say, even though there is one man in Phoenix who intrigues me.

But his name isn't River.

3

GRANT

I slide my duffel bag onto the luggage belt, take the baggage check from the attendant, and give her a grin.

"Appreciate you doing that," I say, nodding toward the bag as it disappears below the airport.

She flashes a quick smile that's gone in a second. "Of course."

It's all in a day's work for her, loading bags, handing out stubs for them. But hell, for me? I'm buzzed, and I haven't had a single drop of coffee. Nor do I want one. I want to remember everything about this moment.

The noise and hubbub of the airport here in San Francisco.

The drone of the announcements overhead.

The click of shoes.

The laughter.

And my four favorite people here with me, seeing me off.

With my grandparents, my sister, and Reese, I

walk to security, backpack on one shoulder, then draw a deep breath as I cast my gaze to the checkpoint and the planes beyond, including the one that'll take me to Arizona.

"I want reports," Grandpa says as he claps me on the shoulder.

I give him a *c'mon* look. "When have I not given you full reports on every single game?"

"More than games, kid." His blue eyes hold mine with that intense look in them that he's shone my way for as long as I can remember. "I want reports on batting practice, on drills, on the coaches, and on the games."

My grandma tuts. "Trevor, when has Grant ever deprived us of baseball reports?"

"Kids change when they go away," he says, all gruff. Sometimes he pretends he's a toughie but—newsflash—the dude is a total softie, and I love him for it. His heart is a big old marshmallow.

My sister barks out a laugh. "Hate to break it to you, Pops, but Grant's been away three years for college and a year in the minors. He's been gone for a while."

He snaps his gaze to Sierra, having none of her logic. "And he's still a kid going away. And you're even younger, so you're a kid too."

She rolls her eyes. "Yes, Pops." But she loves how he looks out for us. How both of them have looked out for us for ages, giving us the only place we could ever truly call home. "Grant's still a kid at the ripe old age of twenty-two," my sister adds with a scoff.

"So young," Grandma says, ruffling my hair.

I *am* young, but not for long. In the majors,

your age flies past you in dog years, and before you know it, you're middle-aged at twenty-nine.

You need to work hard and fast to leave a mark.

Even though I knew I'd be eligible for the college draft after three years, I still wanted to get my degree, so I busted my ass to finish school and still enter the draft when I was twenty-one. I went in the first round, spent a short season in the Cougars' farm league, and now I have the chance to play in the majors.

Reese wraps an arm around me and pulls me a few feet away, dropping her voice to a whisper. "Now listen, I want reports too. But not on the batting practice or games."

I shoot her a knowing glance. "You want the uncensored report on the men?"

She sticks out her tongue. "Yes. Duh."

I pat her head like she's a little duckling. "It's a good thing I love you so much. I must, to tolerate this kind of relentless questioning."

"Oh, please. I'm only looking out for your . . . *libido*."

Laughing, I answer her. "I already told you. I'm not going to do a thing. I am the king of restraint. My libido will be resting in my duffel bag. Side pocket, in fact. Like hibernation."

"Fine, fine, you're a bear."

I crack up. "You saw my chest at the tattoo shop. Definitely not a bear."

Reese rolls her eyes. "Yes, you are not a *bear*, my friend. But," she says, tap dancing her finger on my shoulder, "what is your libido going to do with that big old crush you have on the Cougars shortstop? Is that just going to go into hibernation too?"

I tilt my head back and forth like I'm weighing my options. "It was either that or my powerful mind vise. I opted for the mind vise, and I smashed the crush out of its existence," I say, grinding my right fist into my left palm to demonstrate, and kind of wishing mind vises did exist.

She arches a questioning brow. "Did you now?"

"I did indeed. And seriously, who cares? Crushes are harmless. They don't matter." It's just stupid affection from afar. "Besides, I refuse to crush on another ballplayer on my team—or any other team. I admire his gameplay, but that's all. That's all it can ever be. I am *not, not, not* going to do a single thing with a ballplayer."

Reese's blue eyes are brimming with intensity. "Goals, focus, forward momentum," she says, repeating what I told Echo when I got my new ink the other week.

"You know it. Crushing on a teammate is like arguing with an umpire and thinking it'll work out. You just don't do it," I say.

But honestly, crushing on someone I work with is worse. It can have lasting consequences. It can wreak havoc with how we have to work together on the field, with the focus *I* need to have behind the plate. With, well, everything that matters when it comes to playing the game I love for a living.

"Besides," I add, "if I wanted to hook up with someone, and I do not, there's a whole town of men who are *not* ballplayers." I flap a hand to indicate the landscape of the city in Arizona. "Bartenders, store owners, bankers, mailmen, painters, construction workers, hell, even Echo's brother if I'm truly looking to get laid. What they all have in common is they aren't on the twenty-five-man roster for the San Francisco Cougars." I stab my forefinger against my chest. "I need to be on the roster and stay on the roster. I do not need to fuck the roster."

She holds up her hands in surrender. "I wasn't saying that. As someone who's had her share of crushes too, I was just asking. And don't worry, Grant. You'll be on the roster. I have zero doubts, only faith in you."

But this isn't about faith.

This isn't some breakup I need to get over.

Declan is just . . . some dude I admired.

Nothing more.

I flash her a smile, my best *everything is good here* grin. "I bet I won't even be attracted to him in person," I say, lifting my chin high.

"Exactly! Tons of crushes die a quick death when you meet the crushee. So, there's that."

"Yup. I mean, he's probably a cool guy, but chances are we won't have an ounce of spark."

"It'll evaporate the second you meet him." She throws her arms around me. "I'll miss you."

"Same. But you have college to keep you busy."

"And we all still miss seeing your face around campus, but I'll see you in San Francisco this summer when you're playing for the home team in the best sport there is."

"I. Can't. Wait." I hug her hard, grateful to have her, glad there's someone who knows about crushes I've entertained from afar. Crushes that'll burn to ash any day now, I'm sure.

"Enjoy your spring training with no spring flings, Grant 'Lock It Up' Blackwood," she says.

I let go, return to my grandparents to hug them too, barely giving a second thought to where my own parents are—they're never around—then my sister.

"Good luck in school," I tell her, then turn to Pops. "And I'm expecting another top-ten finish for you in the Napa Valley Marathon."

"As am I," my grandma chimes in, patting his chest. "I want to say I'm married to a top-ten finisher."

Pops drops a kiss to her forehead. "Anything for you." Then to me, he says, "See you soon, son."

My throat tightens with emotions, then I swallow them down and wave goodbye.

I head through security, taking the next step toward the dream I've chased my entire life.

* * *

I settle into my seat, loving the cushy comfort of the first-class chair. It's my first time in the second row.

"I could get used to this," I say to myself as the flight attendant meanders by. He stops in his tracks, then tosses me an inviting smile that's pretty much the equivalent of a full-body eye fucking. Someone is bold, and I like bold.

"Well, I sure hope you get used to it. Would love to see you on another flight," the man says, with a lift of his brow, a quirk of his lips. "Or . . ."

Clever. Way to make the meaning clear without crossing a line.

I scan his name tag. *Dylan*. Then I let my eyes take a one-second tour of his face.

Square jaw, high cheekbones—he's attractive. But do I feel a spark?

My body's not flashing hot. My skin isn't tingling. Which raises the question—is this guy my type? Or not?

Hell if I know. I'm not even sure if I have a type. Except I'm pretty certain *I'm* not a guy who's into one-night stands or banging somebody in the mile-high club if that's what Dylan is proposing.

But is that what he's hinting at? Pickup lingo is still new to me—I spent ninety-nine percent of college either studying or playing ball.

Nah, Dylan's just feeling me out.

And I'd probably need a few dates to see if we sparked. That won't happen, so I find the gentleman's way out. "Thanks. I'll keep that in mind," I say with a grin, and he continues on his way.

This is my MO: flash a smile. Say some friendly words. Be on good terms with everyone.

That's what's gotten me through ups and downs, good times and bad times, hard times and absolutely fucking hard times. When the people who were supposed to stand behind you let you down.

In the worst ways possible.

But that's okay.

I have everything I need now that I'm twenty-two. And this arrow? It's not only about goals and milestones. It's protection.

Sure, things have changed in pro sports over

the last several years. Some players in the NBA, NHL, NFL, and MLB are out now. The closet isn't what it used to be in pro ball—the *only* place for a gay athlete. Leagues, owners, and marketers have embraced the LGBTQ sports nation.

Plus, I'm not even the only queer dude on the team.

I am all the way out, and I'm out on my terms. I don't need a single soul whispering, talking behind my back, or speculating. I don't like to leave it up to anyone's best guess. My Instagram and Twitter profiles are decorated with rainbows.

But even when you're out, people can still trip you up.

That's why I need the arrow for protection.

From the people who let me down.

Those who have, and those who will.

I close my eyes, picturing the arrow going forward, riding that momentum to take me through the next several weeks, then, I hope, on to my first ever baseball season in the Major Leagues. Finally, *finally,* everything in my life feels right, and I don't want anything to change that.

Not even the fact that I have a crush on one of my teammates.

* * *

The next day, I'm a bottle of Diet Coke mixed with Mentos. I rise before dawn, shower, get dressed, and head for the ballpark, all jitters and excitement.

I walk the half-mile from the hotel. The sign

for the ballpark looms high above the gates, graced with the name of the team's first owner.

Helen Williams Field.

The spring training home for the San Francisco Cougars.

It's beautiful, and it beckons me.

Memories flash before me. The time I first picked up the well-worn baseball glove my grandfather gave me. When I threw a ball to him in the backyard. When he tossed it back to me and I caught it on the first try, and he said, *"You're going to be an all-star catcher someday."*

Years of practice.

Sore muscles, broken bones, heartbreaking losses.

But victories too.

High school state championships, college World Series, the Major League Baseball Draft.

As I head into the team's spring training facility for the first time, I take it all in. The plaques, the trophies, the photographs. I'm in the presence of greatness. Just look at the pics of all these guys who've come before me, won rings, snagged batting titles, earned Cy Youngs.

They played here first, took batting practice out on the diamond, and fielded ground balls.

I get to do that now. It's my chance to show my team that I have what it takes to be their starting catcher for the next decade.

Nothing will distract me. Nothing will throw me off.

I make my way down the corridor, my shoes echoing against the concrete, as I say hello to everyone I pass. I greet the groundskeepers, the janitors, the staffers, asking how they're doing. I like to be the one people can rely on for a friendly face, an encouraging word. That's how I fit into the team and the organization.

And with the pitchers too, since they're the guys who have to rely on me most.

Item number one on my to-do list?

Earn the pitchers' trust.

It's mostly just pitchers and catchers at the complex for the first few days, working out on a practice field. I toss balls with the starters, then the relief pitchers, then the team's closer, Chance Ashford. The man has a punishing cut fastball, and I love it.

"I'd like to say that's your secret weapon, but I'm pretty sure all of baseball knows your cutter was forged at the gates of hell," I tell him when he comes off the mound after a throwing session.

He arches a brow, gives an appreciative smile. "So, it's got fire coming off it? Like those car decals with flames? I'll take that compliment."

"Yup. It's exactly like that— nice long tail of fire and all," I joke as we head off the field.

"Excellent." He clears his throat when we reach the chain-link fence. "By the way, I'm going to post a shot on Insta from our practice. I'll tag you in it. Cool?"

"Yeah. Definitely."

"Awesome." He claps my shoulder, his dark eyes intense, his expression serious. "And I saw the flag on your profile. You're all good here. Be yourself, man."

I smile, my chest filling with relief and, admittedly, admiration for this guy. "Appreciate that."

That's all he says, and it's all I need.

Though, I know he's only the start. Can't assume the other players checked me out online. Somehow, I'll need to say something to the rest of the team, just like I did in the minors and with my college team.

I'd rather be the one to say it than have it said about me.

* * *

As the week draws to a close, the position players stream in, some joining us for early practice.

On the first full workout day, I'm early again, leaving the team hotel before the other guys and making my way to the complex.

Once inside, I say hi to Chet, the groundskeeper, then Hope, who runs the ticket office.

I turn the corner toward the locker room, and I nearly run smack-bang into a wall of man. A two hundred pound, six-foot-three mass of muscle, cut abs, and carved jaw.

A man sporting a grin that makes my skin tingle.

The breath flees my lungs. My pulse spikes. So, this is what it feels like to meet your crush.

It feels like your body is alive. Electric. Made of sparks.

"Hey there."

That's it. Two words. They're all Declan says.

But I already know.

This is going to be a big fucking problem.

The sexiest man I've ever seen on TV is worlds hotter in person.

And I was dead wrong when I told Reese this crush would die a swift death in person.

The opposite is true.

The object of my crush stands inches away, with deep brown eyes that travel over me and a body I want to feel under me, on top of me, next to me. I am so fucked.

I haul in a breath.

Time to pretend like I haven't thought of scoring with him so many damn times.

Or that I'm thinking it again right this very second.

4

GRANT

My next thought is, *Impress him*.

I don't mean like if we were in a bar and I were trying to pick him up with wit or banter or a 360-degree view of my arms.

I mean, impress the hell out of him as a ballplayer.

Declan Steele is one of the best in the majors. In his first four years, he's amassed some killer stats, epic plays, and absolutely clutch RBIs, homers, and hits.

He's exactly the type of guy you want on your team, and I want him to like me as a ballplayer.

I want all the guys on the team to trust me.

I go in nice and easy with Declan, homing in on the thing we have in common.

No, not the *gay* thing.

But everyone loves a compliment.

"That was a hell of a double play in that game against the Storm Chasers last fall. The one where you leaped ten feet above the runner as you threw to first," I say, picturing that play perfectly.

Declan raises an eyebrow. His smile spreads slowly, taking its time moving across his handsome face. Then it reaches his eyes. There's a glint in them, along with a crook in his lips.

"Impressed you saw it, rookie," he says, emphasis on *rookie*.

That's got to be good. If he knows it's my first year, he knows who I am.

"You are a rookie, aren't you?" he adds.

Ah. So, it was a lucky guess. The shortstop doesn't know me. I straighten my shoulders instinctively. "Yes, I am," I say, tempted to add *sir*. But this isn't the military. He's not my boss. I do, however, need to show respect for him and the time he's put in. "First time here."

"First time. Gotta make it good," he says in a tone that's a little raspy, a lot sexy. My skin sizzles as I picture other first times.

"So they say," I say, keeping the banter light.

He takes a beat. "And what's your story?"

My story? He asks it like Echo at the tattoo shop. What the hell am I supposed to tell him?

Should I give him my dating profile? Psychological flicks and fast-paced books rock my world, Daniel Craig is hands down the best James Bond, the designated hitter rule is the only way to go, and I'd love to take him out to dinner.

But before I can open my mouth to say something else entirely—because I am not saying any of that, especially the last part—he laughs, then adds, "Your baseball story, rookie. That's all I mean."

I breathe a sigh of relief. "I was in Triple-A last

season," I say, and I make a mental note that he's not one of those guys who follows the minors. That's what I would do if I were him. But, hey, maybe I'd be so absorbed in my own game that I wouldn't have time to worry about who was coming up. That's probably why he doesn't know who I am.

The man has more forward momentum than anyone. He's in a league of his own and doesn't have to peer in the rearview mirror to see who's chasing him.

He scrubs a hand across his chin, studying me. It's not a sexual look. He's not shamelessly eating me up with his eyes. It's more like he's trying to read me, figure out if I have an ego the size of an SUV, if I'm just one of the guys, or a pushover, or somewhere in between. "So, you're a hotshot, then?" Declan asks.

Fuck.

I am doing this all wrong.

I don't want him to think I have a big head since I raced through the minors faster than most guys.

"No. I don't think I am. And I'm also not a shortstop," I say quickly, lest he think I'm gunning for his position.

Then he cracks up, sets a hand on my shoulder, and I go still so I don't give away how much I like that big hand on me. The way he curls it over my muscle. How his palm fits on my body. That's just a friendly hand, nothing more.

Too bad my body doesn't feel friendly with him.

It feels hot.

Hotter still when he says, "Rookie, I'm just fucking with you."

Does he know how much innuendo I can hear laced in his words?

Or is it just me, craving innuendo with him?

Note to self: you seem to have forgotten that your teammate is off-limits.

He drops his hand, then holds it out to shake. "Declan Steele," he says, and I want to tell him, *Dude, I know who you are. I've watched your games, seen your interviews, admired your career. And your deep brown eyes, perfectly messy hair, and chiseled jaw with just the right amount of scruff that blends together into the hottest guy I've ever seen.*

By the way, you might not post shots online of your dates, but I've come across the pics of you having dinner with Nathan Sparks, and all I have to say is this—that guy's a jackass and you can do better.

"Grant Blackwood," I say. "I'm looking forward to playing with you."

And I cringe.

Did that just come out of my mouth? That sounds so filthy. So deliciously, dangerously filthy.

And so wildly inappropriate.

The corner of his lips quirks up. The man exudes confidence. He gives off heady doses of charisma. He's unflappable even as I step in it. "I'm definitely looking forward to playing with you too, Grant," he says, then shakes his head, clearly amused by me.

Which is not the first impression I wanted to make on a teammate.

I have bungled this so badly.

I groan privately, then drag a hand down the back of my neck. I came on to the dude, and I didn't mean to come on to him, and he's going to think I meant something, and I didn't mean anything. Even though some part of my lizard brain means everything because I would love to play with him in the bedroom.

But that is not happening.

That is not what spring training is about.

This is about me meeting a teammate, not some guy I'm hot for.

Ladies and gentlemen of the jury, I'm here to say this—it is seriously hard sometimes being a queer dude on a sports team, even if everyone's cool with queer dudes in pro sports.

Even if I already have sponsors lined up for endorsement deals.

Even if pro sports is no longer a bastion of homophobia, but instead a beacon of rainbow pride, embracing LGBTQ athletes.

I don't want my teammates to think what small-minded people think about gay guys in a locker room—that we're checking out all the men.

I vow to never look at Declan in the locker room.

Right now, I do my best to course correct. "All I mean is I'm a big fan of yours," I say, and yeah, now I sound like a complete tool.

This is awesome.

I love meeting a player I look up to and making a complete fool of myself.

"Big fan," I repeat, owning my tool-ery. "I sound like I'm calling into a sports talk show."

"Long-time listener, first-time caller," Declan quips, then adds, like he's the radio host Jim Rome, "'Welcome to the Jungle.'"

And I relax as he takes the conversational plane in for a smooth landing on the runway, making me feel like it's okay that I put my foot in my mouth.

Like he gets my energy.

He spins around, then he turns back, urgency in his eyes. "Wait a second. You missed the drills, didn't you?"

"What? No, it's nine. First workout is at nine-thirty. Did I get the time wrong?"

His expression turns deadly serious. "Aw shit, man. You missed the early drills. Rookie drills were at eight-thirty. You better get out there now, or they'll make you do all the dirty laundry for the next five weeks."

Panic kicks in, swimming in my blood. I can't fuck up. He points in the direction of the locker room that leads to the diamond. "That's where you need to be. Main field," he says.

"Thanks, man. Appreciate it."

I step away, ready to jet, when he sets a hand on my arm. "Give me your phone, rookie. Skipper will have a fit if he sees you with the phone in the locker room," he says.

"Really?" My brain scrambles, trying to figure out if he's screwing with me. I can't remember the manager mentioning a ban on phones in locker rooms.

"Yes. Go put on your uniform. Get out on the field and do the drills. You can thank me later when the coach doesn't pitch a fit."

I breathe, exhaling heavily as I hand him my phone. I hightail it to the locker room, pull on my uniform, and grab my glove.

I run to the field as the team streams in, but they're not doing drills. They're . . . milling about by home plate.

That's odd.

The third baseman strolls over to me, holding his cap in front of him. "I can do the triple lift," Crosby Cash says by way of greeting. "And I bet all these guys that I can do it. They don't believe me. You in?"

I pat the back pocket of my baseball pants for show. "I don't have my wallet with me."

Scoffing, Crosby turns around. "He has no dough. Who's covering the rookie?"

Seconds later, Declan's voice calls out. "I've got his back. Fifty bucks says you can do it, Cash. You hear that, rookie? We're betting for him."

"Yeah, sure," I say, gulping.

Crosby turns, shoves his hat at Chance. "You in or out?"

Chance grabs a bill from his pocket, tosses it in. "I've seen you fail at it. A hundo says you will again."

"You're wrong." Crosby turns around, pats the weight belt on his waist, then sets the hat on the ground.

"You ready?" The question comes my way from Crosby, and it's time to improvise. I've no idea what the triple lift is.

But I won't let on. "Absolutely."

"Cool," he says, then points to the grass. "Get on the ground. Lie down." I do as I'm told while

Crosby calls out to two other rookies, guys I know well from Triple-A. "Sullivan! Miguel! Get over here too. Grant's in the middle."

Sullivan trots over, his dark eyes eager as a puppy dog's, and drops to the ground next to me. Miguel flops on my other side.

"Hook elbows around the other guys," Crosby says to the three of us. "I'm going to lift you all at once."

This doesn't feel like a drill, but I get in position, the sun shining brightly in my eyes. Crosby leans over like he's about to grab the waistband of my uniform to haul us up over his head.

Instead, Chance sweeps in, squeezing a red bottle at my face.

Before I even blink, I have red goop all over me, my hair, my uniform. I look like a one-man crime scene, and I crinkle my nose at the vinegary smell of ketchup.

Sullivan takes a direct hit of bright yellow mustard next to me, then Crosby is shaking another container on the three of us, dumping an avalanche of baby powder that flies everywhere and coats us in a layer of white talc.

I spit it out, laughing and grossed out at the same time, then Declan gets in on the act, dousing us with a couple of cans of whipped cream, spraying the dessert topping all over us.

My face is covered in condiments. My uniform is toast. But I wipe off the food with a grin.

This is not a drill. It's a rookie hazing.

And I'm loving it.

Even when the manager walks onto the field.

Fisher stops when he spots us, parks his hands on his hips, shakes his head in exasperation . . .

Then laughs his ass off.

I might look like an utter dipshit, but I'm happier than I've ever been in my life.

5

DECLAN

That was necessary.

For the team, of course.

But hey, I don't mind that our hazing helped squash that inconvenient bout of lust brought on by *The Insanely Hot and Adorably Charming Rookie*.

The guy is too cute and too damn likable. Grant is like Captain America, but ten times sexier than any movie superhero.

He needed to be covered in ketchup.

Too bad he can't wear condiments and baby powder for the next five weeks. Maybe that would put a damper on this attraction that sprang out of nowhere.

I'll be fine.

I repeat the reassurance after the rookies return to the field post shower, then as we finish stretching, and again when we trot onto the field to practice throws.

From home plate to second.

Groan.

That means I'll be working with our new catcher, whose number I'd definitely have asked for if I'd met him anywhere but work.

But from this distance, and with Grant wearing a mask, I'll be fine.

And I am for the rest of the morning. Then Coach sends us to run a mile around the field.

I elevate my 'fine' to 'fantastic.'

I'm one of the fastest guys on the team, and catchers are usually slow as molasses from all that bulk. Hell, the backup catcher, Rodriguez, is playing caboose right now, lagging behind everyone.

Grant is going to eat my dust, and I'll be glad for the distance between us.

But a minute later, he's gaining on me, picking up speed as I round the right field corner. "You don't have to race me, rookie," I call as he comes into my line of sight.

"I'm not racing you. I'm just . . . faster than people expect."

I lift a brow. "Sometimes fast is good."

Then I want to clamp my hand over my mouth. Did I not make a decision not to flirt?

One day into spring training—hell, mere *hours* into spring training—and I'm already flirting with him.

Subtly, the devil on my shoulder says. *You're flirting subtly. He probably doesn't even notice.*

Blatantly, so damn blatantly, the angel on my other shoulder offers, adding, *and you should stop.*

"Sometimes fast is everything you need," Grant quips, and I like the devil on his shoulder too.

Too much.

"Truer words," I say, as we round the corner at a good clip. We're quiet for another stretch, but no one catches up to us. The rest of the team is hoofing it, but we're faster, and much farther ahead.

"Fucking sloths," I say, tipping my head toward the guys.

"Better to be a cheetah."

"Always be the cheetah." Then a bird swoops from out of nowhere, landing on the chain-link fence to perch and watch for mice.

"Unless you can be a falcon," I say, and I sneak a look at Grant. "The fastest animal on earth."

"Are they though?" He arches a brow. "Aren't they the fastest . . . *in the air?*"

"Aren't you a wiseass," I say, laughing. "You want to go toe-to-toe with me in bird facts, I will school you, rookie."

"Bird facts?" he asks. "That's your throw down?"

"You weren't so mouthy when you were covered in ketchup."

"And I'm not covered in ketchup now. Hence the mouthiness."

I stifle another laugh. He's a quick talker when he's not so damn nervous. Though, admittedly, he was adorable back in the corridor with his tongue tied and words twisted. And he's adorable now.

Great, fucking great.

But I won't be seduced by his charm. He's just one of the guys. Just another teammate.

"And yes, bird facts are my throw down," I say, and there are reasons for that. Reasons that go way back. Reasons that I will never get into with anyone. But they're real, and a part of me, and they were a shield for a long, long time. "The peregrine falcon is the fastest animal . . . *in the world*. That better?"

"Much better," he says, a smile curving the edge of his lips.

"Gotta say, rookie, I'm impressed you're keeping up. No one keeps up with me."

"What if I told you I'm taking it easy right now?" Grant asks, deadpan.

I laugh. "Wiseass."

But he keeps a stony expression. "Seriously. What if I could run even faster?" He picks up the pace a notch or two.

Holy fuck.

Dude is fast.

But I'm a competitive bastard too, so I push myself, going faster, keeping up.

I want to smack his arm, tell him he won't win a battle of wills, or strength, or fitness.

But he just might.

Grant is as swift on his feet as he is with his arm.

I clear my throat to segue to other topics, but *only* sports topics. "You did good with the triple lift."

"So did you. You had me. One hundred percent," he says.

I smile. "Excellent. I love nothing more than getting the rookies."

He casts a quick glance at me, then swings his gaze forward. "And listen, man. Sorry for the verbal vomit in the hallway. I think I was nervous meeting you. You seriously are one of my heroes in the game," he says, earnest and straightforward, in a voice that does dangerous things to my mind.

Things I can't allow.

"Good of you to say, but trust me, I'm nobody's hero," I reply as we near the end of our final lap. Then I add, "But no worries on the nerves. I was you once. Bright-eyed and eager."

He barks out a laugh. "Is it that obvious?"

I smack his arm. "Absolutely."

Then I wink.

Something I definitely shouldn't do.

What I *should* do is walk away as soon as we finish the drill.

And that's what I do.

6

GRANT

At the end of practice, I shut my locker, say goodbye to the rookies and the other guys, including the veteran Rodriguez, even though I'm competing with him for the starting slot. Declan, though, I avoid, so I don't accidentally gawk at the smoke-show of a shortstop. I make it out of the locker room, but as soon as I'm out the door, I remember my phone.

Shit.

I go back in and scan for Declan, relieved—mostly—that he's dressed. He's parked on the bench by his locker, talking with Crosby and Chance, who slides his wedding band onto his finger. He doesn't pitch with it on.

Other players mill about, chatting as they button shirts and tie shoelaces. Declan slowly turns my way, that easy smile sending a zing down my stomach.

I have got to get it together.

Maybe tomorrow will lessen the impact of

him. Declan is a lot of heat to get used to. Maybe I'll adjust, like inching into a hot tub.

Now I'm picturing the shortstop sinking into a hot bath, and I swear I'm not doing this on purpose.

"Let me guess," he says. "You want your phone back, rookie?"

"I do. Thanks," I say as he stands.

"Couldn't risk you googling the triple lift and finding out we did it last year too." He reaches into his locker and grabs my phone from the top shelf. "Hope you can catch this."

"Ha. No worries there," I say as he wings it my way and I grab the device.

"Nice," he says, and that easy smile of his is the most dangerous thing I've ever seen.

"I do my best."

I turn to go, but before I can leave, Declan clears his throat. "You forgetting something?"

I freeze, my brain cycling through the day. What could I have forgotten? Oh, wait, this has to be another prank.

I turn back around. "To thank you for the whipped cream? It was quite tasty."

Another lopsided grin. Another swoop of my stomach.

He shakes his head then rubs his thumb and forefinger together. "Pay up, rookie."

Ah, right. I grab my wallet from my back pocket and fish around for a bill. My heart sinks as I come up almost empty. "I only have a ten. Can I Venmo you the rest?"

Declan cracks up so hard he has to hold his

stomach. Crosby doubles over in laughter. Chance points at me, barely able to breathe.

Every eye in the locker room turns toward us. Toward me. Or it feels that way—most of the team is here.

"You do that on dates, rookie?" Chance gasps between guffaws. "Ask your dates if you can Venmo the money?"

The heavens part and angels sing. I need an opening to get out ahead of the story of my sexuality, and the closing pitcher just lobbed a slow pitch right over the plate.

I mentally square my shoulders. Not easy to brace yourself for blowback without coming off either defensive or challenging.

"Sometimes when I go on a date, *he* pays for me." I shrug like my heart isn't hammering. "But sometimes I pay for him, depending on my mood."

There's a heavy pause in the locker room. I glimpse a few furrowed brows on the guys, some blinks of adjustment, visible gulps.

Chance just grins at me like we planned this. *I* didn't, but that was a suspiciously perfect setup. But in a good way, I think.

The silence only lasts a few seconds, and it feels damn good when Crosby breaks it. He arches a brow, his tone smooth as butter. "So, Grant, what you're saying is you're quite a *catch* with the dudes?"

I don't look at Declan. I don't even risk it.

But the rest of the Cougars have their eyes on me as I answer Crosby with a casual shrug and a sly smile. "That's what I hear."

"Just one thing, Catch," Chance says, holding

up a hand. The nickname belies his overly serious expression.

"What's that?"

"You like burgers?"

"Course I do."

"Excellent." He sweeps his hand to indicate all the guys in the locker room. "We're going out to grab some grub. And you're gonna pick up the tab. I'm sure that'll be a change for you, but those are the clubhouse rules. Rookies pay."

He finishes with a grin that I match, glad this moment is behind me and I can get on with playing the sport I love.

Forward momentum, it is nice to see you.

"I'm good with that," I tell Chance.

Very, very good with that.

* * *

We go to a nearby burger joint, order, then shoot the breeze about video games and cool tunes. We steer away from talk of baseball, which makes a nice break after a long day of training.

Afterward, we head for the team hotel, the guys dispersing to their rooms, the pool, or the bar. I hang back with Chance and Declan as Crosby looks around the lobby in satisfaction, whistling in admiration as he gets a look at the name above the doors.

Jen Trujillo Suites.

"Damn, the Cougs do love us," Crosby says.

"Because they're paying for our digs this year?" Declan puts in.

"Because this place rocks. Kitchen, bedroom,

and master bath. And it's walking distance to the complex."

Declan snorts. "What, is this your latest endorsement deal?"

Crosby wiggles a brow. "Good idea. I should get my agent on that, stat."

"Anyway, the team isn't paying for it," Declan adds. "Jen Trujillo is one of the team sponsors, so we're here courtesy of her company."

"Well, someone *is* paying for our digs, you turkey burgers," Crosby says, "and it's not me, so I'm calling it a win." He turns to me as we walk inside. "How do you like this place, G-man? You've been here for a week."

Does Crosby's experimentation with alternatives to "rookie" mean that I have a license to come up with my own nicknames for him and the other veteran players? I'm gleeful at the thought.

"I've spent most of it at the complex," I say, "but I can't complain."

I head to the elevator that'll take me to my suite on the sixth floor. Crosby peels away with Chance, pointing a thumb down the hall. "I'm in the other tower. Catch you in the a.m."

"See you then," I say.

They walk away, and I hit the call button and wait for the elevator, figuring Declan will head in their direction.

A few seconds later, though, the shortstop strides over, and the hair on the back of my neck pricks up.

The effect this man has on me is so goddamn unfair. My future looks full of less *hot tub* and more *ice bath*.

"Guess we're in the same tower, rookie," he says, and something about the sexy rumble of his voice tells me everything in my life is about to be ten thousand times harder than I'd thought.

And no ice bath will do the trick.

Not when the way he says *rookie* lights me up all over.

"Welcome to the jungle," I say as the elevator arrives.

He laughs lightly. "It is a jungle in here, isn't it?"

I step into the elevator with Declan, and the doors close on us.

7

DECLAN

Things I'd like to know—why elevators shrink the second you enter them with a guy you're hot for.

Can someone explain that law of physics?

Is it a variation on Newton's Laws? The space between two people becomes immeasurably smaller when you want to get your hands on him?

Yeah, I bet that's a rule of sexual gravity.

Also, Grant smells incredible. All clean and soapy still, even hours later, and that freshly showered smell is my favorite one on a man.

Especially when I can dirty him up.

Damn it.

Isn't that exactly what I'm not supposed to think about?

I blame the elevator. This one feels like it's two-feet wide, and all I want to do is push him into the corner, slide my hands down his chest and get my lips on his.

I clench my teeth.

Will the lust to evaporate.

I've got this. I know what I'm doing. And I sure as shit am not giving in to temptation. I know how to handle the hard stuff. I've been handling it for years, ever since I got my life in order in college. Ever since I decided how I wanted to live—in control, in charge.

This *temptation of the rookie* is nothing.

But a little help comes in handy now and then.

Drawing a deep breath as the elevator chugs past the first floor, I repeat the words I needed back in college. Words that Emma taught me when I was struggling to have the guts to speak in front of a crowd. Doors she opened for me through stanzas, verses, beats.

I start with Robert Frost.

The woods are lovely, dark and deep,
But I have promises to keep . . .

Poems helped me get over some of my fears.

They've given me strength. They've fed me.

This one gives me the courage to say something I don't need to say, but I definitely *want* to say. Grant might admire me for my gameplay, but I admire the hell out of him for what he voiced tonight with one simple pronoun.

Sometimes when I go on a date, he pays for me. But sometimes I pay for him, depending on my mood.

I turn to the man next to me. "That took a lot of guts, what you said in the locker room."

He meets my gaze, the expression in his dark blue eyes serious. "If there's one thing I've learned, it's that I'd rather tell my own story."

There's more there for sure. A conversation I'd love to have if we were at dinner. A deep dive I'd like to take. But I can't, and I won't.

"Couldn't agree more," I say, keeping it simple as I offer a fist for knocking in solidarity.

He knocks back.

But I can't seem to stay away, so I toss out one question. "Spoken from experience?"

"Yeah. Before I was ready," he says, his jaw tight. But then he rolls his shoulders, like he's shrugging it off, or maybe just moving on.

"That sucks, man. I wouldn't wish that on anyone," I say, a pang of sympathy tugging on my heart for whatever he went through.

"That's why I'd rather speak up. You know?" He looks to me, waits, a man-to-man moment. Wiseass Grant has left the elevator. Hell, he hasn't been a wiseass this whole ride.

Solemnly, I nod. "I do. I absolutely do."

He exhales deeply, the sound of relief. "What about you? Did you have to do a big song-and-dance show your rookie season too?"

With a straight face, I answer him. "I did. I chose tap for my routine."

"Ah, so that was your pick in the talent portion of the coming out pageant?"

"Of course. What conveys it better than that?"

"Little else," he says with a grin.

The elevator stops at my floor. As the doors open, I ask, "What floor are you on?"

"Sixth."

I stick my arm between the doors to keep them open. This convo isn't finished. "But in all seriousness, I wasn't quite as smooth as you. Honestly, I didn't know what I was doing." The memory flashes clearly of awkward, unsure me. "I wrote it down. On a sheet of paper. Photocopied it."

His eyes light up with interest. "Yeah? You were going to go the 'letter to my teammates' route?"

The elevator buzzes a complaint, signaling it doesn't want to entertain this talk. The machine wants to send Grant upstairs, but fuck that. Some talks aren't meant to remain unfinished.

I nod to the quiet hall. "Let's let the elevator do its business. Walk with me, and I'll tell you the rest."

He steps out, and we head down the carpeted hallway. I swallow a little roughly, vividly remembering my first spring training four years ago. "I had this whole letter ready to go. *I have a boyfriend, but even if I didn't, don't worry. I'm still me.*"

"And did you share it with them?"

I shake my head. "No. I read it in front of the mirror. Like it was a poem I was practicing for lit class in college. And it sounded so stupid that I crumpled it up and threw it out. Anyway . . ." I heave a sigh and scrub a hand over my jaw. "It took me a while to figure out what to say. I'm not a . . . *sharer.*"

That's the understatement of the year. Of my life.

"Not everyone is. Nothing wrong with that."

"But it was dragging me down, an albatross hung around my neck. So finally, a couple weeks in, I just told the guys when we were playing video games."

"And?"

A small smile tugs at my lips as I remember that night. "Chance said *Cool, and we can talk about that if you want, but I'd really like to beat our roommates in* Madden *first."*

"And did you? Beat them?"

I chuckle as we near my room. "We did. Easier to focus after I got that off my chest. Then Chance asked me more questions. He was engaged then. He's married now to Natasha, but he's been a relationship guy for as long as I've known him. So, he was easy to talk to. Wanted to know if there was someone I was involved with. I said yes. Then he went all Sherlock Holmes and said, 'that must be why you're always talking on the phone at night.'"

"Were you?"

"Yeah. The guy I was seeing at the time was . . . chatty."

"And you're not?"

Laughing, I scratch my jaw. "I guess I'm chatty this second. But no, not usually. And I'm more of a texter, anyway."

"And what about the rest of the team? Did you say something to them?"

"The next day, I said something at practice. It was not my finest moment." I grimace. I'd worked like hell, learning to speak smoothly in front of a crowd, and I wish I'd handled that better. Less . . . chip-on-my-shoulder-y. "I said, 'this doesn't mean I'm checking you out in the locker room.'"

Grant feigns shock. "What? You're not staring at every other guy around you? You don't want to bang everything with a dick? C'mon. If you like dudes, you must like *every* dude, right?"

I smile, digging his sense of humor. "That's the gist of it. So, I asked if they wanted to bang every woman they saw."

"That made it clear, I hope."

I snort. "Not entirely. A couple of guys were like, I'm up for pretty much any chick who wants to sleep with me."

Grant cracks up. "Men. We're pigs, right?"

"Total fucking pigs," I add.

"Did your boyfriend come to games?"

Unfortunately, he did, even after I told him we needed to cut back, that I had to focus on the sport. Kyle would hang around after the last pitch, waiting for me in the parking lot. When I explained I needed space so I could play the game, he went out and got a press pass and used that to get into the locker room after a game.

I shake away the unpleasant memories and tell Grant, "He showed up at *too* many games."

The rookie winces. "Ouch."

"Yeah. Ouch, indeed." I pause, weighing what I'm about to say, and who I'm really telling. It's for me more than him, but I think he'll listen. He seems to notice a lot, to take everything in.

"I'll give you one piece of unsolicited advice," I say solemnly. "Don't get involved with a soul your rookie year. You do not need distractions in your first pro season. It's a make-it-or-break-it time."

He gives an *I've got you* grin, clearly on board. "I couldn't agree more. My best friend calls me Grant 'Lock It Up' Blackwood."

I arch a brow at that. "You don't say?"

I know I need to eighty-six this convo now. By my own advice, I shouldn't give in to curiosity when something about him intrigues me. But how do I resist when everything about him is so damn intriguing?

"Only way to do it, right?" Grant says.

"Only way," I agree. We're at my door and I reach for the key card. "You know, they're going to think that we're fucking."

It's just an observation, but once those words make landfall, I can picture it, crystal clear.

Him. Me. Tangled together in the sheets. Sweat, heat, muscles, moans, grunts.

It's too damn tantalizing.

And . . . I should not have put that out there as a hypothetical.

Now the image of us fucking is playing on repeat in my head.

And it's turning me all the way on.

"Good thing we're not then," Grant says.

"Damn good thing," I echo.

I head inside, shutting the door between us and leaning against it, blowing out a deep breath.

I reach for focus and finish the poem.

And miles to go before I sleep,

Having met Grant, I'm going to have to revise Robert Frost's famous ode.

And miles to go for me to resist.

8

DECLAN

I learned my lesson from Kyle, and from the tons of men and women who came before me, pro athletes who found out the hard way—the way I did—that love and sports don't mix.

To perform at the top, at that one percent of one percent of one percent, you need to laser in on the job.

If love lures you with a whisper or a sexy smile, convinces you to give your energy to it, then more often than not, the sport loses out to temptation.

Sure, there are cases where things work out. Maybe a guy has had a girlfriend or boyfriend for years, maybe since high school even, so by the time he enters his rookie year, romance is the baseline, part of the fabric of his existence. But I suspect those happy endings happen to people who live a charmed life in the first place.

That's not my story.

It might seem like a fairy tale, especially from the outside, and I won't pretend things aren't good right now—fat salary, plum endorsements, a swank house in San Francisco.

But it wasn't always this way.

My mother worked in advertising, penning copy for commercials at an agency in Los Angeles before we eventually moved to San Francisco. She met Tyler there and opened a boutique shop for writing and recording commercial jingles.

My dad was a terrific minor leaguer once upon a time, racking up batting titles in the farm leagues. When that played out, he owned a tow truck business, and that went belly up. Last I heard he was still in the Bay Area—he moved there when I was in high school—and is now with wife number three, trying to start a new towing business with his cousin.

It was a workaday world, growing up. When I was younger, my parents did alright, but no one was getting rich, no one was paying off loans. But my dad was developing other interests—other than baseball, work, for his family. He kept them hidden for a long time, but eventually, painfully, his bad choices spilled over onto my mom, my life, and my sport. Baseball was my one true love, and memories of him showing up at my games in the worst way, over and over again, still make me cringe.

I'd give a lot to erase them, along with the crap that happened after.

To me.

It took me a long time to right the ship after it capsized, but I managed, and I vowed to never forget. To never fall back. I learned firsthand that focus is a rare and precious thing. You need to hone it, nurture it, protect it.

No one else in the whole entire world can do that for you. You can only do it for yourself.

In college, I was damn good at staying zeroed in on my goals, but man cannot live on sports alone.

I'm human. I need connection now and then. And every once in a while, I need some intimacy.

Plus, I suppose I've always been a sucker for a soft heart, and Kyle had one.

He was a friend from college, and the two of us reconnected when I played minor league ball in Bakersfield. He came to some games. We went out. Everything was . . . fun.

Then I went to spring training right as it was getting more intense with him. He was a gentle soul, a writer who wore his heart on his sleeve, poured it into his words.

And into me.

More than I expected. More than I had room for.

I tried to make room for those emotions—talking to him in the evenings after practice, trying somehow to sustain a long-distance thing.

"I miss you, babe," he'd say. "Do you miss me too?"

"Send me a text in the morning, so I know you're thinking of me."

"Can I come see some of your games? I'll catch a plane. Root for you."

Soon, my answers—"Thanks, but my schedule is crazy," or, "I was out for a run at six-thirty in the morning so I forgot to text"—weren't enough.

He wanted more. Wanted to buy a ticket to Phoenix to see me play. Wanted to go out to dinner after a game.

I was stretched thin, with little experience at balancing a boyfriend's needs with my own. I was twenty-two with a pro contract and a future I desperately needed. I didn't know how to manage his hurt. The more he needed me, the less I could give, and the more it weighed on me.

I didn't want to be *that* kind of boyfriend.

Soon enough, the late-night calls and the early-morning pleas affected my game.

There is no room for a few bad games in the Major Leagues. There's barely room for *one* when you're a rookie in spring training.

But I served up two in a row, whiffing at the plate, missing easy grounders, fumbling all over the diamond. My agent flew down from New York, took me to a steak house, lavished praise on me, the kind that warns you that it's the good news before the bad. I girded my loins, and finally, he stared me right in the eyes and said, "You need to get your shit together right now, D."

I gulped. "What do you mean?"

Vaughn raised a solitary finger. "You get one rookie season. Count it. One. It started a few weeks ago. The clock is ticking," he said, pointing to a clock on the wall in the restaurant. I swore I could hear every second, like a bomb counting down. "Whatever is bringing you down, whatever's getting in the way, you need to get rid of it. Trust me. I know exactly how fleeting this job can be." He tapped his right knee. A meniscus tear had shortened his career to three mere years in the

NFL. "I don't want to see you miss your chance," he said, softening.

I broke up with Kyle. Took him a while to get the message, but I stuck to my guns. Didn't look back. The result? I watched my stats soar, and I chose to live with no regrets.

Baseball is *it* for me now.

I don't have a fallback plan. I can't afford to let the game slide. Back in high school I made some foolish choices, self-destructive ones, during a stretch when things were the most beyond my control. But I came back from it.

Baseball has already given me a second chance, and I don't take that for granted.

That's why I gave Grant my warning.

This sport deserves my best years. Deserves his best years too.

* * *

I wake early the next morning and tug on gym shorts, so I can log a dawn run. There's a high school a few blocks away that has a great track. Hardly anyone's on it at six-thirty, so I can get lost in the rhythm of the laps and the music in my ears. With the Arizona sun opening its eyes above the horizon, I crank up the tunes, blasting a mix of Pearl Jam and Nirvana, Soundgarden and Alice in Chains.

Old habits die hard. I grew up with these bands as a teenager, courtesy of my mom blasting Pearl Jam tunes in the house.

As *Black* reverberates, I make out another noise coming from behind. The unmistakable sound of sneakers on dirt. One glance and my skin heats in seconds.

It's not from the sun. It's from the rookie.

AirPods in, he flashes a grin my way.

On the one hand, I wish he weren't here.

On the other, I don't object to the view.

I pull out an AirPod as I keep running. "Didn't peg you for a stalker," I tease.

"I didn't peg you for a Type A, neurotic, early-morning, obsessed-with-performance, extra-exercise runner," he says.

The plethora of words tumbling from his lips makes me laugh. "Really? That was hard to figure out?"

"Maybe because you make it all look so easy."

"I do my best to maintain the illusion. But the way I see it, you've got to put the extra time in. Stay on top of the game."

"Only way to do it. I guess you found this spot too," he says, glancing around.

"Year or two ago. School doesn't start here till eight, so I get the track all to myself most mornings."

"Except today," he says. "Also, for the record, I'd like to say I was here first."

I arch a brow as we round the top of the track. "And how do you figure, rookie?"

"I've been running here the last five mornings. This is the first time I've seen you."

I laugh, tossing my head back. "Because I *just* showed up at spring training."

"Even so. I've got squatter's rights."

"So, you're claiming the entire field. No one else can use it but you?"

"Just staking my claim, if it comes down to it."

"Ah." I stroke my chin as we head along the straightaway, sneakers pounding the track. "You think there might be a scuffle?"

His dark blue eyes twinkle, full of all sorts of mischief. "Maybe. Scuffles can be fun."

I walked right into that one. Now I'm picturing a hot, sweaty scuffle with him after this run. Oh, yes. I'd scuffle with him. Except that's a terrible idea.

I'm quiet for a beat.

Grant shifts gears for us. "What's that you're listening to?"

Music. Playlists. This is safe to talk about. Much safer than scuffles.

I slide into the new topic like I'm stealing second. "Pearl Jam. Ever heard of them?"

He adopts a confused expression. "Gee. I have no idea who they are."

I roll my eyes. "Then I won't tell you Nirvana is on here too."

"Dude, are you from our generation or are you time traveling from another one?"

I jerk my head back. "Well, someone is a smart aleck when he's not handing over his phone."

"Evidently," he says with a laugh, a warm, bright sound, and I want to make him laugh again. It's an infectious noise, and I just dig it.

"Funny, how everything changes when you're not covered in ketchup," I say.

"But weren't you wielding the whipped cream, Deck?" he tosses back. "That's what you were covering me in."

Those words—*covering me in*—conjure up

entirely different ways I could cover him.

Cover him with my body.

Cover him with my hands.

I look away.

"Cat got your tongue?" he asks.

I can't let him win this battle of words and wills. I turn my gaze to him as we run. "No. I'm just thinking of . . . other uses for tongues."

It's too much fun to watch his reaction. To see his handsome face flush with a hint of embarrassment and a touch of something strangely like innocence in his blue eyes.

At last, Grant answers. "That is a nice thing to think about."

His voice is raspy, and he stumbles a little on his words.

The stumble is all kinds of sexy on him.

Fifteen minutes into our run, I'm discovering that our rising-star catcher is a delicious mix of smartass and shy, flirty and a bit awkward.

He's too adorable *and* too hot for words.

Time, once again, to steer the conversation toward safer shores. "I'm guessing you're not listening to 'Smells Like Teen Spirit,' so what have you got on your playlist?"

He rolls with the rerouted topic. "Britney Spears."

I arch a brow. "For real?"

"What?" He feigns surprise. "I don't look like a Britney fan?"

"I'm not going to touch that one."

"Fine. I was listening to Lady Gaga."

I call bullshit on that too. "Really?"

"Don't be a hater. Gaga is awesome. I love her

like crazy."

I groan, rolling my eyes. "Not my favorite, but I'm not a hater. Not of music. Not of anything."

"That's a good philosophy." He looks ahead, rearranges his expression to a more serious one. "And I was listening to Cher, if you must know."

I crack up, a big belly laugh. "Are you running through a list of gay icons?"

"It's a test to see if you pass."

I laugh harder. "Oh man, I don't think that's the best test."

He snaps his fingers, points at me. "You're right. There are much better tests. More fun ones." His eyes glint, and, holy hell, I am in for a world of trouble with him. The flirt is strong in this one. "Don't you worry, rookie. I'll pass with flying colors."

"Good to know," he mutters, then rakes his hand through his thick hair, which flops back on his forehead, all perfectly disheveled.

I nod toward his AirPods. "So, for real, what are you listening to?"

"Nothing . . . at the moment."

I roll my eyes. "What *were* you listening to on that secret playlist?"

He sighs heavily. "I'm listening to a book."

"Did you think I would laugh?" I hold my arms out wide. "I'm not. See?"

"True. You're not. I guess I'll tell you what book, then."

I wiggle my fingers. "Fess up."

He looks straight ahead. "The Major League Baseball rule book."

I gaze heavenward. "Why am I even asking you

questions?"

"Because I'm the most interesting workout buddy you've had in a long time," he says with a confident grin.

We round the corner, our breaths coming fast, T-shirts getting sweaty, and I shoot him a glance. "I think that's fair to say."

He is, and I'm having far too much fun, so I reach for the bottom of my T-shirt, whip it off, and toss it to the ground.

Grant blinks. He lets out a noise that sounds like *ungh,* then looks away, blows out a long stream of air.

"I'm listening to, um, a political thriller," he says, delightfully awkward again.

"Does it have a title?"

His eyes drift down to my chest, before he rattles off the name of what sounds like a James Patterson book.

"Sounds fascinating. A real page-turner. Bet you can't put it down."

His eyes stay locked on me, roaming over my abs.

I shouldn't savor his reaction so much.

But I do.

So far this morning, he's been winning the Flirt Game, but this round goes to the shortstop.

"Some things are hard to look away from," I say.

"I'll say," he murmurs.

He stares shamelessly.

Hungrily.

Making this my best morning workout in ages —and also my hardest.

9

DECLAN

The next morning, I stroll onto the track as the sun peeks over the horizon, pale pink streaks of dawn reaching across the sky. Grant is already there, stretching on the grass.

Good morning to me.

He's bent over at the waist, feet planted wide apart as he twists to the right. Then he switches, twisting to the left.

He rises, shoves a hand through his thick hair, making it all messy.

Messier, I should say.

Mmm.

I'd like to mess it up.

I've never had a type when it comes to men, but I might now, and that type is six foot four and built from pure muscle. Guess I do like a rock-hard body. And athletes are just hot.

"Hey, man," I say as I make for the track.

"Good morning," he says, joining me. I break

into a loose-limbed jog and Grant falls in alongside me.

"Oh yes, it is definitely good," I say, not bothering to strip the flirt from my voice.

"I take it you enjoyed the view. Is that what makes it good?"

"I take it to mean all that preening you did was on purpose?"

"What? Me? You think I'd retaliate because you whipped off your shirt yesterday?"

"I do think you'd do that, because you did do that."

He shrugs, wicked enjoyment on his handsome face. "Payback's a bitch, isn't it, Deck?"

I grin, enjoying the shortened name, the way he dishes out as well as he takes it. "Funny, but right now, I don't have any problems with payback. Not at all."

He laughs, his dark blond hair catching the sunlight, strands of it looking golden. His laugh fades, quickly, though, his voice dipping to a more serious note. He gestures to the gate in the fence around the field. "Did you know there's a path over there that runs along the edge of the woods by the golf course?"

"Arizona has woods? This is news to me."

"Who's the wiseass now?" Grant shoots back.

"Like I said, payback. In any case, are you trying to lure me into the woods?"

He shakes his head, rejecting the idea vehemently. "No. No. No."

I ease up, taking pity on his nerves. "I'm just messing with you, rookie." Nodding toward the gate, I say, "Let's hit it."

"Yeah?" His tone pitches up.

"Yeah." I arch a brow as we peel away from the track. "Are you still nervous around me?"

He pushes out a worried laugh. "No. I don't know. Sometimes. I just don't want you to think that I'm . . ."

"A gigantic flirt?" I supply.

Grant winces. "Yeah. That."

That tugs on the part of me that can't resist a soft heart. "We're good. It's all fun and games, right?"

His answer is instant. "Of course. And I didn't want you to think I was disrespectful when I was, um, stretching."

Yeah, this guy is such a mix of cocky and caring. The most *enticing* mix. "Nothing to worry about. We can shoot the shit and it's cool, and you can stretch and show off your hot body and that's cool too, since nothing is going to happen."

"Right," he says, with a crisp nod like he can't acknowledge the compliment. Maybe I shouldn't have given it to him.

"That was an impartial observation—the hot body remark," I say, easing up. "Purely hypothetical."

He looks my way. "My stretching was hypothetical too."

"There you go again, wiseass."

"Just following your lead. Since, you know, nothing is going to happen."

I groan. Talking about not hooking up still makes me think about hooking up, so I sidestep the topic. "How was your time in Bakersfield?"

"Short but intense," he answers, following the

shift. "Way more intense than I thought it'd be. Know what I mean?"

"I do," I say as we keep up a good clip.

"I knew it was my shot. I had to make it count. Was yours the same?"

"Definitely. Feeling the spotlight. Knowing you're the top prospect. Wanting to prove your worth to the team."

"And keeping distractions minimal. Better yet, non-existent," he adds as the running path dips behind a hill, passing under canopies of trees.

"Couldn't agree more. Learned that rule by breaking it."

Grant tilts his head, his eyes curious. "A guy in every port?"

I shake my head, dismissing that notion. Normally I don't care if a guy thinks I'm a player. For some reason, I don't want Grant to think that whatsoever. "No. That's when I started dating my boyfriend."

"Was he a ballplayer too?"

I snort. "God, no."

Even as he runs, Grant seems to tense at that answer. But I don't need to sugarcoat the risks of dating someone in the same sport. "Getting involved with a ballplayer would be a mistake."

"Of course."

"Anyway, with Kyle, I managed minor league ball fine when we were dating, maybe because he lived close by. It was casual and all. But when it turned more serious, and it was time for spring training, the distraction became too much. I wasn't very good at keeping things light and uncomplicated."

"Are you better at it now?"

I scratch my jaw, but there's not much to consider. "When I get involved, it's not usually for very long, and mostly just during the off-season." I've learned I need limits, even if they're self-imposed. Given the way my parents' marriage imploded with the force of an F5 tornado, I'm best off keeping relationships on a tight leash. "It's just easier that way. Cleaner."

"Less complications and less distractions," Grant agrees.

"That's why I had to end things with Kyle. It was messing with my head," I say. "Worse, it was messing with my game."

I'm saying it for him.

And, even more so, for me. Because as we run and talk about the minors, I need the reminder.

I can enjoy these mornings with Grant as a workout.

And that's the limit.

* * *

The week unfolds like that—extra workouts in the morning as the sun rises then team time after nine.

Drills, exercises, sprints.

Batting practice and field work, then extra time practicing the new rules for sliding into home, meant to reduce punishing collisions at the plate.

I stay in touch with my friends and family—texting baseball updates to Mom and Tyler, trash talking Fitz, and enjoying Emma's funny observations after moving to New York City. (*So much scaffolding! How can there be this many dry cleaners? I am in diner heaven!*)

My favorite text conversation comes from Emma and Fitz in a group chat.

Fitz: I've got a game against Phoenix in March. Want tix?

Declan: Hell, yeah. So long as it doesn't conflict with a spring training game.

He sends the date, and I check my schedule. The timing lines up.

Declan: Center ice, baby. I want center ice.

Fitz: And I want first baseline when you play the NY Comets. Do we have a deal?

Emma: Hello? I'm still here! And I want to go to Phoenix too!

Fitz: Say the word and I'll fly you in, Ems.

Emma: Word.

As I close the thread with *Can't wait to see you,* I smile, glad they'll be in town.

Yes, life is good.

Ticking along.

I'm One-Track Steele—friends, family, baseball.

The one glaring exception? How much I look forward to morning workouts with Grant. How they're becoming the best part of each day for the next week.

Saturday morning, it's a game day, and once more I find Grant on the track, ready to hit the golf course path as the sun rises.

We didn't discuss switching to the golf course. It doesn't take a degree in rocket science to figure out why we gravitated that way.

It's more private, with more shade and less chance of being seen. Even if I didn't find him wildly, insanely attractive, I'm hanging out with the other queer dude on the team. Rumors would fly, and there is no need to fan 'em.

"Have you always been an early-morning-extra-workout person?" I ask.

"Definitely. Gotta stay a step or ten ahead, you know?"

Do I ever. "Work harder and better," I say with a nod.

There's an understanding with Grant that I've only ever had with Fitz—the awareness that we *have* to work harder, have to constantly prove we belong.

Sports has changed so much over the last ten years, thanks to a guy named Sandy Hildebrand who bought the Dallas football team, making headlines then as the first openly gay team owner. Soon, he banded together with other queer business leaders and spoke up about wanting queer athletes to have the same sponsorship opportunities, respect, and chances as straight players. Soon more athletes came out—in high school, college, and the pros.

Still, I feel the pressure of what it means to be part of that change. Of being lucky to be on *this* side of it.

"It's a good pressure though," I say to Grant.

"Same. Reminds me of *Apollo 13*. The movie," he adds.

I jerk my head back in surprise. "Wait a hot second. Are you referencing a movie from the *nineties*? And you said I was from another generation."

"I am a study in contradictions," he says. "It makes me all kinds of fascinating."

"It sure does," I mutter under my breath as we near a small lake along the edge of the course.

"And the flick is from 1995. I've seen it about twenty times because it's my grandfather's favorite movie. There's this line early on when Tom Hanks and Gary Sinise are running a sequence for the moon landing, and Sinise wants to run it again. At first there's some resistance, but then Tom Hanks says, 'Well, let's get it right.'"

"And that stayed with you? 'Well, let's get it right'?" It says a lot about him—about his work ethic, which matches mine.

"It applies to a lot of things. Doesn't matter how much you practice or how many hours you've put in. The goal isn't to check off time on a box.

The end game is doing it till you get it right." He shrugs, but I know what he's saying is important to him. "That's why the early morning workouts. Not to log hours or reps or miles, but to win games."

I nod along. I see it that way too, but I like how he's said it. "Words to live by."

"Movies have some good ones now and then," he says.

For a flash of a second, I imagine watching a flick with him, then turning it off because I'm overwhelmed by the way he smells and how much I want to lick the column of his throat, drag my lips over his jaw, rub my face against his stubble.

God help me.

A caw rends the air—we both jerk our gazes to the edge of the lake as a heron swoops down, joining another one. The male snaps his bill then stretches his neck.

"Ah, the mating call of the heron," I remark. Maybe it should be "Heron help me," because the break in tension has saved me.

"How do you know they're mating?" Grant asks. "They aren't banging. Also, how *do* birds bang?"

This, I can talk about easily. "He's preening for her. Soon he'll bring her twigs. They might even exchange them."

"Ah, the twig exchange. Of course." Grant shoots me an amused smile. "And my other question, Mr. Ornithologist?"

"The how-do-they-bang one?"

"Yes."

"Well, Grant," I sing-song, "when a male bird loves a female bird very much..."

"Enjoy *this* bird," he says, flipping me the middle finger.

We keep that up, running and shooting the shit, and before I know it, I've peeled off an hour. Grant makes these morning workouts something they've never been before—fun.

But are they *too* fun?

I'm here to work, after all, not to get to know this fascinating man.

Should I end them?

Cut them off?

But they have a natural end every damn day, when we join the team for practice. Once we hit the diamond, we're catcher and shortstop again, and that's working out just fine.

That day, the Seattle Storm Chasers arrive for a home game, and we destroy them.

That's all that matters.

Friendship with Grant isn't a detrimental distraction.

These morning workouts aren't hindering my game.

The problem is lying in bed at night, thinking about how badly I want morning to come.

10

GRANT

Like that, we've become workout partners.

Early birds and all.

It's not deliberate. It just happens. We run. We lift weights. We spot each other. One morning, I'm on the bench press and he asks where I'm from. Funny that this hasn't come up in our many conversations.

"I grew up in Petaluma. It's not too far from San Francisco," I say, pushing up the weight bar.

He gives a slow and easy smile. "I know where Petaluma is."

"Didn't mean to imply you didn't know your geography as well as your ornithology," I tease, lowering the bar then pressing it up again. He stares down at me, his eyes roaming over my chest but never straying too far.

"I know my geography just fine. I also live in San Francisco," he points out.

"Yeah, but that doesn't mean you venture to Petaluma."

"I've been there on the way to wine country," he says.

Out of nowhere, envy thrashes in my chest, painful as a cleat in the ribs. This is what happens when you become friends with your crush. I know why he's been to wine country. He once dated a guy who lives there, a chef. I picture him cruising up the highway, laughing with some other guy in the passenger seat, free and easy. He's headed for a weekend getaway. A weekend he could spend with that guy because they weren't teammates.

"Must have been nice. Going to wine country." I push up the bar, doing my damnedest to shove away this dumb jealousy too. "You from there?"

"No. I grew up in Los Angeles, but we moved to San Francisco when I was in middle school."

"You and your family?"

His jaw tightens. "My mom and me."

That's all he says, and I let it go. There's more there, but now's not the time to mine that territory.

Instead, I ask, "You and she are close?"

"Definitely. Me and my stepdad too." He answers, but his tone is clipped. I should change topics, but he does that himself. "Kind of crazy to wind up being drafted to your hometown team."

"Maybe it was meant to be," I say.

"You're someone who believes that?" Declan sounds doubtful. "That things are meant to be?"

"I believe in hard work. But yeah, I think sometimes things are meant to be. I take it you don't?"

He shakes his head. "Nope. Not one bit."

The shadows in his eyes go even darker, and if we weren't treading on dangerous ground, I'd ask what he meant. But I know it's for the best to nip this convo in the bud.

I set the bar down on the holder then sit up, my chest heaving. I'm about to stand when I catch him staring shamelessly at me. My pecs, my abs, my arms. My piercing...

"Like the view?" I ask. I can't resist danger sometimes.

Without a reply, he tips his forehead to the bench, a sign for me to skedaddle. Hoping I haven't pissed him off, I stand quickly, making room for him as he settles in. "You know I do," he mutters, and a bolt of lust slams into me.

We've tangoed, and we've toyed. But that's the first admission that he feels these sparks. This heat. This fire that's blazing between us. It's the first time we've outright fanned the flames.

I throw kerosene on them too. "Look at us... switching positions."

Declan stares up at me, hunger in his eyes. "Is that a metaphor or a challenge?" His voice is husky.

And holy fuck, I am treading on uncertain ground. I've got to be careful. But holding back would be like letting a fastball down the middle pass you by. You have to swing.

"Maybe both," I say as he pushes up the bar.

With a huff, he shakes his head.

Is he annoyed?

Shit. I do need to behave.

"Sorry," I add hastily. "I'll rein it in."

Declan lowers the bar. "Rookie, we are both guilty."

The way he says that—*rookie*—sends sparks down my spine.

"Very, very guilty," I add, and inside, I'm beaming.

I shouldn't be, but I am.

Another lift, another press, another sexy glance. He doesn't talk, just grunts as he lifts in the early-morning quiet of the hotel gym.

When he finishes his reps, he racks the bar and wipes a hand across his forehead but doesn't sit up.

Instead, he picks up the thread of the conversation. "You know how hot you are," he whispers.

"Why would I know that?" I ask, fishing shamelessly for compliments.

He cranes his neck, taking a backward glance at my body. "You've got eyes. You look in the mirror. You know what you see. You know what I see."

Electricity crackles and pops as I croak out, "What do you see?"

He sits, cocks his head, strokes his jaw. His dark gaze cranks my thermostat to furnace hot. "*Danger.* I see danger."

That one word contains multitudes—in it, I hear him saying he wants danger, he craves danger.

But he won't let himself have it.

I want it too, and I'm pretty sure I'm more reckless than Declan. The man seems so in control, and I feel wildly *out* of control with him. But it's a feeling I crave more and more each day, even though I know the stakes. I'm well aware of the risks. We are as taboo as we can be.

I'm not flirting with some guy I won't have to see at work. He's someone I have to work closely with every single game, every single day on the field.

But the field is where I need perfect concentration. A millisecond mistake can cost a game. If my mind wanders to the guy manning shortstop, can I call the right pitch at a critical moment in a game?

No idea.

Trouble is, when I'm near Declan, my body lights up. My skin tingles, and everything inside me spins faster and faster. He's like adrenaline, and I want another hit, then another.

I set a hand on the weight bar, not too far from his. "Our job is dangerous. Standing at the plate every day as someone throws a ninety-five-mile-an-hour ball at you is pretty risky," I counter.

A sliver of a smile tugs at his lips. "Yep. And so is flirting with you."

"You could stop," I offer. I want him to know I'm not going to pressure him. I'm chill with being buds. "Or you could just acknowledge we enjoy some harmless flirting. That's all it is, right?"

Those full lips curve into a grin. His eyes sparkle. He seems to weigh my question in his hand then decide he likes it. "That's all it is, rookie. Harmless flirting."

I hope he's lying, like I am.

When we've finished our workout, he drops a hand on my shoulder like he did the first day we met. No one is around. He curls it tighter, clasping me. I nearly die of pleasure—his touch drives me insane with longing. I want those hands on me, grabbing me everywhere, reckless and crazed.

He squeezes, and that's it. I am gone.

"Tomorrow, I won't flirt with you," he says as we leave the gym, and it sounds like a solemn swear.

One I hope he'll break.

* * *

That night, I call Reese. She answers on the third ring. "I'm studying for a Spanish test, so this better be good," she says.

I play my ace. "It's the report you want. And my report is . . . you were dead wrong."

She's silent for a few seconds. "About what?"

"You said that my crush would go away when I met him in person."

She laughs. "I am pretty sure *you* said that, not me."

"Whoever said it was a dipshit," I say, pacing my room. "Everything about him is intense. He's also sarcastic, and interesting, and smart. And he notices things. And he's the biggest flirt I've ever met."

"So, this *is* a two-way street."

I drag a hand down my face, nodding even though she can't see me. I'm not the most experienced guy. I don't have gobs of sex intel to draw on. But I know a hell of a lot about one thing—trusting your instinct. Everything is instinct with Declan.

"It's not a one-way street at all, Reese. It's like an electrical charge runs between us, and it's frying my circuits."

"But, Grant, are you going to do something

about it?" Her question is an icy-cold shower. It's bracing, and it knocks me out of the haze I'm in.

Ice—we need to keep this thing on ice.

I sink down on the couch, push my head back against the cushion, and heave a long sigh. "I'm not going to do anything. That'd just be dumb. So, I'll do nothing."

It's gut-wrenchingly painful to say.

"But do you want to do nothing?" she asks tentatively.

"Girl, I want to do *everything* with him. Everything I've never done."

She hums thoughtfully. "You need to be careful."

"I'm not going to do anything," I snap, and it sounds like I'm lashing out at her. "Shit, sorry. I didn't mean to take it out on you."

"That's what I'm here for." She takes a beat. "You really like him?"

I shake my head adamantly. "It's fine. I can handle it. Because I'm Grant 'Lock It Up' Blackwood."

She laughs softly. "Are you, though?"

"Fuck, yeah. I've got this. I've done it for years. No one is better at this than I am," I say, full of a bravado I don't entirely feel.

But maybe I need to fake it.

We end the call, and I catch up with some of the other rookies. We hang in Sullivan's room on the second floor, chowing on pizza in between Xbox sessions. Like we did in the minors when Sullivan and I were roomies and Miguel would hang at our place.

Sullivan bests Miguel and me in a ruthless

game on the virtual court, brutal enough to take my mind entirely off that other guy.

After another thrashing, Sullivan sets down the controller. Hip hop blasts from his phone. "Dude, how much better is this suite than our shitty little apartment in Bakersfield?" He's always had a kind of casual cool that makes him easy to hang with. "We've got our Xbox, and pizza and our music..."

"The only thing that would make this better would be a couple of babes," Miguel says. "And you can wingman us like you did in Triple A."

"Gee, thanks," I say.

"With your face and my charm, it's a one-two punch reeling them in," Sullivan says.

I crack up. "You *wish* you reeled 'em in."

"I do have a good face, though. Admit it. Spitting image of Ryan Reynolds," Sullivan says, setting a hand on his cheek and batting his eyelashes.

I snort. "Hate to break it to you... you're more like Ryan Reynolds in your dreams. IRL, maybe his second cousin or something."

Miguel guffaws. "So, if he's Deadpool, can I be Michael Peña?"

I shake my head. "Go for Rafael Silva as a comp. He's much hotter. And if you don't believe me, check out *9-1-1: Lone Star*."

Grabbing his phone, Miguel googles the actor then nods approvingly. "Yes! I will take that comp, thank you very much. I will add it to my Tinder profile. How about you, Grant? You cruising for a spring-training hookup?"

Yes, with our shortstop.

"Nah. No time for that. Baseball is what I'm all

about," I say, underlining that in my head, putting it on a Post-it, and sticking it on my mental fridge.

"True. That's why hookups—and only hookups—are the way to go," Sullivan says. "We need to be all about baseball."

"I couldn't agree more," I say.

I wiggle the controller, asking if they want one more round. We go at it, and this time, I win. On that high note, I yawn and tell the guys I'm hitting the sack.

"Catch you in the a.m.," I say on my way out.

I make my way to the elevator. With another yawn, I push the call button, and when the doors open, I startle briefly. The skipper's in the lift, holding a carton of what looks like Thai food. He gives me a crisp nod. "Hey there, Blackwood."

"Hello, sir."

"How are you enjoying spring training?" he asks as I step inside.

"It's great, sir," I say.

"You're playing well," he says.

I have no choice but to smile. "Thank you. And is that mango in there?"

"Mango sticky rice. The Thai place down the street has it. I get it every night. Reminds me of this spot I used to go to when I played in the farm leagues." He tilts his head, smiles a little. "That was probably before you were born."

I laugh—he's not wrong. Our manager played in the majors for fifteen years as a hard-hitting outfielder before becoming one of the best damn coaches ever, with a killer post-season record. He reminds me of Dusty Baker, in looks and in attitude, and he's the calm rudder we need and want.

"I imagine it was," I say.

"And now this mango sticky rice is my spring training vice. I suppose I'm allowed that at my age," he says drily.

"I'd say you've earned it, sir."

"Mrs. Fisher would have me cut back, but that's why I indulge when I'm away." He brings his finger to his lips. "Shh. Don't tell her."

"Your secret is safe with me, sir," I say as the elevator reaches the sixth floor and I step out.

I take a deep breath as soon as the door to my room shuts behind me.

That was fun with the guys.

I needed it too. It took my mind off other matters, and now sleep will do the rest.

I hit the shower, which always helps me crash. I crank the temperature to high, and it heats me everywhere.

Or maybe my thoughts do that—they return to Declan in a heartbeat. All that time with my buds did nothing to squash this desire.

Not a damn thing.

* * *

A few days later, Declan and I are running along the golf course again, debating a vital topic.

"Pierce Brosnan is underrated," Declan insists.

I scoff. "You're seriously telling me he was the best Bond?"

"I'm saying he doesn't get his due."

"Two words. Daniel Craig."

"I'm not denying that Daniel Craig does a fine job."

I snort. "A fine job? Daniel Craig *is* Bond. There is no question about it."

Declan shrugs easily. "The best Bond debate is not a one or the other for me. You're a one-Bond man? Only loyal to Craig?"

"I'm saying that once you've seen Daniel Craig, you can't go back."

"Nah. I'm all for Brosnan. That's my vote."

"I would say you've got a thing for Brits, but they're all Brit," I say with a laugh.

"I don't have a thing for Brits. Do you?" He sounds more serious than I did, like he truly wants to know my preferences.

I wiggle a brow, fucking with him. "I don't mind the blokes," I say in a terrible British accent.

He cracks up. "That was awful."

"Rubbish. It was rubbish."

"That too, mate," he says in a decent Aussie accent.

"Down under, are you there?" I ask, sliding into an Australian voice and botching it terrifically.

"Wow. You really suck at accents," Declan says.

My big mouth gets the better of me. I don't even think twice.

"I do, but there are lots of other things I don't suck at."

With a slow turn of his head, he locks eyes with me, his deep voice all kinds of raspy. "Such as?"

In for a penny, in for a pound. "Sucking."

On that note, I do my best to leave him in the dust. But he catches up with me. "I thought we weren't going to flirt," he says.

"Is it flirting if you're telling the truth?"

"You are too dangerous, rookie. Far too dangerous."

Maybe I want danger.

"You like danger," I counter, feeling bold.

Declan laughs once, his lips curving up in a grin. "Seems I do."

* * *

The next day, I level-up the Bond conversation. I want to see what will happen if we get personal about our preferences. So, I pull out that reliable but inappropriate icebreaker, "Which *out* celebrities would you sleep with?"

In the gym at the complex, we name them as we lift. It's a roster of a lot of the usual suspects. For athletes, there's former soccer star Robbie Rogers and retired hockey player Brock McGillis, and circling around to actors, we agree on Cheyenne Jackson for sure, and call Matt Bomer at the same time.

We knock fists between reps.

"I would not kick him out of bed for eating crackers," I say. "I'd also kiss him in the morning, and I hate morning breath."

Declan laughs. "Same here. Also, there's just something super-hot about men who know who they are and aren't afraid to be themselves."

Yes, indeed, there is something super-hot about that.

When the workout ends and we're heading toward the locker room, I stop tangoing with danger.

I roll the dice and tell Declan, "Wait, there's one more."

"Who's that?"

I've never felt anything like this spark, this sizzle. It's impossible to turn off when all I want to do is let him turn me on. I feel everything I've ever wanted to feel as a man. *With* a man.

This kind of attraction.

This kind of desire.

I am in its clutches and it can have me, so I say, "There's you."

Turning on my heel, I head into the locker room, buzzed, and I haven't touched a drop of anything.

With my every cell humming, I put on my baseball uniform then go out to the field with the team and stretch. The skipper tells me I'm starting the game today, and our backup catcher, Rodriguez, might come in for the fifth. I thank him, privately hoping his plan keeps me on track to win the starting slot.

After we stretch, we pile onto the team bus for a game thirty minutes away. I sit next to Crosby and chat with him, doing my best to avoid Declan's hot stare.

At the moment I told him, it seemed like a good idea. But right now? Hell, I might have fucked up our friendship.

Feels like a gut punch, and I ask myself if I've fucked up this team too.

Why the hell did I throw that down?

Because I can't handle this much lust?

Like hell I can't.

I put everything else aside, spend the rest of

the ride getting into the zone, blocking out everything else.

I call a flawless game, and I play even better at the plate, clobbering in a three-run homer that puts us in the lead.

I breathe a small sigh of relief.

Maybe I haven't crossed the line.

But there's no time to dwell on it—in the bottom of the eighth, we nearly choke up the lead when Sullivan struggles on the mound.

I've got a hunch about why he's so nervous. I overheard the pitching coach saying that Sullivan was on the bubble for the final roster. His throwing tonight says he's feeling the pressure. He's all over the place, and I've been lunging for wild pitches left and right.

Pushing up my mask, I trot out to the mound and clap a hand on his shoulder. "You got this, Sullivan. Take a breath, block out all the crap, and put that curveball in my glove. That is all you have to do. Nothing else matters."

He huffs out hard. "Thanks, man."

The next pitch is a wicked curve that the batter misses.

Sullivan walks off the mound, not unscathed. But at least we're still in the lead. He catches up to me and taps his glove to mine. "I needed that. Appreciate it."

That's the type of advice my grandpa always gave to me when I was struggling, so I'm happy to pass on the wisdom to a friend. "Anytime."

Chance comes on at the bottom of the ninth to close it out, sealing up a win. We high-five, but when I make my way to the dugout, I look for

Sullivan. "You want to toss the ball when we're back?"

His eyes light up. "You'd do that?"

I furrow my brow. "Did you think I wouldn't?"

He exhales all those nerves in a frustrated sigh. "My head's a mess. That wasn't surprise, that was gratitude, because I'm glad for your help."

* * *

Sullivan and I meet later on the backfield at the Cougars complex, throwing pitches until he feels the mojo again. It's just the two of us, and when we wrap up, we knock fists over a good session.

"You're the man," he says, more relaxed and confident. "Any chance we can meet again in the morning before the first workout?"

"Of course," I say, hiding my disappointment at missing my time with Declan. But then, I have no idea whether he's going to be up for it after this morning.

We head to the locker room, and Sullivan showers lickety-split.

I take my time, letting the water beat down on my head and neck, letting it soothe the aches from the game.

When I turn it off, the locker room has that empty feel.

Can't say I mind it, though.

Wrapping a towel around my waist, I grab another one, drying off my hair before I toss it in the towel bin then turn toward my locker.

Someone's waiting there for me.

"We need to talk."

11

GRANT

I do love a hot pair of wheels, so I tell Declan as much when I slide into the BMW that waits for us outside the complex.

"Sweet ride," I remark, trying to keep my voice steady as I compliment his rental. I slide into the passenger seat, buckling the seatbelt, clicking it in. "I'm going to get one of these someday. You're happy with it?"

I'm spitting out words, any words, because I have no idea what he wants to talk about, but it can't be good.

I glance out the window at the empty parking lot. It's just us.

Even so, there's nothing technically risqué about me heading out with one of my teammates.

"Yeah. It's fine," he bites out.

The crispness in his delivery makes me wince.

Shit. I'm talking too much to cover my nerves.

A whole squadron of them.

But what else would I feel? The man has demanded to talk to me.

And I doubt it's to tell me my comment from earlier was cool or that it rolled off him like water off a duck's back. More likely it's to say, *Stop coming on to me, rookie.*

My brain races through other scenarios just in case I'm reading him wrong.

He can't want to talk about the way I throw to second base.

He likely doesn't need an intro to my agent.

No, there's only one thing he could want to discuss—putting an end to the *I want to sleep with you* talk.

I put on an "everything's fine" face like it's armor.

I did it for years when I was younger—when my parents fought, when they hurled vitriol at each other in front of me, when they went to their room and fucked it out.

Nothing to see here, folks.

Move along.

We are all fine here.

Only this time, there's no escape to Grandma and Grandpa's house or to Reese's home. There is no hiding in the backyard to take imaginary swings with my imaginary bat.

Instead, I am here, next to someone who actually wants to have a conversation.

I'm not used to people wanting to talk.

Declan cruises away from the complex onto the road that shoots us past the hotel.

"I take it we're not going to the suites?" I ask, though, if we were, he wouldn't need his car.

He shakes his head.

"Where are we going?"

He breathes out hard through his nostrils. "Someplace our teammates won't be."

My stomach twists.

This talk is going to be bad.

But I started it. I've got to deal with the fallout. "I heard about a bar called The Lazy Hammock, not far from here in Scottsdale. Do you want to go there?" I looked up the place after Echo told me about her brother. Then I finish the suggestion with a key detail. "It's a gay bar."

"Sounds good," Declan mutters. "Tap it into the GPS."

I do as he asks, and the robotic lady tells us we'll arrive in ten minutes. I slide my palms along my jeans to rid them of the sweat as he drives into the Arizona evening, saguaros lining the road like sentries in the night.

I hunt for something to say, some words to fill the cavernous quiet in the car, something to replace the interminable echo of my mistake.

"So, Sullivan is doing better," I say, my voice raspy with worry.

"Good."

Declan said he's not a chatter. He is proving that tonight.

"I'm going to help him again in the morning. A little extra bullpen practice."

"Bet he'll appreciate it."

He doesn't mention what that means for our routine. Am I the only one who's going to miss not seeing each other at dawn?

I try again to engage him. "So, that was a good game tonight."

His answer is clipped. "Yep."

My throat tightens. I screwed up royally.

I push my head back against the leather headrest. Why the hell did I say that to him earlier? Why did I tell the shortstop that I wanted to sleep with him?

Oh, yeah. Because I do. Because I want it so damn badly. Because the more time I spend with him, the more the desire to kiss him, touch him, taste him escalates. This desire pounds through my blood. It scrambles my brain.

I tug on the brim of my hat, adjusting the bill.

My neck is hot, prickling with nerves, as he turns down another street.

He drives like he plays baseball. No distractions. All focus. Eyes on the road. I guess that's a good thing, but it winds up the tension inside me until I think something will snap.

After a few more minutes of uncomfortable silence, passing some office buildings, a shopping center, and a hotel, we reach the bar, and he parks then cuts the engine. As I get out, he grabs a Las Vegas Hawks ball cap from the console, and he pulls the brim low too. I doubt I'll be recognized, and I'm not sure he will either, but better safe than sorry.

We head inside, where I glance around, taking in the decor, mostly to have something to do.

It's very Arizona meets Florida. Open windows, Jack Johnson playing overhead, palm trees and cacti lining the deck. The place is casual, easygoing, and half-packed. As the host takes us to a table on the deck, we pass the bar, and I catch a glimpse of Echo's brother. He looks just like he did in the picture his sister showed me. His left arm is covered in ink.

He's chatting with a customer—smiling too.

I wish Declan would smile.

We reach the table in the corner, and the host hands us drink menus, then a bar menu. Declan thanks him, and I do the same.

Once he's gone, Declan breaks the silence at last. "How'd you hear about this place? Have you been here before?"

It's a massive relief to be able to answer him rather than ask him dead-end questions. I slide a finger along the T-shirt fabric over my right pec. "The tattoo artist who did my arrow?"

He nods, letting me know he's seen that mark on me.

"Her brother owns it. Runs it."

Declan's jaw ticks. He works the information over, then breathes out hard. "Did you date him?"

"What?" I jerk my head back. "No."

"Did you fuck him?"

What the hell? I shake my head adamantly.

Declan has no idea how far off he is. And I'm honestly not sure if I want to tell him just now or if I'll let loose that little secret at all. I don't know how he'll react, whether it'll turn him off or turn him on.

The man sighs heavily, dragging his hand down his face, over his jaw, running it through that sexy stubble I want to feel against mine. I want him to rub his chin against my cheek. To slide his thumb along my face. To touch me . . . *everywhere*.

I am a tuning fork, vibrating with need, but a red-hot desire got me into this situation. I can't keep acting on it—or voicing it.

After a pause, Declan speaks again, his voice low. "Do you see the problem?"

The tension in me twists even higher. "I honestly don't know," I say, holding my hands out wide.

He rubs his palm along the back of his neck, then his eyes laser in on mine. He holds my gaze, and electricity crackles between us—a hot, sizzling charge. He parks his elbows on the table, parts his lips.

"I'm already jealous of the possibility of you fucking someone else," he says, a plain admission that scorches me.

Declan's jealousy sets me on fire. Every square inch of me burns for him. "You are?"

"I am." His voice is smoke in the desert night. "And what you said this morning?" he prompts, like I didn't remember it perfectly.

"Yeah?" I ask, letting him lead this conversation wherever he's taking it.

"Grant," he says, his tone shifting, full of vulnerability and heat. "It's driving me absolutely crazy."

I don't move. I don't breathe. I don't say a word. A haze envelops me as anticipation builds higher and higher, wrapping me in its naked grip.

He grabs a napkin from the napkin holder, balls it up, rips it. Then he meets my eyes once again, leveling me with a stare that's more dangerous than any he's flashed my way before.

But his words are the true risk as he says, "You and me fucking would be the worst idea ever. And yet I can't get it out of my head."

My throat is dry. I can't swallow. I am an electrical wire. I want to remember those words for the rest of my life.

I want to remember this feeling forever. I've never been this aroused, this turned on.

This . . . *alive.*

Especially when I answer him with the easiest words I've ever spoken. "Same here."

12

DECLAN

Those two words—*same here.*

They echo in my skull, pushing me, prodding me.

Tension lines my body, as want wars with my better judgment.

I shouldn't talk to him like this.

Shouldn't put my cards on the table.

But Grant Blackwood is under my skin.

He's the sexiest man I've ever met, and it's not just his body, his face, or his eyes. It's . . . *him.*

Who he is. How he is.

Maybe talking this out will eject the desire from my head. Maybe acknowledging the white-hot sparks between us is all we need to move the hell on.

Put our lust through its paces. Laugh at it. Remind ourselves why giving in would be the worst idea ever.

"But you're my teammate," I say, presenting it as a logical argument. "We work together, and this wouldn't be some office fuck where we screw in the mailroom and go to separate floors. We share a locker room. We'll share a team plane. We'll share a field. TV networks carry the Cougars. Sponsors endorse us."

I grab another napkin, start shredding it.

"That's all true," he says, taking his time with each word.

"We have a manager. Fisher would not be happy if two of his guys were screwing. Not to mention, we have other teammates," I say, my jaw clenching in between words. "Crosby, Chance, Sullivan." I go around the horn and name the rest of the team to remind myself. Hell, maybe saying their names will free me from this lust as I rip this napkin to pieces. "They depend on us. All of them do."

I link the fingers on both my hands together and hold them up, demonstrating my point. "We are a bond—nine guys on a field. We *can't* give in." I implore him, my voice tight as I do everything to convince him.

But it's not Grant I'm trying to convince.

It's me.

Because the way this man looks at me, with sex in his eyes, dirty deeds on his lips, makes it nearly impossible for me to resist.

"I know we can't, Deck."

That. Right there. His boy-next-door voice. That's part of why I want him so much. I shake my head and laugh futilely. "Even that gets me going. The way you say my nickname."

A smile curves his lips. "Deck." He's all gravelly

and raspy, enjoying knowing what it does to me, and it does the trick.

"Mmm. Like I said . . ."

Grant jerks his chair closer to the table, licks the corner of his lips, and murmurs, "The way you call me rookie . . ."

My neck heats. My blood incinerates. "You like that?" I take a beat, lingering on his gorgeous face, the blue flames in his eyes flickering higher. "*Rookie?*"

He shudders, nodding. "Yeah. Makes me hard."

"Jesus . . . fuuuuck." I am broiling. "Do you get what I mean? Do you see the problem?"

"I do, Deck. I do."

A bolt of heat slides down my spine. "I'm trying to tell you all the reasons why this is a bad idea, and now all I can think about is your cock."

He shifts in his seat and swallows visibly, his Adam's apple bobbing. I want to lick it. "Pretty much all I'm aware of too," he whispers. "Safe to say all the blood in my body went straight to my dick when you said you were thinking of us fucking."

I groan.

He shudders at the sound, his lips parting, his shoulders rising and falling.

"Dear God, I am going to climb across the table right now," I warn.

"I think you know I won't stop you," Grant says.

And that is my reminder—I have to be the strong one. I have to be strong for both of us. I've got to look out for the rookie.

I let out a long exhale and lean back in my

chair, searching for something else to focus on, when the man from the bar arrives. Ink crawls down one arm, and his smile is bright.

"Can I get you two a drink?" His voice is cheery, and it helps break me out of the haze.

"Iced tea for me, please," I say.

The man shifts his gaze to my companion. "And you?"

"Diet Coke, please," Grant answers.

"Great. Can I interest you in any food? Our Sonoran sandwich is pretty darn good, if I do say so myself. The barbecue sauce is to die for."

"I'm not sure yet," I say, and the guy nods, then glances once more at Grant, his gaze snagging on the bands on Grant's biceps that look like water.

The man's smile deepens, his eyes flickering with recognition. "Oh, wait. You're Grant, aren't you? My sister mentioned you to me. I'm River. Welcome to Arizona."

"Thanks. Good to be here."

River's eyes return to Grant's arm. "I heard you were a regular at Ink Lore. My dad did that one, right?"

Grant smiles and taps his arm. "Yeah, he did the bands a couple years back. Echo did my newest one a month ago, and I love it."

"She's a rock star of tattoo artists, but she works all the time. I keep telling her to get out of the shop and get some vitamin D. *Go for a hike, Echo*! She's like a ghost, that girl," he says with a laugh.

"All that time in the chair, though, is working for her. She's super talented," Grant says. For a second, I wonder if he'll lift his shirt, show his arrow to this guy.

I grit my teeth. He better not.

The man taps his finger on the table. "Glad you could come by The Lazy Hammock."

Something snaps. "He's with me," I bark out, jealousy ravaging my insides.

With a sweet grin, the man turns to me. "No worries, hun. I'm not hitting on your guy. Not my style."

And I'm an asshole. I just snarled at the owner. It's not like he's some random dude flirting with Grant while I'm off taking a piss.

"My bad. Sorry. I just . . ." I don't even know what to say. I don't normally react like that. Hell, I *never* react like this.

"No worries. But I do understand why you'd feel possessive." The guy dips his voice to a conspiratorial whisper. "If he were mine, I'd make sure no one got near him either. Now, why don't you two let me know if you decide you want some food. I'm River, and I'm happy to help."

He leaves, and Grant smirks. "You're just a little jealous."

"I'm a prick too, it seems," I mutter.

"Yeah, but it's sexy," he says. "Your jealousy."

"Is it?"

"Very, very sexy." He nibbles on the corner of his mouth.

All the breath leaves my lungs as a hand slides onto my knee under the table, just below my shorts. He's touching my leg, and I want to pounce on him. I push my knee closer, letting him know he can touch me all he wants. He takes my invitation and spreads his fingers wider. And now I know my knee is an erogenous zone, and Grant Blackwood has claimed it as his own territory.

"If we slept together," Grant begins. "Would you want to . . .?"

I finish for him. "Fuck you?"

"Yeah."

"Yes. I would."

He nods. "You seem like you'd want to top."

But he's only half-right. "And the next night, I'd want you to fuck me."

Grant blinks in surprise, then he curls his big palm tighter, covering my knee. "You would?"

"I'm vers, rookie. All the way."

"You are?"

"One hundred percent. Best of both worlds," I say. "God made sex with a man the most pleasurable thing ever in existence, and I don't want to miss any aspect of it."

"Jesus," he says, gripping my knee tighter, clutching it.

"What about you?"

He hesitates a few seconds before he answers. "Same."

I lower my hand under the table, reaching for his, taking it in mine. Our fingers slide together, and my entire body becomes a lightning rod. We clasp fingers, and it feels like a prelude.

Like it's just the start.

That's the good news.

And that's the bad news.

Seconds later, River returns, and we let go. The owner sets down the drinks. "Here you go. Did you two decide if you want food?"

I shake my head but smile to make up for my earlier behavior. "Not yet. Promise to tell you soon, River."

As I lift my iced tea, Grant looks at the glass. "Is that because you're driving?"

"Yes, but if you're asking whether I drink, then no."

"I had a feeling."

"Why?" I ask, curious.

"You've never had a beer when we've played video games with the other guys."

"You noticed?"

He nods. "I kind of notice you," he says, a little embarrassed. He lifts his Diet Coke, takes a drink.

"You can order a beer with me. I'm cool with that. I don't expect you to make the same choices I do."

He smiles, soft at first, then full wattage. It's infectious, and it warms my soul. "I'm good, man. Also, I think kisses taste better this way."

He lifts the glass again, his blue eyes twinkling above the rim as he knocks some back.

"Who's the flirt now?" I ask.

"Both of us," he says when he puts it down.

And now I'm thinking about kissing.

How he'd taste.

How he wants me to kiss him tonight.

He's practically taunting me.

But someone has to lay down the rules. I bet Grant would strip naked for me if I asked him to. I bet he'd blow me in the car if I said the word.

It's not that he's submissive.

It's that he's eager. He's hungry. He's fucking

horny. So am I. But someone has to pump the brakes.

"Grant," I say, more serious now. "I don't think it's a good idea if this goes any further."

His face is stony at first. He swallows, a little roughly, like I've wounded him, and he needs to shake it off. Then he shrugs, shooting me that magic grin as if this decision is no big deal. "I figured you'd say that. So, does that mean we can finally order? Because I'm starving."

I crack up, laughing so damn hard. "Yes, let's get some food."

* * *

An hour later, we leave, stopping to say goodbye to River on the way out.

"Come back anytime," he says from behind the bar. Then he quiets his voice. "If you want to keep a low profile, we've got your back. Happy to do that for our guests who need it. I can make sure you get a corner table away from anyone else."

"Appreciate that." I wonder what I did to deserve this dude looking out for us. Nothing, but I'll take it.

Grant offers him a fist for knocking. "You're a good one."

River knocks back. "Anytime."

When we get to my car, I have this impulse to open the door for Grant.

That's how I like to treat my dates.

I head around to his side, behind him, reaching around his arm before he can open the door. He turns, spins, shoots me a *what the hell* look. "What are you doing?"

We're inches away. The closest we've ever been. I can smell the shower on him still. The soapy scent of his neck. His shampoo, some classic barbershop scent that's all man. The vein in his neck pulses. The heat from his chest warms mine. My brain goes haywire, but my arm stays still, my hand on the door handle. "I was going to open the door for you," I say, awkward and uncertain.

"You don't have to open my door," he says. "I'm a grown man."

And just like that, he makes it clear. We're equals. However this plays out, we're equals.

I swallow, my throat tight. "Shit. Sorry."

"No biggie."

His eyes drift away like something has caught his attention. I follow his gaze. A couple leans against a truck several feet away, wrapped up in each other, kissing soft and tender, but with the kind of passion that could turn hot and frenzied any second.

Grant and I look back at each other at the same time. Our eyes lock. I don't move. He doesn't either.

Neither one of us speaks, but our eyes say the same thing.

We could be those other guys.

We could kiss here in the parking lot.

He could open his door, I could open mine, and we could drive somewhere.

Get in bed.

And if we were anyone else, that's where we'd be tonight.

In bed. Fucking. All night long.

But I have to see him tomorrow morning on the field.

I step away, even as it pains me, even as my libido screams, flailing and kicking, telling me to stop protesting, to just give in.

I don't.

I go around to the driver's side, get in, and turn on the engine. I take off my cap, toss it in the back seat, and turn on a playlist, hitting random.

Guns N' Roses.

Grant lifts a brow. "'November Rain?' Seriously?"

"I'm old school."

"So old school." With a laugh, he shakes his head, then stares out the window, humming along to the lyrics.

I drive away, but each second that ticks by makes my chest squeeze. It's like there's a rope around my heart, tightening like a noose.

I can hardly breathe.

It's unbearable, the thought of this night ending.

I glance over at him.

Is he thinking the same thing as the miles unfurl?

I breathe out hard, fighting like hell to focus on the road, and I do my best. I swear I do. But when he slides one hand absently along his jeans, I'm obsessed with it.

How his fingers felt in mine under the table.

How good it would feel to have his hands on me.

Mine on him.

The GPS interrupts Axl Rose, telling us we're two miles from the hotel.

Two miles.

Those words reverberate in my skull, a warning or a countdown.

The thought of going back into this hotel in less than two miles without tasting his Diet Coke kiss is killing me.

Making a split-second decision, I hit the right turn signal, pull onto a residential side street, then cut the engine. It's quiet enough. No one's out.

He jerks his gaze to me. "Why'd you stop?"

I meet his eyes. Lift my hand. Hold his face. His breath hitches.

I slide my thumb along his jaw. Grant moans softly, and everything feels right in my world.

"Fuck it." I inch closer, lick my lips. "Kiss me, rookie."

He smiles. "Hell, yes."

13

GRANT

My lips crash down on his.

Flames lick every inch of my skin as I taste the shortstop's lips for the first time.

I don't play around. I don't tease or toy. I take his mouth hostage as I pour all my lust into a white-hot kiss with Declan Steele.

I grab the back of his neck, jerking him closer, claiming his lips.

It's rough and fevered, everything I imagined a kiss with him would be.

Exhilarating.

It's utterly exhilarating.

Declan's stubble scrapes my cheek like sandpaper, and I lose my mind. Need grips me, so I drag him closer, my thoughts becoming a hazy blur as pleasure blasts through my body, filling every single cell.

Weaving my hands into his hair, I swallow down a harsh groan. His hair is soft and thick, and, holy fuck, it's between my fingers. My God, he's *here.*

Kissing me like I'm the only man he's ever wanted.

I know that's not true. I damn well know that. But at this moment, all I feel is how much he wants me. It washes over me. It rolls off him in waves as our teeth click and our tongues skate together.

He knocks my cap off, sending it skittering to the floor, his fingers diving into my hair too.

We grab, take, devour.

My God, he tastes so good. Like fantasies becoming real. Like I've imagined kissing should be.

I've kissed before, but not like this.

This feels like sex.

Especially when he pulls back and lets out a wild groan of pleasure that makes my balls tingle.

"Love the sounds you make," I rasp.

"Yeah?"

"I do. A lot." I pant, jerking him close again and slamming my lips back to his.

"*Yes . . .*" Declan gasps into my mouth.

My cock twitches in my jeans, and I'm leaking already. I'm so fucking turned on I don't even know what to do.

I can't stop kissing him. Can't stop touching him.

I tug his bottom lip between my teeth, and I moan so damn loudly I'm sure the house at the end of the block can hear. Sure, too, that I don't care.

Especially when Declan unleashes a hard, shuddery breath as I lick the corner of his lips, then as I flick my tongue right there, and once again as I dive back in for another hungry, heated round.

His moans and murmurs are the sexiest noises ever.

I can only dream of how much louder he'd be if we were fucking. How much more erotic his sounds would be. How fantastically filthy.

But I guess it'll have to be okay that we won't be screwing ever. I don't know how I'd survive sex with him since kissing him is already the hottest thing I've ever experienced.

It feels like I'm fucking his mouth, and he's fucking mine right back.

The trouble is this damn console in the middle. The steering wheel by his arm.

I break the kiss, eyeing the back seat. It's roomy enough, and I like his BMW even more now.

He sees my glance and doesn't hesitate. "Go."

"Yes, sir," I tease and nearly vault up, scrambling between the seats, diving onto the leather, stretching out and kicking his cap from the seat to the floor. He's right there with me, following me and reaching for the bottom of my shirt. Sitting up, I whip it over my head.

"Fuck. Yes," he says, then takes off his. I'm in jeans, he's in shorts, and this is heaven.

We slam together again. Side to side, we make out like crazy as he takes over, plundering my mouth with his wicked tongue, kissing me ruthlessly, and jerking me close so our chests touch.

And then, holy fuck, I nearly come through my clothes when our cocks align.

"Deck," I moan, feeling both utterly helpless and completely horny at the same time.

He growls against my lips, then devours me again as he grinds his erection against mine.

Pushing.

Pressing.

Giving.

Taking.

My entire body is short-circuiting from the intensity, from the sheer volume of pleasure annihilating me.

His strong arm snakes around me, his big hand covering my ass. He hauls me even closer, sending a spike of ball-tightening arousal all the way down to my toes.

His other hand travels up my chest, stopping at my left pec, where he flicks my nipple piercing.

"Ahhh," I gasp, breaking the kiss since I need a moment to let the pleasure radiate.

"I have wanted to do that since I first saw it."

"Do it again," I beg, desperate.

Declan does, and desire pummels me in a blissfully beautiful wave. Then he scoots down, kissing my chest as he goes, till his lips make contact with my nipple, and he tugs on the barbell with his teeth.

Another bolt of lust crashes into me. Another feral moan spills from my lips.

My cock aches, and I can feel another drop of pre-come on the tip. I'm not far off.

I want release so badly.

Want his as well.

I have no clue where this is going. How far we're taking a kiss that's already sped past kissing.

But I also know I don't want to have sex in the back of a car.

And I don't want to blow him on the side of a road either.

Back in high school, I messed around with girls in cars before I learned I only wanted to mess around with guys.

And I don't want this to feel one bit like confusion.

Because it's not.

It's clarity.

It's intensity, and it's everything I've wanted, and then it's even better when he slides me under him.

He pushes up, then stares down at me, lust scorching his irises.

Then, he tilts his hips and grinds down hard on my cock.

"Oh God," I grunt, my dick thumping against my jeans. I wrap my hands around his big biceps and blurt the truth. "You need to stop, or I'm going to come in my pants. I'm that turned on."

He releases a sharp, hot breath. Then another. But he listens, moves off me, and mutters, "Wow . . . you are just . . . wow."

As I swing my legs to the floor and sit up to rest my head against the seatback, a wild grin plays on my lips.

I'm *wow*.

Holy shit.

He's wow.

I drag a hand through my hair, trying to calm

down, to cool off. I glance up at the windows. They're covered in steam. "Dude, your car is like a sauna."

"So am I," he says.

"Me too. I'm going to jerk it so hard tonight when I get back to my room."

He spreads a hand across my abs. "To me?"

I laugh. "Yes, dickhead. To you."

"Mmm. Your hand on your cock. I would love to see that."

"Maybe I'll show you," I tease, pushing up.

My gaze catches the digital display on the clock. It's close to midnight.

I flashback to a few nights ago. Coach in the elevator. The mango rice. His midnight snack.

An alarm rings in my head, and I sit bolt upright. "We need to go. Fisher usually comes back with his mango rice in a few minutes, and I don't want to run into him."

Declan frowns in confusion, and I explain as we grab our shirts and yank them on.

We climb into the front seats, and Declan wipes the steam from the window before he turns the ignition and peels outta there.

I comb my fingers through my hair, but when I flip the visor to check out the mirror, my face is whisker burned. "We can't walk in together like this. Not tonight."

"I know. I'll drop you off a block away so no one sees you get out of my car. Then I'll park, and you'll go in first. Put your cap on," he says, pointing to the floor.

I grab it, pull it on, then stretch my arm to the backseat. "Same for you. Your hair is a mess."

A grin tugs at his sexy mouth. "A good mess," he says, and that makes my stomach flip. "Put it on me."

I put the cap on him as he drives, and the moment is strangely intimate as I adjust it by his ears.

"If anyone asks, you were out for a walk," Declan continues. "And just to be safe, I'll come in a few minutes later. I'll say I had to go to CVS for something."

"Sounds like a plan."

He slows the car as we near the hotel, shooting me a once-over. "Not gonna lie. You look like sex, rookie."

I chuckle. "Not gonna lie. I feel like sex too."

His sly grin makes me smile too.

A minute later, he pulls up, and I get out without a second glance, walking the final block to the hotel entrance in the warm Arizona night, my erection finally, *finally* disappearing.

The glass doors slide open, and I go inside. The hotel is quiet, but I take the stairs anyway, just to be safe.

Just in case Coach's spring training vice lines up timewise with mine.

When I hit the sixth floor, I turn down the hallway, then blow out a long breath as I reach my room. I shut the door in a daze.

Did that just happen?

And what will happen tomorrow?

No idea, but I know this much. Tonight, there's something I plan to tell him.

Because I know now exactly what I want, no matter the risks.

I haven't forgotten how forbidden we are. He's more off-limits than anyone else in the world. And really, of all the queer men on the planet, why does the guy I want so damn badly have to be my teammate?

I wish I knew.

But one thing I do know with absolute certainty.

I want to sleep with Declan. I'm ready.

There are no questions.

I take a piss, wash my hands and strip out of my clothes.

When I sink down on the bed, my mind returns to the car.

Tonight was the hottest night of my life and he didn't even touch my dick. As I replay what we did, I'm instantly aroused, and my reaction to the shortstop validates what I'm about to do.

But first, I'm going to give him what he wants.

I grab my phone.

14

DECLAN

I cut the engine, but I don't get out. I just breathe.

I rest my head against the back of the seat and stare out the windshield. A desert willow tree looms at the edge of the lot, and as I study the leaves, how they blow faintly in the night breeze, a pair of unblinking eyes watches me from a low branch.

An owl.

Rare sighting in Arizona. Rare sighting anywhere.

But only if you don't look.

I always look.

When I was a little kid, I used to believe the owls were looking out for me. That they'd invite me to their homes, take me under their wings, so to speak.

It was a vivid childhood fantasy, one I needed for my own escape from my father and his habits.

My fantasies are different now, but even so, I'm still drawn to birds.

Some say owls are a sign of wisdom.

I'm not sure I was wise tonight.

Others say an owl means you should face your fears, reveal your secrets.

What was once my biggest secret—liking men—I revealed, so I've got no worries there.

I draw a deep breath, staring at the winged animal. The owl doesn't look away. His eyes are challenging, like he can see inside me.

Like he knows my new secret.

Knows that I am struggling mightily. That kissing the rookie did nada to get him out of my system. I *only* want more of him.

And yet, I need to be strong.

I've got to live with this struggle, find a way through it. It can't be harder than the other shit I've dealt with. From my father, to my own fuck-ups, to being one of the first openly gay athletes in baseball.

Even to Kyle and the trouble that came with the end of that relationship. The trouble that rattles through my life now and again, like late last season when I ran into him as he was signing up for a membership at my regular gym in San Francisco. He acted surprised that I worked out there. But it turned out my trainer had posted a pic of our workout online as he was hunting for other pro-athlete clients.

I chatted with Kyle to be polite, and he quickly mentioned he was single again. And did I want to go out for a drink? Or a *not-drink,* he added, since he knew I didn't touch the stuff.

I declined, found a new gym, and hired a new trainer.

But that's the last I heard from Kyle. As for Nathan, he never tried to get in touch with me after that epic fight on my front steps earlier this year. Emma told me in a text that his show was renewed and he was going to start shooting in Georgia next week, once he finished his *family time* in Florida.

They're both in the past, where exes belong.

Now, I need to do better. Be better.

I'm here, living the good life.

I can't just risk it all because Grant would be a good lay.

Ah hell, he'd be a great lay.

My skin burns as the images flash past me.

That man.

That sexy, flirty, outgoing man.

I let out a long, heavy sigh.

The owl hoots, the sound reminding me that some say owls are harbingers. They warn you of trouble.

Thanks, owl. But I can see the trouble clearly myself.

I unbuckle and get out of the car.

Sometimes an owl is just an owl.

But either way, I need to cool it. I need to resist Grant.

Tonight needs to be in the past.

Tomorrow I'll reset.

Keeping my shit together is my specialty.

But as I cross the lot, tossing my keys up and down in my palm, my gaze strays to the hotel windows. I count up to the sixth floor, wondering where Grant is, what room he's in, and if he's taking matters into his own hands right now.

My cock twitches at the thought right as my phone bleeps.

Grabbing it from my shorts pocket, I slide a thumb across the screen. A notification pops up from the man who commands my thoughts.

My messaging app shows a preview of his text.

Grant: You've got to check out this movie clip. It's the one you wanted to see.

My skin tingles. My mouth waters. I'm Pavlov's dog.

I stop in my tracks, shove a hand in my pocket, hunting for my AirPods but coming up short.

If this is what I think it is . . .

I hustle to the lobby, my thumb hovering over the screen, eager, so damn eager to play it.

My room is too far away.

It's going to take forever to get there.

I want to see this clip *now*.

But I can't take a chance.

Nope.

I jam the phone in my pocket, stuffing it deep, but I keep my hand on it, protecting it. Like it's a treasure, a precious artifact I've discovered.

When I step into the lobby, a basketball hurls my way. Instinct kicks in, and I palm it, then look up at the shooter.

"Nice reflexes, shortstop," Chance says, striding in from the outdoor pool, Crosby by his side. They are wearing swim trunks.

I grimace privately.

Love these guys, but I want to be alone with this . . . message ASAP. I toss the ball back to Chance. "I do my best to keep them up. You playing Marco Polo?"

Crosby mimes dunking a shot. "Nope. We found a way to combine pool and basketball because we're brilliant like that."

"Maybe you'll even start a league," I toss out.

"Goals," Crosby jokes.

"Feel free to join us tomorrow, man," Chance offers.

Saved by the bell.

"I'm there," I say. It'll be good for me to spend time with them, rather than obsessing over the catcher I want to eat for an appetizer, dinner, and then dessert.

Crosby furrows his brow, then tips his forehead to the doors. "What are you up to? Hot date, Mr. No Dating During Spring Training?"

"Ooh, busted," Chance says with a grin.

A worm of annoyance wiggles through me. I'm about to lie. I abhor lies. They're everything I strive to avoid.

My chest squeezes and I ball my fists, thinking of that owl.

Just like I did when I was younger. When I had to tell lies about my father. Lies when he missed my games. Lies when I was late to practice.

But I couldn't lie anymore when he showed up at my games drunk. When he practically stumbled onto the field, reeking of tequila sometimes, beer others.

I hate lying.

But then, if I were seeing some guy in town,

would I tell Crosby and Chance? If I were dating River, would I advertise them of that?

I decide I would not.

So, this is not a lie.

"Just went to CVS to get some shit," I say, though I'm empty-handed. For all he knows I bought condoms and they're in my pocket.

Which reminds me . . .

"Anyway," I say, pushing out a yawn. "I'll see you tomorrow."

They say goodbye and amble down the hall. I stab the button for the elevator, and it arrives instantly.

Anticipation winds through me as the doors close. I'm a horse at the gates. I'm champing at the bit.

Once the elevator chugs upward, I grab my phone, turn it to mute, and click open the message, hitting play.

One second in, I go up in flames.

"Oh, fuck me," I mutter as the video plays.

I shut it down right away so I'm not sporting a raging boner as I walk along the hall. But I write back quickly.

Declan: Gonna watch this in 30 seconds. But I need to know—did you finish? If not, wait for me. I'll send you something in a couple of minutes. Something you can finish to.

Grant: It's Dirty Christmas morning! I'll stroke it slow and easy, but don't make me wait long. I'm dying here.

Declan: You have my filthy word.

A minute later, I'm in my room, shorts unzipped, hand in my boxer briefs, stroking my cock as I watch the sexiest video ever.

Grant is a goddamn porn auteur.

Has he done this before? Shot videos of himself? The dragon of envy thrashes inside me again.

But screw jealousy.

This video is *mine*.

And it is off the chain.

His fist curls nice and tight around his thick cock. He's all lubed up, slick and hot. One hand slides up and down that fantastic shaft, slow and sexy, gripping the base, then squeezing his way up the head, sliding over his crown, pushing out a drop of liquid arousal on a guttural grunt.

"Yes, rookie. Stroke that beautiful cock," I urge as I watch his moves, as my own hand travels up and down my pulsing length.

He moans and pants as he works his shaft, shiny with the lube, making it feel even better for him, I'm sure, and making me think of lubing him up and guiding him into me.

I shudder, a groan ripping through me as I jack harder.

The video lasts forty-five filthy seconds, and I am halfway there already, hard and horny and utterly amazed at this guy's guts, at his confidence, at his ballsiness.

And speaking of balls, oh yes, do I ever want to get my mouth on his.

I write back, dictating because I don't want to stop touching myself.

Declan: I'm on my bed, hand down my shorts, watching your video, stroking my dick, wanting desperately to taste your come . . .

His response is short and crystal clear.

Grant: Show me.

Declan: I will.

Grant: Wanna see you come. I want sound.

Declan: You a porn director?

Grant: I just know what I want.

I angle the phone on a pillow by my thigh, turn it to selfie mode, then video. I grab some lube from the nightstand, coat my dick, and I go to town, jacking it fast, recording every second. Every noise I make.

"Yes," I grunt. "Fucking yes. Unghhh."

My fist is a blur as lust torches my veins. As I picture Grant straddling my chest, his gorgeous cock hovering above my lips, then I see him plunging it into my mouth.

"Ah fuck," I groan.

I thrust up, hips jerking as I unload on my chest, moaning and groaning till I drag a finger through the mess.

I hit end, then I send the video and grab a tissue to clean up.

I lay there, spent. Exhausted. Blissed out.

Sixty seconds is all it takes for my return delivery.

His text arrives, and I click so fast on the video.

He's faster, harsher, louder than me, and hell, I feel like I could come again just watching him.

He grips tight and rough, moaning and cursing, hand flying until he comes buckets on his chest.

I am enrapt.

Utterly enrapt in the sexiest selfie I've ever received.

The filthiest too.

But it's not even the dirtiness that turns me on. It's the fact that he did this, that he sent it, that he threw caution to the wind like this.

I'm about to reply when a new message lands on my phone.

No video this time.

Just a text.

The preview says only: *hey, I need to tell you something.*

My brow furrows. That feels like the start of bad news.

Of a tough conversation.

Like *Hey, I don't think we should do this again.*

My heart stops, stutters, then speeds up again in the span of several seconds. I swallow roughly, nerves thrumming through me.

I don't want that outcome. I don't want his stop sign.

With a deep, fueling breath, I click open the message.

Grant: *Hey, I need to tell you something. I need to tell you what I was picturing there at the end. What I've imagined every time I've jacked off since I met you.*

This is hard for me to say, for a lot of reasons, but partly because I know I talk a good game. I may act like I know what I'm doing. This isn't easy, but I'm telling you anyway since I want you to know what I was thinking.

I was thinking how much I want to sleep with you. Yeah, that probably won't surprise you at all. But maybe this will.

I've never had sex before. With anyone.

And now I want to. With you.

15

GRANT

My phone rings a minute later.

I answer it faster than I can swing a bat at a cutter.

"Rookie," he rumbles, and my chest flutters.

"Hey," I say, giving him my chillest voice. Can't let on I'm a mess of nerves.

"Did you think that would turn me off? That you're a virgin?" He dives right in, and the thoughtful tone settles me somewhat.

"Or freak you out? I don't know. Maybe one or the other. Maybe both," I say, the words pouring out in a rush. "I mean, you asked if I was vers, and I said *same,* and I don't want you to think I'm a liar, now that you know I haven't topped or bottomed," I say in another fantastic display of blurt-dom. I'm a master at that with him, it seems.

"You think you have to have had sex to know? You know you like men. But you didn't need to sleep with a man to figure that out, right?"

"Right. True," I say, because once I figured out

for sure I liked men and only men, I knew I'd want to sleep with a man someday. "And porn helped. I've watched a lot of it."

"Good. Porn is great for many things, including figuring out what turns us on. But real sex isn't like porn."

My stomach churns, but I've come this far, so I say the next thing. The hard thing. "I have no idea what real sex is like."

"Nothing wrong with that," he says, his voice warm, kind of inviting. He makes me want to open up more as he says, "You figure it out in your own time. What do you like watching?"

That's easy. So easy. "I'm pretty simple. Hot guys, ripped bodies, blow jobs, rim jobs, flip fucking," I say, and holy hell, that was like a ten-ton truck driving off my chest. I feel a million times lighter. I've never said that out loud to another person. Never told a man what I fantasize about. But I fantasize *a lot*. My mind is a very active land. "And when I watch, I can put myself in all the roles. But I don't know if that means I'm vers. I mean, maybe I am. I think I could be. I just don't want you to think I lied to you."

"I don't think you're a liar for saying you're vers even if you haven't had sex. Sex is in the mind. Some men learn if they like to top or bottom or both from experimenting, and some men know it intrinsically."

Relieved, I drag a hand through my hair. "Right. But..."

I'm not even sure what I'm trying to say.

Except, what I want to say is, *will you please sleep with me? Will you teach me everything you know about pleasing a man and being pleased, and I'm dying here because I'm twenty-two and I'm ready, I'm so damn ready.*

And I want it to be you so badly.

Instead, I wait. Something I know all too well how to do.

"But what, Grant?" he asks gently after a few seconds. "Am I turned off? I am not. Am I freaked out? I am not. Am I curious about you and your choices? You bet I am."

A wave of relief washes over me. "Good."

"I want to know you. I want to know why you held out. I don't think it's that you're waiting to get married," he says, laughing.

"Yeah, that's not it," I say, laughing too. But before I can open up the book and tell him my story, I want to know his. "I'll tell you, but first . . . how old were you?"

"I was seventeen," he says, in a voice laced with regret.

"You sound like you're not crazy about that choice," I say.

"I was drunk. It was stupid." He inhales sharply.

His decision not to drink makes more sense. That must be when he stopped. "Did someone take advantage of you?"

"No. It was just me being an idiot."

"I can't picture you ever being an idiot, but I suppose we all are at some point," I say.

"Definitely."

"Did you lose it with a guy or a girl?" I ask, a little unsure if he's talking about gay sex or all sex, so it's best to ask.

He's quiet for a beat. With a sigh, he says, "Both."

It's like someone just banged a cymbal. I scoot up in the bed. "Whoa. Not what I expected to hear."

"Figured I'd surprise you," he says drily, but not like he's trying to amuse me by dropping that news. He's simply sharing. "We were messing around, the three of us. A guy I knew and his girlfriend. They liked to . . . mix it up."

"Wow," I say, feeling so vanilla, so boring. "Was it . . . did you . . .?" I can barely finish my questions. I'm not bothered that he slept with a girl. I'm trying to wrap my head around how he's so much more experienced than I am. "Did you like it?" I manage to ask.

"With her? Not really. With him? Hell yes," he says.

"Then why did you say you were an idiot?"

"Because he wasn't interested in me. He was doing it for her."

"What?" I furrow my brow. "That does not compute."

"It was her thing. He was bi, and she liked to get it on in threesomes, so they did. I was their . . . extra. Their plaything."

I scrub a hand across the back of my neck, trying to understand what went down. "So, you had sex with both of them?"

"Yes. I fucked her, and he fucked me," he says plainly, laying it out, and the image is weird. I can't see the Declan I know doing that. Not that there's anything wrong with it—people like what they like. Polyamory is cool, if that's your jam, as long as everyone consents. But it doesn't seem like it was his jam. Maybe because his focus on me at The Lazy Hammock was so single-minded. Maybe because he's got a jealous streak—one that turns me on. That's what's odd. Declan seems like a one-man kind of guy.

Declan swallows audibly, then, in a voice brimming with vulnerability, asks, "Are you turned off now? Freaked out?"

I sit up straighter and answer from the gut. "No. God no. I'm not. I'm just trying to . . ." I trail off, searching for the words, then finding them easily. "Understand you."

"Good," he says, in a softer tone, like he's grateful for my answer. "And honestly, I did it because I was attracted to him. I think I knew I was gay. I think I knew I was only attracted to guys. But we were all out one night, drinking. And they made me an offer. They said, 'We've been wanting to do this.' Her parents were out of town, and they asked me to come to her house, and I was so—I don't know—intrigued by him that I said yes. So, I had sex with both of them."

"Did you regret it in the morning?"

A long sigh is the first half of his answer. "I guess I could say I felt used, but honestly, I chose it. I said yes. I was into him, and I was very, very curious. But yeah, I regretted it when they went at each other right after and said I could leave." He ends on a note of annoyance, but one of shame too.

"Jesus, man. That sucks," I say, feeling a pang of sympathy for him and his less-than-great first time.

"It did. But I learned a lot too."

"Like what?"

"That I liked touching him. That I liked it when he touched me. I'd been pretty sure I wasn't bisexual at all, but that encounter solidified it for me. But the next morning, I did regret it."

I relax, feeling free. Unjudged. He's speaking so openly with me, and I'm into it. "I'm sorry you regretted it," I say.

"Regret sucks," he says, then pauses. "Your turn. Why did you wait? No opportunities in college or some other reason?"

I flash back to the way I grew up, to the noise and the fury, the moans and the groans. The things I overheard that went beyond sex. Now's not the time to unload chapter and verse of the *I had shitty parents* saga, but he was frank with me, so I give him some of the same. "My parents had me when they were young. They were teenagers. And they fought all the time. And fucked all the time. And it was just . . . hard . . . really hard. I didn't want that—the kind of relationship you wind up regretting."

"That does sound rough."

"I also didn't know right away what I wanted. I fooled around with girls first, back in high school. Mostly because it was easy," I say.

"Because that's what society expects?"

I shake my head, picturing those days, those times. "Not really for that reason. Honestly, it was because I spent a lot of time with girls. I've always had a lot of female friends. My closest friend is Reese—she's two years younger, and our grandmas are best friends, so we pretty much grew up together. Nothing happened with her, but I was friends with a lot of her friends and always enjoyed hanging out with them, talking to them. So, I thought, *maybe I like girls.* I mean, I could tell who was pretty, but I guess in the same way I could tell a sunset was pretty. So, I went on some dates to see if I was straight."

"How'd that work out for ya?" he deadpans.

"Fan-fucking-tastic," I say, smiling, then I continue. "And after that, I thought maybe I was bi."

"Are you?"

It's funny that he asks. I want to say, *"Dude, can you not tell how much I love dick?"*

But that's not the point. You can love dick and love pussy too. But I only love one.

"No. My dates with girls were pretty so-so. Fooling around with a girl always felt like a shoe on the wrong foot. Or like I was standing in front of a crowd and didn't know what to do with my hands."

He laughs at that last one. "Like Will Ferrell in *Talladega Nights*. 'I'm not sure what to do with my hands?'" he says, imitating the movie star's race-car driver when he does his first TV interview.

"Exactly."

"And what does messing around with a guy feel like?"

That's easy—so damn easy. "Like playing baseball. Like hitting a home run. It's not at all like looking at a sunset."

I can hear him smile. Hell, I can feel it. "Mmm. Couldn't have said it better myself."

"And I figured out I was into dudes and only

dudes at the end of high school. That's why I got the piercing. Just kind of a personal marker, to honor what I'd learned about myself."

"That's a damn good reason."

"But it's not like I was showing it off to guys all the time. College was insane. I was on scholarship and wanted my degree before I entered the draft, so I was trying to finish in three years. I was either studying or playing ball. It sounds cliched, but I barely had time to breathe."

"Let alone figure out how to breathe when a dick is lodged in the back of your throat," he teases.

That brings on a smile. I fucking love his sense of humor. It keeps me sharing, wanting to hear more of it. "Then I went to the minors and then here."

"Have you ... done anything?"

"You mean did I lie about being good at sucking?"

"Listen, rookie. Being good at giving head is something I can teach you if you want to learn," he says, and my pulse spikes from the offer. "So, I don't care if you said that to flirt with me. I'm asking because I want to know you."

My heart thumps a little harder over his last few words. Funny that talking so honestly about sex makes my chest warm. "I've done the whole blow job and hand job thing plenty of times. Yes, I like sucking cock, and I think I'm good at it, but feel free to be the judge of that yourself," I toss out, pretty pleased with my flirt game.

Declan laughs. "Nice way to say you want to suck my dick."

"You know I do."

He hums, low in his throat. "I want to see you on your knees taking my dick between those lips. Want to see you crawling up on the bed and settling between my thighs to swallow my cock," he rumbles, and my dick springs to life again.

"That's where I want to be," I say. I'm not turning back now.

"I know. And you know I want that too." He breathes out hard, taking his time. "And everything else."

Which is a perfect entry point. Or reentry point, I should say.

"So," I say, circling back to my original question, girding myself to put my loins on the line. "Will you let me? Do that and everything else?"

I brace myself for his answer.

16

DECLAN

Will I let him?

My God, I want Grant Blackwood with a ferocity I've never felt before. I want him more than anyone else. Ever.

But I've met regret. I've confronted it in the harsh light of day. I don't want him to regret me when the sun comes up.

"Grant, you know how I said I regretted my first time?"

"Yeah. You think you'd regret me?" he asks quickly, anxiously.

This guy. He has the guts to show me his desire, then to ask the toughest questions.

Does he have any idea how endearing that is? How attractive he is on so many levels?

I close my eyes, squeezing them.

Is that part of my hesitation?

That he'll be more endearing than I imagine?

I shake that off. Focus on the physical. Open my eyes. "No. Not a chance in hell I'd regret you, rookie. But I don't want us to make a decision right now. And most of all, I don't want *you* to regret me." I turn to the digital clock. "It's late. It's well past midnight. You've got to work out with Sullivan in the morning. You're not going to get much sleep at this rate. As much as I want to head upstairs to your room right now and show you exactly how much I want you, I also think you should sleep on this."

"You're worried I'm making this choice in the heat of the moment? Because we messed around tonight?"

"Somewhat. I don't think that's a bad reason to make it. All I'm saying is midnight is for regrets. If you want to make a choice this big, you should make it in the daylight. Does that make sense?"

"I want to say no. But I get it. I do."

"For the record, I think it takes serious cojones to do what you did. To say what you said," I tell Grant.

"You've seen my cojones. They're very serious."

I laugh hard. "That they are, my friend. That they are," I say, when my mind jumps to tomorrow. "Hey, do you need someone to join you with Sullivan? You'll want a hitter, right?"

"That'd be great."

"You've got one then."

"We're meeting at seven-thirty."

"I'll be there," I say.

"Night, Deck," he says, soft and tender.

"Sleep well, rookie," I say it back the same way.

* * *

I stride up to the plate, adjust my batting glove, nod at the catcher.

Grant's mask is pushed up on his forehead, his hair sticking through the cage. His expression is all business. "Don't go easy on him," he says.

"Not in my nature," I say.

"Good." Grant pulls down his mask as he crouches behind the plate, glove between his legs.

I take a few practice swings outside the box, loosening up. The sun rises on the horizon, bright and bold.

The sky is blue and it's a new day, full of new chances for baseball, for life.

And no regrets, I hope.

In a few hours, we'll host the Texas Scoundrels for a game. Will Grant know by then if the daylight gives him the same answers as the nighttime?

I'm tempted to steal a quick glance at the man behind the plate, but I don't. Best to let him make this decision entirely on his own.

I draw a steady breath and visualize putting on my blinders.

Getting in the zone.

At this moment, here on this field with the sun on my shoulders, my world narrows to baseball, only baseball. And just like that, everything feels right.

That's how this sport has always been for me. It's been the solace from any storm. It was the escape from my home when I needed it. It was my joy, my respite, my freedom.

I settle in at the plate, adjusting my stance, digging in.

Ready.

Grant must give Sullivan the signal because the rookie pitcher pulls on the bill of his cap, nods, then lifts his glove.

He goes into the windup and fires off the white orb that whizzes right past me.

Damn.

With a thump of ball against leather, Grant fields it.

I don't even swing. That ball flies by too fast.

Grant tosses it back out to Sullivan on the mound. Sullivan paces then settles again on the rubber.

He sends the next pitch straight down the middle; I can see it in my crosshairs. I put my weight into the swing, slicing the air.

"Strike!"

I turn around. Crosby clenches his right fist, jerks it high like he's the umpire.

"No shit," I say to my teammate.

"I call 'em like I see 'em," he says with a shrug. Then his eyes light up, and he smiles. "Want a third baseman? I can also cover second. And I can cover shortstop."

"You're taking over for me already?"

"Maybe I am," he says.

"We can always use another player on the field," Grant says.

"I'm there," Crosby says and trots out to shortstop like a kid in the park.

I settle back in, and when Sullivan goes into the windup, Grant's words reverberate.

Don't go easy on him.

Never.

The ball whizzes down the line, and I connect with a satisfying *thwack*. The grounder skitters across the field and Crosby scoops it up easily, smothering it with his glove.

I curse but then return to the plate.

"Give us another grand slam like you did in September," Crosby shouts.

Laughing, I roll my eyes. "If only it had gotten us all the way," I shout back, then turn to Grant. "Game against the Aces that clinched a playoff slot for us last year."

Grant nods, a spark in his eyes. "Yup. You hit a slider off the Aces star closer to win the divisionals, and no one threw a slider to you the rest of the month."

I whistle in appreciation. "Damn. You do know the game."

"I do. Now get your ass in the box and hit."

We keep it up like that for several more rounds. I get a few solid hits and put one over the fence. Sullivan strikes me out a few times and walks me once.

All because of Grant, who's unflappable. He calls the right pitch at the right time, guiding Sullivan. Crosby and I trade off, with Crosby taking some swings, working the pitcher as I field.

It's teamwork. It's four guys playing pickup baseball like when we were kids, a ragtag bunch helping each other out, playing a game—loving a game.

It's no regrets.

At least, that's how this last hour has been for me.

I hope it's that way for Grant too.

When the session is over, the rookie pitcher is smiling again, a grin of gratitude.

"Keep that shit up," I say to Sullivan. "We need a good right-handed reliever."

"Thanks, Declan," he says. "And it is a hell of an honor to play with you. You've got serious game."

"And you are doing much better, Sully," Crosby says, knocking glove to glove. "Good job putting in the time."

Those words tap on a recent memory. "You know how the saying goes," I say. "Well, *let's get it right*." Out of the corner of my eye, I see a smile tugging on Grant's lips.

Let's get it right, indeed.

Today was a test—of concentration, form, focus.

And if I'm grading myself?

I was not one bit distracted by Grant. That's got to be a good thing, as I weigh what to do with his offer—an offer that's already making me revise my rules about getting involved with ballplayers.

Rules I need for my own sanity, so my emotions don't rule me, so my cravings don't defeat me.

But then, Grant is making me rip up all my rules.

17

GRANT

I am not looking at the clock. I am not staring at the time.

I'm only checking my phone for the tenth time to see if Reese scored a big guest for her podcast. My friend started her sports interview show this year as a junior in college, and she's already killing it, racking up downloads and fantastic reviews.

When I click on my text messages as I leave the locker room after the Texas Scoundrels game, I refuse to let it get me down that Declan hasn't texted me about my offer.

Hell, I refuse to let it get me down that we lost the game when a Scoundrels home run sealed it for the opponent. And that after an endless at-bat when my pitcher and I just couldn't get in synch. He shook off sign after sign until I called for a curveball, and then the hitter went long.

Did I call the wrong pitch, or was it just one of those games? But close games happen, so I decide to let it go.

I should do the same with Declan and my offer. Except, am I supposed to text him?

Ugh. I have no idea how this shit works. I made the offer, so am I supposed to make it again? *Hey, dude. Called it! I still want to bang you like a screen door in a hurricane.*

Time to focus on anything else. Like Reese and her good news. I click on her message.

Reese: Slam dunk! I nabbed Zayden Wilson, basketball star and NBA rookie, for my podcast!

Grant: Course you did! You're a rock star! So proud of you.

Reese: Thank you! I love that you always support my crazy endeavors.

Grant: They're not crazy at all. They're very you. And you are an awesome podcaster and interviewer. Maybe someday you'll have me on.

Reese: Duh. Of course I want you on.

Reese: Also, any news on the report front? :)

As I leave the complex, I tap out a reply.

Grant: We kissed. But I don't think anything more is going to happen.

. . .

My finger hovers over the send button, but some strange sensation in my chest keeps me from sending it. Is it a weight? Or a worry?

I don't know, so I don't hit send.

Trying to figure it out, I read the draft one more time, and my face goes hot. I glance behind me, like someone can see me, read what I'm writing, tell what I'm thinking.

Like it's written in my eyes and on my features too.

That's when I know why I don't hit send.

Reese is *my person*, and I tell her nearly everything. She was also the first person I came out to. I'm not at all ashamed of who I like or what I want and especially with her. But this situation with Declan feels too new, too uncertain. I don't even trust what's happening in my own mind, so I don't know that I can share it with my best friend. Whatever is or isn't happening with Declan feels intensely private. Incredibly personal. It's not for anyone else but the two of us.

And for some uncomfortable reason, I have this sinking feeling that it's happening *only* in my head.

That I'm about to be rejected, and I don't know that I want to serve that intel up even to Reese.

Maybe it's because tomorrow I'll need to adjust.

Reroute back to the way things were.

Workout buddies?

Fine. I can do that.

Teammates?

I damn well better buckle back into that role because I suspect that's where I'm headed. Just a gut feeling.

I hit delete and write a new note.

Grant: There's nothing to tell at the moment. I'll keep you posted, babe.

Reese: You better!

I close the thread, a smidgen of guilt wedging itself under my skin for not confessing.

But what would I confess to? That my head is a ball of confusion over what happens next?

Where exactly did we leave off?

Is there a website with a how-to guide for making a deflower-my-dick-and-ass-please offer to your teammate?

Grinding my jaw, I pop in my earbuds, and I get the hell away from the hotel, the complex, and all the confusion.

We have a free afternoon, so I wander in the Arizona heat, sunglasses on, listening to a wild thriller as some swaggery dude named Jack or Stone or Blade tries to evade Interpol and find a stolen cache of radioactive diamonds.

The escape does the trick.

But only in short spurts.

I can't entirely stop thinking about Declan. I

feel stupid for thinking about him so much. Utterly stupid and young.

Like a puppy dog.

I need to shake him off, get him out of my mind.

When I reach a sprawling park, I break into a jog, then pick up the pace and go for an impromptu run in the middle of the day, jogging past cacti and desert flowers, around trees and along red rocks.

The one thing that always works for me is moving my body.

Eventually, a half hour or so later, my thoughts of him settle down. Even out.

Whatever will be will be, and I'm good with it.

I'm not going to text him because I don't know what to say.

When I finish the run, I return to the complex. I'm near the Helen Williams sign when my phone flashes with a call from my grandpa—as if he can sense from California that I need someone familiar.

A sense of homecoming threads through me, comfort that comes from the person who's always been there for me, and I answer with a happy hello.

"Nice double," he says as I head to the backfield.

"You saw the game?"

"Hello? Streaming. Ever heard of it?"

I smile as I climb the steps in the empty bleachers, then grab a seat. "You guys didn't ever like to miss a game, did you?" I ask, stretching my legs out in front of me, sitting in the afternoon sun, the mountains in the distance.

"We watch most of your games, kid." He clears his throat. "Now, my daily report. I'm waiting for it."

Leaning back, getting comfortable, I give him my report as I've been doing every day since I've been here. I tell him about the hitters, the pitchers, the coaches, the skipper. About the fans and the guys. About Sullivan, Crosby, Chance.

I leave Declan out. But that's okay. There are plenty of other things to talk about.

"And what about you? How's all your running going? Ready for the Bay City marathon?"

There's a pause before he answers. "Doctor says I might need knee surgery."

I sit up straighter. This is the first time he's mentioned anything. "Yikes. What's that all about?"

"Apparently, two marathons a year is a lot on a body. Especially an old one like mine," he says.

"You're not that old."

"'Not that old' is easy to say when you're as young as you are."

"When will you have it?"

"Not sure," he says.

"I want to be there."

"You do baseball. You let me take care of my knee."

"Pops, I want to support you. Just let me know when it's going to be. Try to schedule it when I'm in town," I say, halfway to begging.

He laughs. "When? In between your home games? You're going to be busy the second you get back here. You'll be on the road. And I am going to be okay. Trust me."

I swallow roughly, wishing I could help him out. "But—"

"But your grandma will be here. I'll be fine."

"Does insurance cover it?"

"Probably, but it's insurance. Who knows? I'll look into it."

"What about PT? Do you need PT afterward?"

"Kid, I just saw the orthopedic surgeon the other day."

I sit up straighter, resting my elbows on my knees. "Let me pay for the PT. Insurance doesn't always cover that. I want to."

"You're so damn stubborn."

"I wonder where I got that from," I deadpan.

"Your mom," he says with a laugh, then clears his throat. "By the way, I saw her recently. She said she wants to come to Opening Day when you're playing in San Francisco."

I cross my fingers. "We don't even know for sure I'll make the roster."

He scoffs. "I have faith."

"And I appreciate it," I say, and though I don't want to assume I'll make it, things look good so far.

He takes a beat, then adds, "And she wants to come with Frank."

It's like I've been sucker-punched. "Is she with him again?"

"Seems she is," my grandpa says with a sigh.

"Guess she can't stay away from that guy. I haven't seen him since the end of high school. Haven't seen her in a while either." My gut twists again, but this time there's no confusion—my parents always have that effect on me. "And she wants to come to my games? Now that I'm this close to the majors?" I say, frustration lacing my tone. "She didn't come to any minor league games."

He sighs. "She's complicated."

"I know."

"So is your dad."

"Did he ask for tickets too?"

"No, but he's pretty busy with Cammi," he says, and I guess that's wife number three or girlfriend number twenty. Hell if I know. I stopped trying to count.

My throat tightens, and images of Mom and Dad flitting in and out of my life, Mom singing in clubs, Dad trying to play guitar, flashes before me. My mom is barely thirty-eight years old, same as my dad. They're not together. They haven't been in years. Both have dated plenty since they split. Mostly jerks. The only one I ever got along with was Frank, the guy my mom was briefly married to when I was in high school. Till he opened his big mouth about me.

But I don't want to deal with them today. With a painful wince, and a promise to myself, I let go of the knot of emotions the people who gave me DNA stir up in me.

"Tell Grams I love her, okay?"

"I will, kid. Anything else interesting happening at spring training?"

The back of my neck pricks. My senses trip.

Part of me wants to tell him. Part of me wants to sit down at the table with him and my grandma and have a chat. Talk to them openly, like I did when I was in high school. They were the next ones I told after Reese. They were so damn cute. My grandfather said, "When you meet some guy who steals your heart, I want an introduction so I can make sure he's good enough for you."

And my grandma said, "And don't you dare settle for anything less."

But *this*? This whatever-it-is with Declan? This is not a stolen heart. This isn't anything.

There's nothing to tell.

Even though I'm dying to speak. *I met a guy. He revs my engine. He makes me laugh. He gets me. He's so easy to talk to. He understands me. We've been through the same things. And I want his yes. But am I supposed to give him mine again?*

All of that is stuck in my chest where it belongs.

Instead, I say, "My coach has an addiction to sticky mango rice, Pops. He gets it every night at midnight. I think he gets it because his wife isn't around."

My grandfather chuckles. "So, he's cheating on his diet on spring training. His wife doesn't know about his secret mango sticky rice addiction. That's rich."

We have a laugh, then say goodbye, and I check my phone one more time and find it empty.

A little like how I feel.

Since this feeling is bugging the crap out of me, I return to the hotel, go straight to my room, and flop down on my bed, kicking off my sneakers.

I stare at my phone, tempted to text Declan, but no words seem right.

I have no clue how to navigate this stuff, and I don't want to say the wrong thing.

Especially when so much is on the line.

My career, my future, my team.

It's all too much.

I turn off my notifications and crash.

18

DECLAN

I hit the gym that afternoon, running through those Nautilus machines with Chance.

Or really, next to him.

Music keeps my mind occupied, my headphones playing Nirvana's "Come as You Are," then Alice in Chain's "Would?" before I go to my hair metal bands with Guns N' Roses.

Which reminds me of someone.

Of soft hair, and five o'clock stubble, and lips so lush I lost my mind. I flick over to "November Rain," and that's the dumbest gym decision ever because now I'm replaying last night, remembering how Grant went after me during that tune like I was his meal.

He mauled my lips, and I wanted every second of the kiss attack.

I blink, trying to send the tasty reel to the trash can in my mind.

But even when I switch songs to something

newer to vacuum up the memories, to Jordan Davis and Luke Bryan, my thoughts return to Grant and our talk last night. To the way he opened up to me, and how I did the same. To how effortless it was to connect, to tell him my story, and to hear his.

Everything about the man intrigues me, especially his boldness.

And my God, I hope he won't regret me if he decides to go through with this.

This thing I desperately want.

And there I go, popping wood.

I sit up on the weight bench so my semi is less noticeable and distract myself by firing off a note to Emma. She dragged me to a Guns N' Roses cover band in college, so my playlist is a perfect entry.

Declan: Remember Arrows and Daisies?

Emma: Worst cover band name ever.

Declan: Could have been Ammo and Lilies.

Emma: Fine. That might have been worse. Also, it's funny that you wrote to me.

Declan: Why's that?

Emma: I just bought a peach.

I laugh then type out a reply.

Declan: Do you dare to eat it?

Emma: I did. I ate it. I always take the Eliot dare.

I laugh over our private poetry jokes, this one courtesy of T.S. Eliot. Emma turned me onto the poet in college when I needed to conquer my fear of public speaking. She was a lifesaver. I wouldn't have been able to survive those classes without her, and she helped me see my way into T.S. Eliot's *The Love Song of J. Alfred Prufrock.*

As I make my way through the rest of the machines, I let a few lines from the poem play in my head.

I grow old . . . I grow old . . .
I shall wear the bottoms of my trousers rolled.
Shall I part my hair behind? Do I dare to eat a peach?
I shall wear white flannel trousers, and walk upon the beach.
I have heard the mermaids singing, each to each.

Drawing a deep breath, I ask myself some of the same questions. Not about a peach, but about a person.

Do I dare to tell the rookie that I want to take him up on his offer more than I've wanted anything from any man in ages, but the barest chance he'll regret me eats me alive?

I need to know he's not just thinking with his dick.

Well, he *is*.

But I want to know he's making decisions with his big head, to make sure he's thought this through.

When I finish my workout, I find one more message from Emma.

Emma: PS: See you in a couple days!

It takes a second, then the lightbulb flicks on.

Declan: Yes, the hockey game. Can't wait to see you.

Emma: I have a thing in LA after, so it's perfect. I'll be in for a night then go on to California.

Declan: Excellent. Let's grab a bite before.

Emma: As if I'd let you get away with anything less.

Declan: You let me get away with nothing.

I send the last note then drop my phone in my pocket, done with the workout. Tugging out my headphones, I tell Chance I'll catch up with him later.

The pitcher points a finger at me. "Pool tonight? You still there?"

"I'm there."

"Excellent."

I ask how Natasha's doing, and he tells me she's keeping busy but eager for spring training to be over.

"And then you'll be on the road," I add.

He shrugs. "The life of the ballplayer."

"Indeed, it is."

Chance clears his throat, lifts his chin. "Hey, what do you think of the team? You think it's coming together?"

I get why he's asking. Couple of guys were traded at the end of last season—notably, our longtime catcher, traded because of Grant. But also, our former catcher was older, getting rickety in the knees, and missing more games. Rodriguez is a solid backup, but he's thirty-two and he's always been a backup.

"Our new catcher specifically, you mean?"

"Well, yeah."

"I would think you know him better than I do. You throw to him. What do you think of him?"

Chance grins. "The dude is like a sunrise."

I shoot him a *what-the-hell* look. "A sunrise?"

"He's steady and calm, and he's always there. You can count on him."

I remember Grant's comparison of women to

sunsets, and I hold back a snicker that Chance wouldn't understand. I guess Grant and I have a private joke now.

Actually, Grant and I have a lot of private jokes, a lot of private moments, and maybe, we'll have a lot more in the future.

"You like him behind the dish?" I ask, stripping any laughter from my tone.

Chance nods enthusiastically. "I really do. He's like the ocean breeze, guiding me home."

I crack up. "You want to go for a triple metaphor? Maybe he's a mountain too."

"Let's call him Mountain Man," he says. Then, more seriously, he says, "But, no joke, he has a gift."

"Yeah. He really does." I tilt my head, searching his expression. "Why did you ask me, though?"

I suspect Chance gets the unspoken question. *Are you asking me what I think of him because we're the two queer dudes on the team?*

He scoffs. "Because you work out with him every morning? Duh. You know the guy."

I let out a held breath. "Right, yeah. He's a good one. Hell of an addition to the team."

I leave, texting my mom as I make my way through the complex. I haven't checked in with her in a few days, so she replies quickly.

Mom: I've cleared my schedule for Opening Day.

Declan: As you should. I'm getting you tickets on the first-base line.

Mom: Where else? But the game seems so far away.

I look at the calendar on my phone. Three and a half weeks since I got to Phoenix, one and a half more to go. Anxiety knots in my chest—there's so much I want to happen at spring training.

Declan: It'll be here in the blink of an eye.

Mom: And Tyler and I will be there too. We'll always be there.

That's one of the truest things she's ever said. I feel it deep in my soul, and that means the world to me. She was there when Dad left, cheering at all my games, taking me to early morning practices, and weekend tournaments all over the state. She stepped up as *both parents,* with Dad hardly around.

Then later, when I struggled with the aftermath of a visit from my father, she was there too. Some shit went down at the end of my senior year, and that's when I caught a glimpse of my own self-destructive potential. Mom did, as well, and she helped me get on a better path.

Declan: Love you, Mom.

Mom: I love you too.

I reach my room, and as I open the door, I find a new text.

It's not my mom.

Speak of the devil.

Anger lashes out of nowhere—anger I haven't felt in years. Fury and shame and guilt wrap around each other into a treacherous ball that slams into me like a rogue pitch.

"Are you kidding me?"

I shut the door and open the text from my dad.

He hasn't written to me in months. Not since he needed help paying his credit card.

Dad: Hey, kid!!! Miss you like crazy! How's it going? I checked the spring training blogs. You're killing it.

On the surface it's innocuous, just a note from a dad checking in with his son. But a headache blooms behind my eyes.

I sigh, leaning my pounding forehead against the door as I weigh my options: ignore it, ignore it and delete it, or engage with him.

I want to ignore it, but he's not asking for anything. He's still my dad. The least I can do is let go of my anger and reply to his message.

. . .

Declan: It's been good.

Leave it at those three words and hit send. His answer pops up quickly.

Dad: Proud of you. Have I told you that lately? I don't think I tell you that enough.

The pain throbs in my head, and I pinch the bridge of my nose. He wants something. I know he wants something. I swallow roughly then reply.

Declan: Thanks.

Dad: You're doing so well.

I grit my teeth. The hammering moves to my temples, a persistent banging. Inhaling deeply, I choose directness.

Declan: Dad, do you need something?

Dad: Just to tell my son that I love him.

My hand tightens on the phone. Fingers wrapped around it, I squeeze so damn hard it should break. I might smash it to smithereens.

This is so typical of him. Reach out, drop a line, say something nice. Then I'm the asshole for being curt. I'm the shitty son for doubting him. But feeling shitty about it doesn't change the feeling he wants something more—that this is just him buttering me up.

I inhale. Exhale. In. Out. In that measured pace, I recite the opening lines of Prufrock.

Let us go then, you and I,
When the evening is spread out against the sky.

Loosening my grip on the phone, I leave my room, head to the stairwell, bound down the steps, stride straight out of the hotel, get in my car, and drive to the foot of a hiking trail. At the trailhead, I park and get out, lean against the car, and name all the birds I see.

A cactus wren. A sparrow.

A woodpecker on a saguaro.

He takes off when I walk closer.

I get it, woodpecker. I understand why you show off those wings. That's all I wanted when I was ten, eleven, twelve, thirteen.

Finding a seat on a rock, I close my eyes.

I learned to recite poetry in my head because I was terrified to speak in public. I hated crowds, hated people looking at me. I was petrified at what they might think. I saw the way other kids in middle school stared at me any time my dad showed up at a game. I saw the way kids and adults looked at me with pity, feeling my shame.

I saw them turn away.

There by the saguaro, I go through the whole T.S. Eliot number, slowing at the line *Do I dare to eat a peach.*

When I finish, I slide open my phone and reply to my father at last.

Declan: Love you too. Appreciate the note.

One of those things is true.

Closing the thread, I drag a hand through my hair, hating lying.

I want truth.

I don't want the bullshit of Nathan and his *I won't do it again* empty promises, and I don't want the pop-up-out-of-nowhere style of Kyle, reappearing at whim, asking for another chance.

I want a man who knows his mind and who speaks it.

I flash back to yesterday. How Grant put his wishes out there for me the morning he said he wanted me.

I'm pretty damn sure Grant Blackwood knows his mind. I feel confident it's not changing. But more than that, I don't want him to do all the work.

And I want to say something that is wholly true. That doesn't have a single shred of a lie in it.

I send him a note.

. . .

Declan: There is no way I will regret you. The question is—do you still want me to come over tonight? Say the word, and I am there.

19

GRANT

Three hours later I roust my tired ass out of bed.

Spring training is exhausting.

Can't remember the last time I slept so long.

I roll over, yawning, and catch a glimpse of the clock.

It's eight, so I drag myself upright, brush my teeth, pull on board shorts, and head down to the pool. Crosby invited me to join him tonight, and I find him and Chance horsing around in the shallow end with some of the other guys, including Rodriguez, who slides a hand over his shaved head when he comes up from underwater, tiny droplets beading over his Black skin.

"You're gonna love our pool basketball," Crosby shouts, right before I cannonball into the deep end.

When I come up, the waves still rippling, I arch a brow as I swim to the middle where there's a net strung across the glistening water. "This is just pool volleyball," I point out.

Chance scowls at me. "Dude. Don't be a buzzkill."

Crosby seconds the indignation. "It's our version of basketball, and it's awesome."

I laugh. "Fair enough."

"Young guys. What do they know?" Rodriguez quips.

I'm glad that the guy I'm vying against seems cool with me. He's a good catcher and an even better person—he's an advocate for both foster kids and adoption, since he was adopted and I respect the hell out of how he puts his heart back into the world.

But no matter how cool he is, I want him to be *my* backup.

I zone in on the game, spiking a ball over the net. Crosby jumps, slams it back to me, and I serve it right back. We've been playing for a few minutes when Declan strides out to the pool.

I don't pay him any mind. No more than anyone else. Clearly his answer to my offer is no, and that makes him just another one of the guys.

I'll survive. All baseball all the time—that's how I should be. How *he* said I should be.

We all goof off, and as the clock ticks closer to nine-thirty, Chance calls it a night. "Don't know about you all, but I need my R and R," the pitcher says as he clambers up the ladder.

"Because you're old," taunts Crosby, who's maybe twenty-two or twenty-three, at the most.

Chance arches a brow. "If memory serves, it wasn't too long ago when it was you covered in ketchup and baby powder."

Crosby grins evilly. "And since then, I've belted thirty homers a season."

Declan clears his throat. "Thirty-five for me."

"I'm twenty-six years old, just like our shortstop," Chance puts in. "If that makes me old for hitting the sack at nine-thirty, fine. You can have an old all-star closer or a tired and drag-ass closer."

Crosby straightens in a snap. "Go! And say hi to Natasha from all of us. Sleep well. You're our secret weapon."

Chance nods sagely. "I thought so. I'll pass on your regards to the wife."

"Hell, I guess I should have hit the hay at seven since I'm the old fogey," Rodriguez remarks.

"Six-thirty for you, old man," Crosby teases, and Rodriguez flips him the bird.

I take this as my cue to get out too. Some of the other guys stay, but Declan heads up the steps, water droplets sliding down his muscular back.

I jerk my gaze away, say goodbye to the others, drying my hair and tossing the towel in the bin on my way into the hotel.

A minute later, I'm waiting for the elevator when footsteps grow louder behind me. I step in, Declan right behind me.

The doors close, and it's just us. He stares at me, his brown eyes intense. "You didn't answer my text."

His text? I knit my brow, confused, and shake my head. "I didn't see it."

He drags a hand through his wet hair and sighs heavily. "Rookie, you're killing me."

That nickname sends a buzz of electricity

down my chest, straight to my balls. But I won't make any assumptions. Won't rub up against him like a cat in heat. "I took a nap. I crashed. I left my phone in my room. But why am I killing you?"

"Why?" He glances at the buttons on the elevator panel. We're near the third floor. "Because I want to see you tonight."

It's embarrassing how much my stomach flips. "Yeah?"

"Read my message when you get to your room."

Like I'd do anything but pounce on my cell. "Give me the SparkNotes."

Declan looks like he wants to drag me into his room right this second, slam me against the wall, and punish my mouth for that request. "It says I have no regrets. But I want to make sure you don't either?"

Scoffing, I stare at him. "Do you seriously think anything changed for me?"

He lets out a breath. It sounds like the biggest relief in the world. "No. Were you waiting for me to say the word?"

No point pretending otherwise now. "Honestly?"

"Yes. Honestly."

"I kinda felt the ball was in your court, Deck," I admit. The truth has gotten me this far, and it sounds like we're going farther. I keep my foot on the pedal. "You know I'm all in. So now the question is—your room or mine?"

A sexy rumble falls from his lips. "I'll come to you."

And on me, I hope.

As the elevator doors open, I give him my room number. "I want to rinse the chlorine off me. Give me ten."

"Leave your door ajar so I can get in quickly."

"Will do."

I head down the hall. The second my door shuts, I dive onto my phone, turn the notifications on, and read his message.

I feel like I've won the sex lottery.

I punch the air, strip out of my board shorts, and hit the shower.

Ten minutes later, dressed only in a pair of basketball shorts, I open the door a crack, using the lock to leave it open.

When the door creaks after a few seconds, my lungs burn with anticipation.

Declan steps inside, flips the lock the other way, and kicks the door shut.

Excitement burns in me like jet fuel as I watch his every move from a few feet away. I lean against the wall, ready to fly into the stratosphere.

I'm ready for anything.

In no time, he strips off his T-shirt and kicks off his flip-flops. His dark eyes travel down my chest, my crotch, my legs, then back up to my face as he flares his nostrils and stalks over to me. "We should talk. Set ground rules. But I need a minute with my hands on you, rookie."

"That sounds like the start of a great conversation," I tease.

"Yeah, let me say *this* first." He runs his hands down my chest, over my abs, his thumbs sliding along the grooves. My whole body shakes.

Declan leans in and brings his face close to

mine, and my breath catches. I groan, ridiculously loud.

His eyes turn savage, then he drops his lips to my jawline and kisses along it, under it, down my neck. It's mind boggling. I'm crackling everywhere as he licks my Adam's apple then kisses up to my chin, where he stops, loops a hand through my hair, and clasps the back of my head. "You are so damn irresistible."

"Don't resist me." My voice barely sounds like my own, yet it's the truest statement I've ever breathed.

His eyes lock with mine; his irises contain a thousand dirty wishes. "And I am going to make you feel so fucking good. I'm going to do things to you that blow your mind. I'm going to make your toes curl, your knees weak, and your dick weep with pleasure."

His filthy, beautiful promise electrifies me. But what if I can't do the same to him? What if I'm no good?

But I've come this far. I'm not going to back down. Not from the act, or from the words.

"I want to make you feel good too," I say, letting him see beyond my bravado. Stripping bare. "I want you to teach me how to make you feel good."

"I will." Declan's eyes darken, glimmering with heat. "But know *this*—you already do." He slides his hand along my right arm, traveling over my muscles, down to my hand. He brings my palm to his crotch, then presses it against the hard ridge of his erection.

"Oh fuck, oh fuck, oh fuck," I gasp as I feel how hard he is. How big he is.

"You feel that?"

My throat is dry. All I can do is nod and gasp out a husk of a *yes*.

He crowds me, stepping closer. "You make me so fucking hard. You turn me on so much. You already make it so good for me," Declan says as he licks a path up to my ear, biting the earlobe while I fondle his cock, his length pushing through the thin fabric of his shorts.

I want more.

I want *skin*.

What's the point of clothes anyway? They're all coming off soon.

I have no idea what we're doing tonight. I have no clue if we're going all the way or some of the way. But I know this much: I want my mouth on Declan.

I push both hands into the waistband of his basketball shorts, shove them down and let them fall to the floor. Then I stare at his erection, thick and hard and pulsing. A vein throbs in the middle of his cock. The head is engorged, like a dirty invitation for my lips.

My mouth isn't dry; it's watering. I grasp him, gripping his hard-on, feeling that hot, smooth skin, and the virile strength underneath.

Everything about having Declan in my hand is intoxicating. It fries all my senses. It sends my system into overdrive.

Growls tumble from his lips with each stroke of my hand on his shaft. I give a few tight pumps then I drop to my knees. But right before I put my mouth on him, he ropes a hand through my hair and stops me. "I'm giving you one minute."

"Why?"

"Because," he says, gripping my hair nice and tight, then sharing his plans for us. What he wants to do next.

Something I've never done.

Something I want desperately to do.

I shudder everywhere, and my dick leaks.

"Have you done that yet?"

I shake my head. "No."

"Do you want to?"

"Hell yes."

The images he evokes are so arousing. Because they're a promise. A roadmap. A blueprint of what I'm sure is going to be one of the best nights of my life, ever.

And it starts with me taking Declan Steele into my mouth. With wrapping my lips around his pulsing length and tasting him for the first time, salty and musky and everything I've imagined and more.

I draw the head of his cock into my mouth with a groan.

"Yessssss," he rumbles.

I let go to lick a stripe down the underside, cupping his balls, then sweeping hot, wet kisses all over his shaft till I'm out of my mind with lust. Till he is too, judging from his moans. With a fist wrapped tight around the base, I bring him back into my mouth, and I don't take it easy.

I take it all, dragging him to the back of my throat in one long, hot haul.

"Your mouth," he grunts as his hands curl tight

around my skull. "Your irresistible mouth. Want to fuck your lips, rookie. Shoot into your throat," he says, and my dick throbs, hard and heavy between my legs.

I suck harder, hoovering him deeper as he unveils filthy promise after promise.

"But not yet. Know why?"

I shake my head and flick my tongue along the length of him.

"Because I need you naked and under me. Naked and over me. Because I need this insane body against mine," he says as he pumps, thrusting his hips mercilessly into my mouth.

My head is a hazy blur, and my nerves spark and crackle.

I loop a hand around to his ass, grabbing a muscular cheek, slamming him harder into my throat.

His growls and grunts are everything I've wanted, and we've only just begun.

Then Declan stops, curses, and drags his cock from my mouth.

I rise, feeling heady and powerful and a little crazy.

Feeling like a whole new part of my life is starting tonight.

20

DECLAN

I literally have to pry myself away from Grant.

He's too sexy.

"I need some space, or I will throw you on the bed and fuck you right now," I say, grabbing my shorts and yanking them back on.

"That doesn't really make me want to give you space. Just saying." Grant's all deadpan as he sasses me.

I toss him a look and head to the chair a few feet from the bed. I half want to sit next to him because I want my hands all over him, but I also think a buffer is a good idea while we lay down the law.

He goes to the mattress. Sits on the edge. Gestures to it. "This help? Got enough distance from the virgin you want to fuck?"

A wave of lust crashes through my body. This man and his mouth will be the death of me. He knows how to play me so well. Knows what words turn me on.

I lift a brow. "Aren't you funny when you get a little taste of my cock?"

He shrugs with a smirk. "I wouldn't say it was *little.*"

I laugh then shake my head and shove a hand through my hair, try to reset for a few minutes. "Baseball has rules," I say, focusing on the important matters. This is like the safe-sex talk. Gotta have it first. "We need them too. We're teammates, and we'll still be teammates after we screw," I say, as matter-of-fact as I can.

He nods in agreement. "We will."

"So, we need to agree. No clinging, no asking for more—none of that shit." Grant might be one hell of a guy, but that doesn't change my position on dating.

Grant scoffs. "Dude, I don't want a relationship."

"Good. I don't either. Second." I lift a finger. "No one can know. No one can ever know. This stays between us." I gesture from him to me.

He flubs his lips. "Obviously. I'm not about to go into the locker room and boast about us banging. Also, pretty sure no one wants to hear."

"Agreed."

Grant lifts his chin, humming thoughtfully. "I've got one though."

"Lay it on me."

His blue eyes lock with mine, the intensity in them searing. "When this ends, it ends. We move on. We don't talk about it. We don't reference it. We don't flirt on the diamond, off the diamond, on the bus, on the plane."

He draws a line in the sand, one I didn't expect

from a twenty-two-year-old. I admit, a part of me was worried he'd grow attached. It's good to know we're cut from the same cloth.

This line makes all the sense in the world. I need to adhere to it as well, no matter how endearing the man is.

I'd do well to remember that. To remember I need to resist his big heart, his clever mouth, his wide-open attitude.

Best to focus on the expiration date, and on the physical. "So, how about this for the rules of engagement? You tell me what's on your list of things you'd like to try, and when we check them all off, we're officially done, and we move on?"

He lists the things he wants to try, and even though my chest heats and my skin sizzles, I keep my cool.

"You good with those?" he asks.

"I'm very good with all that," I say in the understatement of my lifetime.

I am not only good with his list, I am infinitely aroused by it. By the specificity. By the details. And most of all by the fact that we're going to work our way, one by one, through his filthy wishes.

"Just so I'm clear—you've done hand jobs and blow jobs. Anything more?"

His face is stoic at first. He swallows. Shakes his head. "No. At least not with another person. I've played with butt plugs on myself."

"And you liked that?"

"I did."

"Mmm," I say, wildly turned on as I picture his

dirty list. "So, everything on your list is new to you?"

"It's all new," he says, chin up, eyes glimmering with lust. "And when we reach the end, we're done."

"When the lessons are over, they're over," I reiterate, though at the moment I'm not thinking about endings. I'm thinking about beginnings, and coming together, and coming on each other, and in each other, and holy hell, it's time to turn the oven off.

I am roasted.

Grant breathes a sigh of relief, clearly glad I'm onboard.

I am, all the way, but there's one last thing. "I've got one more request, but it's not quite a ground rule. More like a wish."

"Hit me."

I run my hands along my thighs, drawing a deep breath.

This next one matters *a lot*. I can't entirely explain why. I'm not sure myself. But I don't want to dive into sex tonight. I want the exploration, the discovery—for him, but also so I can experience it through his eyes, through his touch. "We take our time over the next few nights. Work our way up to sex. Get to know each other's bodies. Do the things you're dying to do."

A wicked grin curves his lips. "I get it. You want to drive me crazy."

I laugh. "Pretty sure you do that to me too, rookie."

"So, we've got a deal?"

"We've got a sex deal," I say, and that's enough

space and talk. I rise, cross to the bed, park my hands on the mattress, and dip my face to his, running my nose along his neck, inhaling that barbershop smell.

Grant shudders as the tip of my nose slides over his skin. "I want to get to know your body now," I murmur. "To touch you. Please you. And I want you to do the same to me."

"Oh fuck," he groans, his hands flying to my hips.

I grin like a cocky bastard. He's so damn frisky and his eagerness is the hottest thing I've ever seen. I sweep my lips along his neck. "All day long, I've thought about you. I can't stop thinking about what you told me."

Grant's fingers curl nice and tight around my hips, digging in. "That I'm a virgin?" He seems to enjoy saying the word, knowing what it does to me, how it rolls down my spine like Christmas lights flickering on, foot by foot, row by row, till I am all lit up.

"It's driving me wild," I murmur, running my lips down his neck. I brush them up to his ear, nip on the lobe. Then I pull back, meeting his hooded gaze. He sits straighter, his chest close to mine, heat simmering between our bodies. His eyes shine with lust.

"I want it to be so fucking good for you. I want you to have the first time I never did," I tell Grant.

"So, you're a gay sex revisionist?"

I laugh. "Maybe I am. But mostly I want to watch your face as you experience the greatest pleasure ever," I say, dragging my hand down his chest. He trembles as I go. "You're going to love it so much. Sex is fucking spectacular."

"How good?" he asks in a heady whisper.

"Nothing on heaven or earth is better. And I want to be the first man to fuck you, and I need to be the first man you fuck."

Grant lets out a long, staggered breath. "I can barely keep up with you. I'm having an out-of-body experience from the way you talk to me."

"Then you're really going to like what we do next."

21

DECLAN

Our clothes vanish in a heartbeat, and I am on him.

I climb on top of Grant, straddling him and dropping my mouth to his for a hot, searing kiss.

My cock bumps against his stomach. Valiant fucker wants to get right next to his shaft. But I hold off, waiting, teasing, so I can kiss him some more. Work him up.

Work him over.

His dick pokes me in the thigh, jerking against me. A slick of pre-come slides over my skin, and I love it. I love how aroused he is, how turned on I am, but I keep my body above him. A little space creates a lot of want.

I want him writhing for me.

I suck on his lower lip, eliciting a throaty rumble from the man, a shudder of his shoulders. Flicking my tongue across his top lip, he thrusts up under me, seeking contact. Begging for touch.

I don't give in. Instead, I devour his mouth, my

tongue tangling with his in a battle for dominance as his hands explore my chest. His palms curl over my pecs, slide down to my abs, trace the outline of my stomach.

Each touch makes my skin light up.

His fingers dance lower on a hunt for my shaft again, but just as he gets close enough, I slide down his body.

Drop my face to his chest.

Plant a soft, tantalizing kiss on his pec.

Grant groans, twisting under me.

"Mmm. Need to do this again," I say. I tug on his nipple piercing and his hips shoot up.

"God," he grunts, sounding lost, utterly lost.

I smile against his chest. "I'm learning things about you, rookie." Another lick, another flick.

"Yeah? Like what?"

I raise my face. "I think you like nipple play," I say with a dirty grin.

"I think you're right," he rasps out.

"But do you like this . . . ?"

I make my way down his body, sweeping slow, lingering kisses on the ladder of his abs, the dip of his V, then along his pubic hair, dragging my nose through the wiry, dark blond hair, indulging in a long, deep inhale till I'm dangerously close to the cock that I want to suck.

My whole body thunders with want.

My lips ache to draw him in deep.

"Suck it, please," he moans, pushing on my shoulders.

I want to give in, but I'm dying to give him something he's never had, and I won't deviate from the plan. "Uh-uh. Not yet. We made a deal."

"Does the deal involve you torturing me?"

I kiss his hip, getting drunk on the taste of his skin, that showered, soapy scent that makes me crazy. "Do you dislike my brand of torture, rookie?"

I punctuate my question with a brush of my tongue across his abs, then down to his pubic bone, so my jaw bumps against his hard cock.

"You. Are. Killing. Me," he growls.

I laugh lightly against him, then give in for a second, kissing the tip of his dick. Just the tip. That's all. But the salty taste of his arousal is a jolt to my senses.

A hit of the best stuff.

It invigorates me, trips all my switches. I am a slot machine hitting the jackpot, clanging and flashing.

I kick the tease-him plan to the curb and cover his body with mine, our cocks lining up like horny soldiers falling into formation.

"Ohhhhh," he rasps, his lips parted, his breath coming in harsh stutters.

His hands fly around me, grabbing my ass, tugging me closer. He grinds up against my dick, his sliding right next to mine, the friction making my balls sizzle.

"Do that again," I tell him.

He does as he's told.

"Yes. God. I want this so much," Grant says, and every single word sends sparks shooting across my skin.

Knowing he's saying them for the first time, that he's feeling this for the first time, that he's never rubbed off with a man before is such a high.

But I want it to be even better for him.

I want him to be in control.

And, not gonna lie, I want to watch him as he takes over. As he experiences the power shift.

I push up on one arm and reach for the lube on the nightstand with the other. "Get on me," I murmur, then I flop onto my back next to him, the bottle by my side.

The man needs little instruction. In an instant, he's lowering his big body onto me, and oh yes, I like athletes very much.

I've never been with a man the same size as me, the same width and breadth. Never been with someone with shoulders like Grant's, a chest like a wall, abs cut from the same daily regimen.

And I like it very much, especially when that fine dick rubs right against mine, making me hotter. Hornier. Ready to take us over the edge.

"Let me help us out," I say, breaking contact for a second.

"Right. Yeah." He blinks as I grab the lube, flip it open. Rising up so he's on his knees and I'm on my back, he watches me with avid eyes, like he's never seen anything as enticing as me slicking up my hand.

"Love it when you watch me, rookie," I whisper as I reach for my cock, stroke up and down, my breath coming in fast, hot pants.

Then, I wrap a hand around his dick for the first time. "Nice to meet all of you," I say as I weigh that big cock in my palm.

His eyes float closed, and I stroke him, as his moans fill my chest with pride, fill my body with pleasure. I up the ante, taking both our shafts in my palm, my fist sliding up and down.

I stare at his carved chest, his cut abs, watching as pleasure ripples down his body.

"Wrap your hand around mine," I tell him.

With one hand on my knee, he wraps his other fist over mine, and we jerk together.

"Yes, fucking yes," he grunts as we go, finding a rhythm for a few quick pumps.

Then, I give him a new instruction. "Now rub that beautiful cock against mine, rookie."

Grant covers me again, slides his arms under me, loops them around my shoulders, and unleashes all his desires on me. I grind up against him, and he pushes down, pumping and thrusting. I make room for him, legs open, hips jerking, dicks rubbing.

He doesn't say a word, but he can't shut up. He's all grunts, and sighs, and moans. It's the sexiest song I've ever heard. His noises, his breaths, his growls of desire.

But I know he likes it when I talk. Good thing I'm a chatty guy in bed. "Mmm. You feel so fucking good like this, rookie."

"Yeah?"

"So good," I say, gripping his ass, tugging him tight, letting my finger drift down his cheeks to the seam. "Tomorrow, I'm gonna play with this perfect ass."

"Oh God, yes, please, yes," he pants as he grinds and thrusts, and we are covered in sweat and lust, in longing and lube. It's intense and exhilarating and so damn good.

"I'm close, Deck," he grunts.

That's my cue. Another bit of lube in my hand, then I shift our weight, sliding out from under him, moving us side to side. I reach down, grab our cocks, wrap my hand around our pulsing shafts.

His eyes are glassy, lost in another world as he swings his gaze down to our dicks, shiny and hard. I jerk us together, my hand a blur, my fist a tight, hot machine. I am aching to come. But I want to come with him. I want him covered in him, me, us.

My balls tighten. Pleasure twists and writhes in me as Grant grips my hip, his fingers curling tight.

"Give it to me," I rasp, urging him on.

His lips part; his face contorts in exquisite torture. He twists his hips, spearing his cock into my fist.

"Gonna come," he grunts, thrusting in my hand and growling in my ear.

That's enough for me too. My nerve endings are on fire. My climax marches through my body, storms through my cells.

He unloads on my stomach in hot, white jets, and seconds later, I return the filthy favor, spurting all over him as wave after tsunami wave of pleasure wracks my body.

"Fuuuuuck," I groan as I shoot onto his chest. "Yessssss."

He answers me with a shudder, an *oh God*, and then a long, satisfied sigh. A pause, a breath, then he says, "Holy fuck. Did that happen?"

I can't talk yet. I'm still basking in the orgasm. In the shudders. The shockwaves. My eyes are closed, and my body is floating, and I feel incredible.

When my eyes open, I am looking at the most gorgeous man I've ever seen.

And he looks like all my dirty dreams, with eager questions in his blue eyes.

I answer them instantly. "You were perfect," I tell him.

"I was?"

I nod, then jerk him against me, so our release smears together.

He rubs that hot body against mine, getting in on the action.

When I stop, I slide a hand down, swipe a finger across his abs, dragging it through the mess.

I bring it to my lips and suck off the taste of us. Then I stare at the man in bed with me. "Want to know what we taste like?"

He trembles, his eyes shining with a fresh new round of lust. I lie on my back, gently bring him onto me, and give him my lips.

He sinks down, our two spent dicks resting now as his lips find mine and he tries something else entirely new.

This kind of a kiss.

Grant is more tender. He's soft and sensual. He lingers, exploring my mouth like it's the first time he's kissed me.

These kisses feel like they're happening to me for the first time too.

22

GRANT

Declan waves a hand at my right pec. "So, what's the story with the arrow? Were you an archer in a past life?"

Laughing, I park my hands behind my head, but don't answer right away. I'm kind of amazed he's still here ten minutes later.

What's the protocol on that? Are we screwing around more tonight? Is this pillow-talk time? Pillow-talk-before-more-sex time? I have no clue how *this* post-hookup stuff works. But we're still naked in bed, albeit cleaned up, courtesy of a washcloth break.

I thought he'd leave after that—tug on his shorts, give me a tip of the cap and say, "See you tomorrow, rookie," then wink and shut the door, leaving me to my thoughts.

That's what most of my hookups have done.

They've been quickies.

Trading BJs in college.

Quick hand job for quick hand job.

But they never lasted. I didn't have the time or the inclination to pursue anything more. Or the skills, to be honest. I don't *do* relationships because I've never *done* relationships.

I've never had a boyfriend.

Is this arrow question normal post-hookup talk? Or maybe post-sex-Sherpa talk?

What am I supposed to make of this guy lying next to me asking about my ink, wanting to know me?

It's all so uncharted. But it's also cool.

And natural too, like I'm just lying in bed chatting on the phone or FaceTiming a friend. Gone are the nerves and excitement of sex for the first time, the worry whether I'm doing it right. Now it's just us connecting, and I like it. I like it a lot.

"Was I an archer in a past life?" I repeat as I run my finger across the artwork Echo made. "Maybe I was. Maybe I was the god of archery."

He seems amused. "Were you Apollo once upon a time?"

I preen a bit. "If I were to be any god in a past life, it would totally be Apollo."

He chuckles. "Somebody thinks highly of himself."

"Dude, it's not because he's hot. It's because he was clearly one of the gay gods."

Declan tilts his head. "Have you studied the gay gods?"

"I was a history major in college. So, I took Greek and Roman history, and that got me interested in taking a mythology class too."

Declan pushes up, resting on his elbow on his side. "Tell me more about all the queer gods, then."

This, I can do. I know how to talk about history. Plus, Declan has such a casual way about him, especially when he asks questions the same way he does when we work out in the morning. "Apollo had lots of relationships," I say, shifting to my side too. "With lots of men and lots of women."

"So, he was the original fuck boy?"

I crack up. "I'm sure that's his nickname on Mount Olympus. Anyway, he was quite generous with the gift of his body. But one of his most important lovers was a nature god, who was also a Spartan prince named Hyacinth."

His expression is dubious. "So, the fuck boy's favorite lover was named after a flower?"

Shaking my head, I laugh. "Actually, I believe the flower was named after him. Legend says a dark blue hyacinth sprouted from Hyacinth's blood when he was killed."

"Did Apollo kill his lover, or was it one of those crazy god-gets-jealous-and-accidentally-offs-someone things?"

I tap my nose. "Good guess. One of the stories of Hyacinth's death is that Zephyrus, the Greek god of the west wind, was jealous of Hyacinth's relationship with Apollo. So, when Apollo was teaching Hyacinth how to throw a discus, the god of the wind blew it off course and killed Apollo's lover."

Declan mimes an explosion. "Wait. Wait a hot second. Not only was Apollo gay, he was part of a three-dude love triangle?"

"Homosexuality has been alive and well for centuries. And in spite of the debauchery, the infidelity, and the raging jealousy, the Greeks were pretty good flag bearers for LGBTQ back in the day."

"Things you learn," he says, a little delighted. "I suppose we owe them a debt of gratitude." He presses his palms together prayerfully and gazes heavenward. "Thank you, Apollo."

"Gods and poets, right?"

"Yeah, there were definitely a lot of poets who traveled on this side too." His eyes go thoughtful for a few seconds, like he's lost in time. "I think there's a hyacinth in a T.S. Eliot poem. *The Waste Land*. 'You gave me hyacinths first a year ago . . .'"

I quirk a brow. "From Guns N' Roses to T.S. Eliot? You're quoting poetry now, shortstop?"

Declan rolls his eyes. "I took a couple poetry classes in college. Helped me a lot with some stuff. I'm not *just* a jock. But I know the body might make you think that." He gestures to his firm, fit frame. Then he points to my arrow again, seeming determined, almost like he doesn't want to linger on the topic of poetry. "All right, Apollo. What's the story?"

"I got the arrow about a month ago. Right before spring training. It's all about forward momentum. Focus. Goals. Funny thing, though—I planned to get this long ago."

"You had a tattoo picked out when you were a kid?"

"Yep. My grandpa is covered in them. The dude has a full sleeve on his right arm," I say, running my hand down my arm to demonstrate. "I always loved his tattoos, and I used to trace them when I was a kid."

Holy hell, it is as easy to tell Declan these

things as it is to talk to Reese. For a second, I wonder if I'm saying too much, but the eager spark in his dark brown eyes tells me to keep going. It's like the coach waves me past first and I'm running hellbent toward second.

"I love ink that means something. So, for me, when I was five or six and I knew I wanted to be a baseball player, I told myself I was going to get a tat if I ever had a chance at making it to the Major Leagues."

Declan smiles. "That is awesome dedication from a very young age."

"I'm sure it was the same for you. Well, maybe not a tattoo. But didn't you know that you wanted to play ball?"

He laughs softly. "Absolutely." He inches a little closer, his voice turning reverent. "Do you remember the first time you stepped up at the plate when you were a little kid? And you dug in there, staring down the pitcher?" He sounds mesmerized, lost in time.

I nod, a tingle running down my shoulders as I picture it. "Like it was yesterday."

"Yeah, and it was just magic, wasn't it?"

I shake my head, amazed. "Nothing like it."

"It was all I ever wanted to do." He takes a beat. "Now, what about this?" He slides a finger down my bicep to the bands, black ink sketched like water, with waves. "Water is life? Go with the flow?"

"Sort of," I say, a touch embarrassed. "It's kind of cheesy."

He wiggles his fingers. "Bring on the Swiss, rookie."

"My grandpa has this one. On his arm. It's the first one I had done."

"Did you want to be like him?"

"Yeah. He took me to his shop. And he's an athlete too. Not pro, but he runs marathons, and as I said, I always liked his ink as a kid. So, I wanted to have the same."

He smiles. "Not cheesy at all. More like . . ." He stares into the distance. "Like a strawberry. *Sweet*."

"Okay, now you're making fun of me," I say, but I'm smiling too.

"Nah. I think it's cool. I like that you have the same one." His fingers travel down my arm to the compass tattoo near my wrist. His touch warms my skin. "And this one?"

I swallow. Do I tell him? This one is even more personal. But he seems determined to know its meaning, since he doesn't wait for my answer. He asks another question. "Is it for travel? Did you just want to see the world?"

"No. It's a reminder," I say, a little heavily, wondering if I should voice it. "To find my way out of the dark."

Declan shifts, studying me more intensely, his brow furrowing. "Is this about being gay, like how you came out? Or something else?"

Lord knows it *could* be about the way I came out. Or really, the way I was outed. But nope, that's not what this is.

"It's not about sexuality." Dragging a hand through my hair, I push past the discomfort. "It's just shit from my parents. I told you they weren't happy with each other. They weren't happy with a lot of things. There were things they said to each other in the heat of the moment that were hard to hear." The words taste like acid. Something black and tar-like twists inside me as memories jostle to the front of my mind, the terrible things they said to each other.

About me.

About my sister.

I swallow those down, tucking the dark truths into the far corner of my mind where nobody can know them.

His voice softens to a warm rumble. "I'm sorry you went through that. It's not easy." He sounds as if he understands what it's like to have to deal with shit.

Something in me wants to get to know Declan more. "Spoken from experience?"

"Yep. Absolutely." His eyes darken, and so does his tone.

I'm tempted to ask about his family, but that would be way too much for tonight. It doesn't seem like he wants to talk about that either.

His eyes stray to my mountain tattoo. "And what about this?"

"Actually, this is the one that's for adventure and travel," I say, easy and breezy now, because that's the nature of this ink in some ways. "When I was a kid, we didn't go to many places. I never got on a plane until high school for state championships. And when Reese and I were younger, we used to plan all the places we would go."

"What made the list?" he asks, more curiosity in his tone than I would have expected.

"Back then, we didn't care. We would pick the globe, spin it, and put a finger on it. And then we would just pretend. When we were really young, we would grab our backpacks and wander down the street pretending we were escaping to China or Alaska or Canada. Then later, we would talk about what it must be like to live in New Zealand and Australia. Honestly, I just wanted to get away."

Declan heaves a sigh, drags a finger absently down my arm. "Man, do I ever know that well."

This is my chance to understand him. Maybe he keeps mentioning it because he wants someone to open the door for him. But I'm not sure how much I want to hear or how much he wants to say. I take only the most tentative of steps. "You were trying to escape from shit at home too?"

"My dad." The word contains the weight of the world.

"You don't get along with him?"

"I *did*. Incredibly well. For a long time. When I was really young, he was my hero." Shaking his head, Declan blows out a long breath. "He was a ballplayer. A Minor Leaguer for a couple of years. A coach. But things changed . . ."

He's quiet for a bit, contemplative. I don't push. I don't know how to ask or if I should.

"He left when I was at the end of middle school. And honestly, Grant, it was for the best."

It's as if Declan just skipped a period of his life in that pause. Maybe that's the span he wanted to escape from. "Did you see him again?"

"Sometimes. He would show up now and then. He lives in Oakland now, and he still gets in touch when it's convenient for him, usually to ask for stuff. Know what I mean?"

Do I ever. "Sounds a bit like my mom. She just

told my grandpa this week that she wants to come to my first Major League game, assuming I make the roster. She never went to a single one in the minors. My dad is just the same. So yeah, I know what you mean."

He settles back into his pillow, hands behind his head, staring at the ceiling. "It sucks, right? When I was younger, I wished I could fly away from it all sometimes."

A few Declan puzzle pieces snap into place. "That's why you like birds," I say.

Shifting back to his side, he taps my temple, a smile playing on his lips. "You're too observant for your own good," he says and yawns. "Damn, I'm tired. That was a day."

A second later, he gets up, pulls on his shorts, and pads to the door.

My chest tightens.

Did I say the wrong thing? Did I push too hard? It didn't even feel like I was pushing, but now he's staring through the peephole, his attention elsewhere.

"Crap. Some of the guys are wandering down the hall."

My stomach twists, and I swing my legs out of bed, grabbing my shorts, so I feel less . . . well, naked. "Are they coming to my room?"

Declan shakes his head but walks back to the bed. "No. They're just going by." He kicks off his shoes, shucks his shorts, and stares at the king-size mattress. His eyes flicker with vulnerability. His voice dips to a gentle tone. "You mind if I crash here for a bit?"

I half want to say, *"Weren't you just about to leave? Wouldn't you rather go?"*

"Of course." I don't mind at all if he crashes, but I'm not ready to unpack why it doesn't bother me.

"I'll set my alarm. We're going to work out, right?" His voice wavers the tiniest bit at the end like he really wants me to say yes to a workout. Like he needs reassurance that tomorrow we're doing the same thing we did before we messed around.

I smile. "Yeah, we are."

"Good," Declan says.

I figure he'll close his eyes, turn the other way and crash. But instead, he cups my cheek, brings his lips to mine, and whispers a kiss across them.

I shiver down to my toes.

His kisses are electric—even the soft, sweet ones.

"Mmm. Your lips taste so damn good, rookie," he says. "I'm not sure I've ever enjoyed kissing as much as I do with you."

I close my eyes so he can't see how happy those words make me, and I sink into the softest, sweetest goodnight kiss I've ever had.

But then, I have nothing to compare it to—a goodnight kiss is another first. I let myself enjoy it for several delirious seconds that spill into a minute, maybe more.

Soon, Declan breaks the kiss, glides a hand softly down my chest, and crashes into sleep.

I don't.

My brain is a maze, and I'm trying to find my way through twists and turns, past dead-ends, around bizarre angles. I'm trying to navigate all this newness.

A man in my bed.

My teammate asleep next to me.

My first sexual encounter like that. My first, too, where we were both that close, touching each other at the same time, coming at the same time, kissing after coming.

I run my finger over my bottom lip, replaying tonight, his body on mine, the heat between us.

I return too, to our kisses. I've never kissed anyone that much.

I drag a hand through my hair. I need to stop thinking about how good those kisses are.

He snores slightly, scoots closer, and drapes an arm across my chest with a soft murmur. I both hate and love how good that makes me feel. How my chest goes all flippity-flop.

But mostly, I love it, and I fall asleep just like that, with his arm around me.

* * *

When I wake, Declan is gone, but there's a note from him on my phone.

Declan: See you at dawn, rookie.

Somehow, this makes me as happy as the sex.

23

GRANT

When I find Declan on the track the next morning, he gives me a chin nod. "Morning."

"Morning," I say, unsure what happens next. Do we just start running? Do we acknowledge last night? Do we flirt still?

I have no idea how anyone navigates trysts, let alone a tryst with your teammate. Then he says, "Apollo," and shoots me his cocky grin that's so damn sexy.

I grin right back. "Hey—"

He holds up a hand. "Don't you dare call me Hyacinth."

I smirk. "He's also known as Hyacinthus. That better?"

He shakes his head adamantly. "Don't even think about it."

"Well, I won't invite you to throw the discus with me then either," I taunt.

"Thanks. Appreciate that."

Declan nods toward the track, and we start running. "Sleep well?" he asks.

"Very," I reply, my lips twitching.

"Yeah. Me too." His mouth curves up the slightest bit as well.

I pretend I don't notice, but my pulse does. It speeds up long before the cardio kicks in.

We run along the track, then he gestures toward the gate and we take off through it, heading for the golf course. Along the way, we pass the lake. This time, the heron is doing more than preening. It's rubbing up against another heron.

"Dude, *that's* Apollo," I say, tipping my forehead to the scene near us.

"I think Apollo is banging his Spartan prince," Declan quips.

"Is it any surprise? Those herons were hot for each other."

"I feel like I understand birds even more now," Declan drawls.

"The birds and the bees," I add.

We laugh and kill thirty more minutes like that. Like friends, not like lovers. It feels right, a necessary antidote to last night. Something about the talking then felt almost too close.

Everything about my life right now is new.

My job.

My career.

My totally-awesome-for-the-first-time-ever sex life.

But Declan is the first guy who's ever spent the night, and I don't need to make stupid mistakes with him.

Being friends, though? This I know how to do. "Friends" is also what I'll have to be with Declan when our affair ends in only a few more nights.

Because it *will* end, but he'll still be around. I'll still be around. And we'll have to get along. So, I have to be careful with him.

When we finish our workout and return to the complex, he catches my eye again and lowers his voice. "Your room tonight? Ten?"

I grin. I can't help it. I really want to see him again.

But before I can tell him so, he wiggles a brow, licks his lips and says, "You're looking forward to that too?"

It's the *too* that makes me shiver. Before I even have to say yes, that's an admission that he's on the same page as me.

"Yep," I say.

"Catch you later," he says, and relief flows through me.

We can do this.

We can be friends in the day. We can be lovers at night. And when it ends, we can be friends and ballplayers.

Nothing will go wrong.

* * *

Except baseball.

We lose the game against the Chicago Sharks that afternoon, and by an embarrassing amount.

It's not just a rout, it's a clubbing. I whiff at the plate every time. My pitchers roll over too, throwing softballs down the middle that the Sharks clobber over the fences.

Maybe I called for the wrong pitches. Did I set the target too low?

But it's spring training, and I've played well until now, so I hope no one's too worried.

We return from the Sharks spring training home, pile off the bus, drop our bags on the field, and run a mile.

"Burn off the loss, men. Burn it off," Fisher says.

I run.

We all run. Heads down.

No one pairs up.

One by one, we trudge through the dugout and into the locker room. I've just grabbed my bag when Fisher calls my name.

"Blackwood. A word."

Tension slides down my spine. *A* word is never a good word.

I wheel around, following the manager back out to the field, joining him at home plate. The hitting coach is there too.

I drop my bag by my feet. "Yes, sir?"

His gray eyes remain locked on the rest of the team headed inside. Once it's just the hitting coach and me, Fisher says, "How are you doing?"

Is this a test? I've never liked pop quizzes.

"I'm well, thanks."

I'm also tense in every single muscle in my body.

"Everything is good?" he asks next.

Why is he asking me if I'm good? Why are we

having a random conversation after a shit-tastic game?

"Everything is great."

"You fitting in?"

Ohhhh.

Is *that* why we're talking?

"Yes, sir," I say, my stomach curling. I hope this isn't the *be nice to the new queer player* moment.

But I know I should be grateful I'm playing now rather than five or ten years ago.

The skipper scrubs a hand over his chin. "Good. Is everyone...?"

Oh man, he can't even finish the sentence. I wince but try to fight it off. I hate this shit. It's so awkward for everyone, but for me, it dredges up all the crap I thought I was past. The moments I had no control over, the times when others took ownership of my identity. My skin crawls with uncomfortable memories, but I remind myself this doesn't have to become another one.

He clears his throat, starts over. "Is everyone treating you right?"

I exhale. Fasten on a smile. "Yeah. It's all good, sir."

He swipes one palm against the other. That's done. "Excellent. I like the way you're working out."

Some of the tension unwinds. This is just a politically correct conversation. A moment to be diplomatic. I can live with that. He probably wants to be a better ally. He's in his late fifties, so I bet this is still all new to him. New generation, new effort. I get it.

This, too, is why I'm out, openly out. For

chances like these—to speak freely with others, to allow them to speak freely with me.

"Glad to hear," I say with a smile, because that's how I choose to be. No snark, no pushback—just be me, and be authentic.

I bend to pick up my bag, figuring we're done, but he keeps talking. "But could you take some extra time with the hitting coach right now?"

I freeze, midway to the ground. "Extra batting practice?"

"Yeah. It'd be good for you. Especially as we figure out our roster."

I rise, leaving the bag there, unsure what to do, what to think, except this is part of the test for the starting slot. But this is batting practice, not catching practice.

He claps me on the shoulder. "Thanks, Blackwood." He walks off and I turn to the hitting coach, who strides over from the edge of the field.

Coach Tanaka is gruff and no nonsense. He nods at me and says, "I'll be back. Give me ten."

And I freak the fuck out.

Why the hell does the hitting coach want to work with me? I pace around the field, fishing my phone from my bag as Tanaka heads inside.

With the speed of a falcon *on* speed, I call my agent in New York.

Haven answers right away. "What's going on, Grant?" Her calm voice does nothing to soothe me.

"Dude, what is going on? Why does Fisher want to have the hitting coach work with me?"

"I don't know. Your batting average is terrific. You're batting over three hundred," she says, heading straight for stats, since stats are everything.

"So, what the hell?"

"I don't think it's anything to worry about," she says. "But I'll do some digging. And don't you go googling yourself."

That's the advice she's been giving me since she signed me. "I won't, but here's the thing." I shake my head. She's wrong. "My gut is telling me something else is going on, Haven. Why the hell would he want to work with me? There's something he's not happy with. Is Rodriguez moving up from backup? I thought this was my spot to win. Can you find out? Are they going to send me down?"

Panic kicks in. I can't be sent down. I have plans. Big plans. A future. I only want to go up.

"Grant, the team has you in its sights as its new starter. I don't think there is a thing to worry about, but I'll make some calls. See what's going on."

"Thanks, Haven," I grit out.

I hang up, tossing my phone in my bag as Tanaka strides over to me at home plate. "You ready?"

"I'm ready."

For the next hour he takes me through my paces, works with me on my hitting, on my stance, on my swing.

Over and over.

When we're done, he's as stoic as Fisher.

"That'll do," he says, in a monotone that gives nothing away.

That'll do?

That's what the farmer said to the pig in *Babe*.

But at least then, it was a compliment.

This is a *non-compliment.*

I stand there, trying to make sense of what just went down.

I thought I was having a great spring training, especially for a rookie.

But now I have no clue.

And no idea what this means for the starting slot.

Especially when Tanaka walks off the field, gives me a curt nod, and says, "Thanks, rookie."

I don't like the way he says *rookie*. I don't like the way he says it at all.

I definitely don't like being left in the dark. This moment feels all too familiar—other people knowing secrets about you, whispering them privately, leaving you to guess.

I head to the locker room, stalk into the shower, and let the hot water rain down over me, letting it wash off my annoyance and my frustration.

It doesn't do the trick.

Instead, my gut twists. My jaw clenches.

My brain races three laps ahead, trying to figure it out but coming up empty.

When I walk into the locker room, it echoes.

I'm all alone.

And something about that feels like an omen.

* * *

I get dressed quickly, grab my phone and my wallet, then head out of the locker room, calling my agent once more, "Did you find out anything?"

Haven is warm and reassuring as she says, "I talked to the GM. He says all is well."

I wince, stopping, sinking against the wall, closing my eyes. "But isn't that the kiss of death before you're sent down?"

"Grant, let me work this. Don't jump to conclusions," she says.

"Okay. Thanks." I hang up because there's nothing else to do.

I head into the hotel so I can call someone to talk, but I quickly veto Pops. I don't want to stress him. Not while he has to schedule his knee surgery. Maybe I'll try Reese.

On my way to the elevator, I bump into Sullivan, who's strutting down the hall in his cool cat mode. "You, me, C and C. They invited us to pool tonight."

"Who's that?"

"Crosby and Chance. They look like . . ." He furrows his brow. "Ah hell, I don't know how to do your celeb comp thing. Two white dudes who look like all-American ballplayers. Maybe you've heard of them? Those guys want to go out to play some pool," he says, miming pulling a pool stick behind him and smacking a ball with it.

Right—C and C. I should have figured that out. But my mind is elsewhere.

"Come with?" he asks, back to his smooth style. Glad to see he's doing better after those wobbly games.

"Yeah, sure," I say, answering quickly.

Pool is better than sitting here moping and stressing and not wanting to bother anybody.

"By the way, I'm pretty sure Ryan Reynolds's

second cousin is fifty times hotter than I am, so thanks for the tip," he says with a wink.

I laugh lightly, but it fades quickly since my mind is elsewhere.

"See you at nine," Sullivan adds and struts off.

Nine. Fucking nine.

I groan, a huge sigh of disappointment. I can't tell him I have someplace to be at ten. That'd look suspect. I can't say I'll play pool at nine, but I have to be somewhere else less than an hour later.

And I can't get out of it.

When I reach my room, annoyance is hitting sky-high levels in me.

I'm annoyed at myself.

I'm annoyed at the world.

I'm annoyed at the fucking game.

I sink down in the chair and send a text to Declan.

Grant: Hey. Can we push tonight back a bit? I'm going to play pool.

I say *going* rather than *I've got to*.

I don't want it to look like my friends are an obligation. I don't want it to look to him like I would've canceled to see him.

But I would have.

He writes back right away.

Declan: At the Cactus Club. Yeah, I'll be there too.

. . .

A grin tugs at my lips.

Grant: Cool.

Declan: Want to see how good I am at acting like I don't want to fuck you?

As I read his text, I smile big and wide and genuinely for the first time in hours.
I write back.

Grant: Dying to.

Declan: Considering how much I want you, it'll be a goddamn master class.

24

DECLAN

This is great practice.

This is what we'll have to do in a week.

Then, come April, we'll be traveling together on the team plane. Going out after games sometimes.

We'll need to blend in.

So, as I line up the shot at the Cactus Club, I don't think about who Grant is texting on his phone.

Nope. I don't care if his attention is elsewhere. Just like I wouldn't care if Crosby was keeping himself busy.

But Crosby is not.

Crosby is all teammate tonight as he tosses down a fifty-dollar bill. "Fifty bucks says the shortstop and I kick all your sorry asses," he says to the other rookies.

I glance over at him as I line up the shot. "You're so damn lucky I let you be my teammate at pool."

Crosby laughs. "Because there's no way I'd win without you." Then he wiggles his fingers at Sullivan. "Come on. Pay up too. Bet's for everyone."

Sullivan shoots him a dubious look. "Wait. This is another rookie prank, isn't it?"

"I bet it is," Miguel puts in, arching a smart-aleck brow.

I toss a shrug Crosby's way. "Guess they won't find out until the end of the night."

Grant's hanging out by the end of the table when he looks up from his phone. "Bullshit. This isn't a prank," he says, one of the first things he's said all night.

But I am *not* paying attention to him.

I am playing a game.

I aim, shoot, and send the ball into the pocket.

"Woohoo! My teammate can handle a stick," Crosby says, thrusting his arms high in the air.

I bark out a cough then give him a side-eye stare. "Oh no you didn't."

Crosby's face goes slack. "Oh shit, man. I'm sorry."

I crack up, offering him a hand for high-fiving. "Don't be sorry. You're not wrong."

Crosby rolls his eyes. "Of course you know how to handle a stick, you big stud."

"And you're an ace with the . . . *glove*," I say, laughing, but I don't risk a single glance at Grant.

Not one.

I take a few more shots till we miss. I grab my iced tea, and Crosby lifts a beer as Grant strides to the table with Chance, who is a steely-eyed mofo. This will be good practice for me too.

Watching and talking and *not* thinking about seeing Grant later.

Not at all.

I lean back against the wall and toss out a critical issue for debate to the guys. "LeBron or Jordan?"

Sullivan snaps his fingers. "Oh, man. That is a tough-ass question, but it has got to be MJ all the way. He did not lose a championship."

"Nope. LeBron. Better stats," Miguel puts in, punctuating his point with a stab of his pool cue to the floor.

That sparks a great basketball debate for another round as Grant lines up at the corner of the table, calls the shot, then pulls back the stick and smacks the white ball against the black one, sending it home, and winning the game.

I want to shout, clap him on the back, and say *good shot.*

Because I *want* to whoop and holler for this guy. But I've got to treat him just like any other teammate. He's just another guy who played a solid round of pool. "Good game," I remark.

He nods a thanks. That's all.

Damn, he is good at ignoring the hell out of me too. I guess he could also teach a master class. He's been doing it all night long.

I'm good with that.

So good with that.

He clears his throat and lays down the next debate as he racks up. "Who would win in a game against the '27 Yankees. Us or Murderers' Row?"

"Us," Crosby says in a second.

"Nah," I say, shaking my head. "Them."

Chance hums thoughtfully. "And why is that?"

I hold my hands out wide, like it's obvious. "Because you don't disrespect Ruth and Gehrig."

Grant cracks a smile. "Damn good answer, man."

If we were alone, or hell, maybe if we were at The Lazy Hammock again, I would toss out a joke. I would say something to him like, *"And I'd also bet on them too, because I don't think Ruth wanted to fuck Gehrig or vice versa."*

Then Grant would say, *"But what if he did? What if Ruth and Gehrig were really messing around after a game?"*

We'd have a laugh as we ate our dinner on the deck, the warm night air surrounding us, the palm trees swaying. We'd be in the corner table that River hooked us up with.

It'd become our thing. Grant would call me Ruth and I'd call him Gehrig, and we'd joke about it the next day as we went for a run.

Maybe he'd even become my off-season guy. The one I poured all my energy into after October. I'd remove my baseball blinders and give him the best of me for a few months.

I'd take him out, take him home. Be seen or not be seen. I wouldn't have to care. We could just . . . *be*. No need to post selfies of our dates, but no need to sneak around either.

For a fraction of a second, hell, for more than that, I look at Grant like that's where we are.

Out together.

Then in bed, alone.

I look at him exactly the way I shouldn't. Like he's my lover.

And that's no good.

I need control. Must have it. Like I have at the plate.

Don't swing at just anything. Don't let bad calls get to you.

That's how I've been.

And so, I *do* need to think about Ruth and Gehrig. Anything but Grant.

Except when the rookie catcher lifts a drink and brings it to his mouth, my eyes sail to the bottle.

Diet Coke.

I swallow roughly, itching to touch him, aching to taste his Diet Coke lips. I want to take him in my arms and kiss the hell out of him.

I practically break the stick in my hands because there's so much tension flowing through my body.

Then Grant sets down the bottle, reaches into his pocket again and grabs his phone. He turns away, tapping on it once more.

I force myself to look away too.

Practice. This is practice. Doesn't matter if Grant's on his phone, if Chance is on his phone, if Sullivan is on his phone.

It's not like I'm jealous.

It's not like there's some other guy he's talking to.

I'm not worried about that.

But I do want to know why he's distracted.

When it's time to go, I'm no closer to finding out because half the gang piles into my car, the other half into Chance's rental.

Grant's not with me, so I chat with Sullivan and Miguel.

My crew walks through the door of the hotel at 10:31 and I make a show of yawning. At 10:33, I'm in my room. At 10:34, I text Grant.

At 10:35, he replies that the hall is empty, but to give it five minutes anyway.

I do just that and at 10:40 I leave my room, head for the stairwell, bound up the steps to the sixth floor, and push on the door. I glance right. Left. Right. Left.

My heart skitters, pulse pounding.

Coast is still clear.

But my heart won't calm down. It's not from the exertion. A two-flight jaunt is nothing. It's beating fast from the secret.

From the sneaking around.

And the chance that we could get caught.

I suppose we could book a room at another hotel, but we'd still have to slip out and sneak back in. So even if we were elsewhere, it's six of one, half a dozen of the other.

I act like I'm doing nothing wrong as I stroll down the hall and head for his room, taking one long glance behind me, making sure no one is around when I reach his door.

I push it open.

Once inside, I slide it shut, lock it, exhale.

Do my best to leave the tension behind me. I made it here, safe and sound, unscathed. To my secret hideaway where no one can find us.

Grant's waiting for me on the edge of the bed.

"How's it going?" I ask.

He shudders a sigh. "I'm a fucking mess."

My heart thumps with worry, as I head to the bed and sit next to him. "I noticed."

"You did?" His voice is stretched thin with worry.

I run a hand down his thigh. "I kind of notice you," I say, softly, repeating his words back to him. Speaking my truth.

"You do?" He can't seem to mask the smile.

"Yeah, I notice you, Grant Blackwood." I squeeze his thigh. "What's on your mind?"

I hope to hell it isn't anything involving us.

Because right now, right here, all that pretending, all that practicing, and all that rapid heart-beating disappears.

This is where I want to be.

25

DECLAN

Grant drops his forehead into his palm. "Skipper called me aside after the game," he says.

"What'd he say?"

Grant adopts an older voice. "How's it going? Is everyone nice to you?" He lifts his face, rolls his eyes. "Like he has to make sure no one's going to beat me up for sucking cock."

I sigh sympathetically. "Some of these older guys . . . it's hard for them, so they think they have to be extra nice. We have to remember it wasn't always this way. Hell, it wasn't this way for a long time." I tilt my head to the side, studying his face, the way his brow creases with worry, how his eyes are etched with concern. "But is that what's bugging you? Because honestly, you seem pretty tough. I don't buy that one awkward exchange with the coach is turning you into a 'fucking mess.'" I sketch air quotes. "Your words."

Grant shakes his head. "He had me stay for an hour of extra batting practice with Tanaka. Said he wanted to work on things with me. I keep thinking it's a sign, right? I'm the rookie they bet on. The horse they can't make run, and I'm not performing so they're giving me extra laps, extra runs, before they decide if they're going to let me go or not."

Oh, man. This guy.

My chest squeezes for him. "Is that what you think?"

The catcher shrugs, a little helpless. "Well, yeah. I've been playing well during spring training, and then I had one bad game, and all of a sudden, they're all over me saying *you've got to work on things*. So, I bet not only am I not winning the starting job, I'm getting sent down. I called my agent, and she called the GM, and he said everything is fine. But that feels like the kiss of death. It's like when a boss says *he has my full support* and the next day, they fire you."

I set a hand on his back, run it up and down for reassurance. I'm about to tell him what it means when he builds up a new head of steam.

"I don't want to get sent down, Deck. I really don't. I want to prove to everyone that I can do this," he says, a pained expression in his eyes. "You get it, man, right? I mean, we have to work that much harder than the others. Just to prove we belong."

A fist grips my heart, clutching it. "I get it. One hundred percent."

"I want to just fit in. Feel at home. Not feel like I have to work ten times harder. But I *will* work ten times harder. I have worked ten times harder. Know what I mean?"

I squeeze his shoulder. "You know I do."

The rookie drags a hand roughly through his hair. "This is what I worked my ass off for, all those years. To build a new life," he says, his voice strung tight with desperation. The sound of it makes it clear baseball is way more than a career for him—it's a reinvention of his soul. I understand that deeply.

Innately.

I understand too, that I alone can put him out of his misery.

In a soft but clear voice, I cut in. "If I could get a word in edgewise, I'll let you in on a little secret."

"If it's the answer to this, I would love that," he says, sounding thoroughly miserable.

I ruffle his hair. Stifle a grin. "It means they like you, rookie."

He jerks away. "What? No way."

"It means they absolutely like you. Want to know how I know?"

"Yes."

"They asked me to do that my first spring training. It's a sign. They're asking more of you and want to know how you handle it when you have to take on more responsibility. More time. More practice. It's not bad, Grant. Not at all."

"It's good?" His voice is full of wonder and hope.

"It's very good."

He breathes out the biggest sigh of relief I've ever heard. "Are you sure?"

"Positive. Even if they ask you to catch a scrimmage."

"Wait. The bullpen catcher and minor leaguers

on the roster have been catching most of the inter-squad games. Should I be worried if they ask me to catch one?"

I smile, shake my head. "No. At least, I don't think so. I mean, they asked me to take extra batting practice, not catching practice, for obvious reasons. But my point is—it's a good thing. They want to see you play—see how you perform. You've been starting most of the games, and they want to know you can handle the rigor, the attention, the bruising, punishing schedule."

"I can definitely handle it," he says, a note of pride returning to his voice.

"I know you can. But they want to know too. It's a good thing."

"Promise?"

"Promise." I hold out my hand for him to shake.

He takes my hand. Tugs me toward him. "Thank you," he says in a rush of gratitude-tinged lust.

Grant kisses me deeply and passionately, exploring my mouth. Grabbing my face. Hauling me up on the bed. Pinning my wrists above my head. Pushing up on his arms. Staring down at me, playfully angry. "You let me get all worked up."

I chuckle. "You worked yourself up, rookie. I had to talk you down first."

"Before you could tell me the secret," he says with narrowed eyes.

"I wanted to tell you, but you needed to talk it out."

"I needed to know," he grumbles, but does so with a smile. Then, with a deep exhale, he runs his hand through my hair, his touch surprisingly gentle. "I guess you knew what I needed."

"I think I did. I was glad I could give it to you," I say.

"I was a mess."

I laugh lightly. "I know. You were all nervous and twitchy at the pool hall."

He arches a skeptical brow. "But I thought you were ignoring me?" he asks, back to sassy, cocky Grant now.

My eyes sweep up and down the man above me. "Have you seen you? You're hard to ignore."

He hums. "How hard?"

I raise my knees, plant my feet on the mattress, yank him down between my legs. "Feel for yourself."

"Mmm," Grant murmurs, slamming his pelvis against my cock that's warming up to come out and play.

"Yeah, you're getting good at that, rookie."

"At dry humping you?" he asks with a laugh.

"At showing me what you want," I correct.

"It's easy with you," he says, swiveling his hips, grinding his hard-on against me.

I loop my hands around to his firm ass, sliding them down the back of his shorts, grabbing that hard, muscled butt of his. Angling him just so, in the perfect way for him to ride my cock someday. Someday soon. "Why is it easy with me? To show me what you want?" I thrust up, like he's riding my dick, and hell, that is a fine image.

Grant lets out a long, hot shudder. "Don't know," he says, all husky as he works his ass against the ridge of my erection.

"You don't know?" I challenge, squeezing that flesh, my fingers drifting down the seam of his ass—my playground for tonight.

"Maybe because you want to give it to me? That's all I can figure," he rasps out.

I smile. Wickedly. "That's a good enough reason," I tell Grant on an upthrust, one that I hope lets him feel how hard I am for him. Then, I bring his face down to mine, and whisper across his lips, "I'd like to introduce myself to your prostate tonight."

Grant lets out a staggered breath. "Yes, please. Yes."

I tug at his shirt. "Off."

He nods savagely, slides away from me, and sheds his shirt, shorts, and boxer briefs.

I do the same, grab the lube from the nightstand, and climb on top, straddling him.

My dick slaps against his stomach, then I nod. "Gimme room. Want to be between your thighs."

He widens his legs. "Like this?"

"Feel free to raise your knees. I want access."

With zero fear, only excitement, Grant lifts his knees, plants his feet down, widens his legs.

I can't resist giving him a preview. I kneel between those muscular thighs, slide my hands up the back of them, lift his legs up in the air, and get him in the perfect position for a pounding. "This position?"

"Yeah?" His voice is dripping with sexual intrigue.

"It'll be one of your favorites."

"For topping or bottoming?"

"Mmm. Bottoming. Feels so fucking good. I

love being on my back." I rock my hips, thrusting my cock in the air, gripping his thighs harder, pushing his legs farther apart. "The way you are right now? How does it make you feel?"

"Honestly? A little vulnerable," the blue-eyed man beneath me admits. "But turned on too."

"Good. That's how *I'm* going to feel when you fuck me like this," I murmur.

He stutters out a breath. "This is how you want it when I'm inside you?"

I stare down at Grant, my blood roaring. "Yes," I say, since I want to wind him up, turn him on, get him seeing all the ways we can fuck. With no limits on roles. I might be teaching him, but I want him to discover how we can turn each other on. All the ways we can trade off. "That's how I want you to fuck me for the first time."

He just groans—a long, needy groan that makes my balls tingle. That lights me up. I slide my hand down to his ass, my fingers teasing over his skin. "Want to know why it's going to feel so good for me?"

"Yeah?" he says, like he's hanging on every word.

"Because I can look at you the whole time. I can see your face, the pleasure on it as you drive deep into me. Because I can enjoy the view of your body. And, when you fuck me like this, you can nail my prostate so damn good." The glassy look in his eyes tells me he likes the sound of all that. "Let me give you a taste of how good that'll feel."

I let go of his legs, settle between them and grab the lube, as Grant slides a hand down his shaft, playing with his balls.

As I set to work on his ass, I stare at the sexy sight in front of me. This man I didn't know a month ago. A man who has become a friend. A man I care about in ways I never expected.

A man I want to take to the edge and back.

So I begin.

26

GRANT

The internet is my best friend, my study companion, and my research guide.

I'm so glad I was born in this time for so many reasons, but among them is the vast array of opportunities for self-directed education. I've learned about bodies.

Explored my own body too.

I've fingered myself.

But no one has touched my ass till now.

As Declan drizzles lube onto his digits, my chest turns into a furnace. I'm already halfway to blast-off from his filthy words and his dirty talk when he cups my balls in one hand and roams his other down to my hole.

He skates his fingers across my ass and I tremble, heating up all over.

"You like that?" he rumbles.

"I do," I pant.

"Me too," he says in a throaty purr as he teases,

one finger playing right there, another rubbing my taint.

I groan, struck speechless by the feelings, the sensations.

He laughs, a sexy, satisfied kind. "I know, right? So, so good."

"So fucking good," I echo, then all I can do is pant as I writhe and twist underneath his touch.

"And I've only just started," he says as he strokes me, pushing the pad of his finger against my entrance right as he bends his face and kisses my inner thigh.

And holy fuck.

I arch up from the twin—no, triple—dose of pleasure. Of hands cupping balls, fingers playing around my ass, and his perfect lips fluttering near my cock.

Then, Declan adds more lube, and returns to my ass. He pushes one digit inside and enters me for the first time. It makes me shiver but it burns too, and for a second or maybe more, I tense.

"You okay?"

"I'm good," I say as I breathe deeply, let my legs fall apart more. Give the pleasure room to take over, and it does.

Declan drops a soft kiss to my knee, then continues working me.

Pressing.

Teasing.

I squeeze my eyes shut as the unholy sensations roll through me like a heat wave.

One that's scorching me as he takes his time.

As he plays.

As he explores.

He pushes in farther while bringing his mouth to my cock, drawing the crown past his lips.

His finger's in my ass, his mouth is on my dick, his hand is on my balls, and it's official—I incinerate.

I become a five-alarm fire.

"Oh, fuck yes," I growl, bumping my ass down on his hand, seeking him out, wanting him, needing him.

He murmurs around the head of my dick, and he goes deeper into my body at the same time. "You got me now. Want another finger?" he whispers against my dick.

I melt from desire. I am a raging ball of need, and lust. "I want your dick. Give me your dick," I beg, getting lost in the haze.

He lets go of my cock, shakes his head. "I know you do, babe, but we're going to work up to it. Need to open you up first. Fuck you with my fingers." He slides another one in. "I want you to feel what it's like when I do this first," he says, and with some kind of voodoo magic, he crooks his fingers just so inside my ass.

Yup. He just introduced himself to my prostate and I am very happy to make his acquaintance.

Pleasure torpedoes each cell in my body. I shake everywhere, head to toe and back. "Yes, yes, yes."

It's a chant, a plea, a desperate cry. I'm begging for anything and everything from this man.

My eyes fly open, and I stare at Declan. He's nibbling on the corner of his lips, his eyes dark and dirty. His face is twisted with pleasure as he adds more lube, then a third finger.

Sparks of heat dance around my ass. Heat and tingles and insane pressure.

I nearly lose my mind. I forget where I am.

I'm desperate, so desperate for more. I push up on my elbows, wanting to get closer to him. "Fuck, babe. It's so good," I pant out.

Like he can read my thoughts as they're forming, he leans forward, fingers still in me, his other hand on my cock. He takes my mouth with his, kissing me as he finger fucks me. His tongue delves into my mouth, his lips fusing with mine.

All this contact is like a high-voltage charge rushing through my body. Then he breaks the kiss, whispering, "I fucking love kissing you. Love it all the time."

"Me too," I moan as he returns to kneeling between my legs and I fall back down to the pillow.

He plays, he strokes, he crooks.

My hands slide up and down my chest, traveling over my nipple piercing, pinching it.

"Oh, hell yes. Play with yourself as I finger fuck this stunning ass," he urges.

Easy enough. I tease at my nipples as he bends a finger just so.

My eyes lock with his dark brown irises. Flames lick my skin. "Jesus, this is . . ."

"Yeah, it is . . ."

Then he bends his face toward me, takes the crown of my cock in his mouth and sucks hard, unleashing another jolt of pleasure in my balls, my ass, my dick.

My hands fly to him. They curl around his head, holding him, one palm sliding down between his shoulder blades. I push him deeper onto my dick, making him take me far into his mouth.

And he takes. Oh yes, does he ever, finding room for my shaft in his mouth. With loud, wet slurps that make my whole body sizzle, he sucks me to the root. Then, the man crooks a finger inside me, and my climax announces its intentions.

It's coming and it's not stopping for anything.

It barrels down my spine, rattles through my bones.

And I explode.

My orgasm owns my body. It steals my thoughts. It takes me over all the edges everywhere.

"Yes, fucking yes," I grunt, coming harder than I ever have before. I come for days and he takes it all.

Groaning as he sucks me down.

And I'm just gasping.

Panting.

Moaning.

And writhing in the aftershocks of this brand-new bliss.

But he's not done with me.

As soon as he swallows my release, he pulls off my cock with a smack of his lips, eases out his fingers, and then flips me over to all fours. Moving behind me, he smacks my ass, then grabs my cheeks with both hands, squeezing rough and hard, pulling me apart.

I look behind me, and the sight is phenomenal.

It is all my fantasies. It's what I've imagined for

years. A man I want. A man I trust. A man I connect with. And he wants me with the same ferocity.

This is what I've waited to have someday.

Some night.

And maybe I can have it tonight. *Now.*

I shudder, picturing what might happen next. Hoping for it. "Are you going to fuck me?"

Declan shakes his head. "No," he says, emphatic. "But I do want to give you a teaser."

He grabs my ass even harder, then slides his hard cock along my crack: up, down, up, down.

"Fuck, yes," I groan, swaying against his length, craving more of it.

He echoes my sentiments with growls and grunts of his own as he simulates fucking me.

Sliding a hand up my back so possessively, Declan pushes down between my shoulder blades, giving me the best trailer of the hottest movie ever.

I bow my back, raising my ass higher, letting him know he can have me whenever he's ready. I ache everywhere. My balls, my cock, my ass. My God, this is insane. This intensity. This longing. It's like nothing I've ever felt. It's like a full-body possession. Like desire owns every cell inside of me, like it's twined in my DNA. "I want you to fuck me so bad," I say, begging.

He grabs my shoulder, gripping it hard, then covering me with his chest. "Trust me. It's all I want too, and I'm going to make it so good for you," he murmurs in my ear, then he moves off me, falls to his back and thrusts the lube in my hand.

"It won't take me long," he says.

I follow his lead.

He gave me the map. He handed me the instructions. So, I return the favor. Lubing up, teasing, toying, then pushing a finger inside his body. And it feels incredible when I watch his reaction.

His face is exquisite torture, excruciating bliss, and his mouth is dirty magic.

Yes.

Do that.

Fuck yes.

More, more, more.

I don't want to screw up, but I'm not sure I can, because he showed me exactly what to do. But I add little changeups as I learn his body, as I discover he wants it a little deeper than he gave it to me, a little harder, a little more pressure. I listen to his cues, and I give him what he seems to want, what he seems to need.

I feel like a king when he thrusts up, moaning and groaning. Then begging.

"Suck me off," he says hoarsely.

In a heartbeat, I bring my lips to his dick.

I draw him in, nice and deep, sucking his fantastic cock with everything I have. He pummels my mouth as I fuck his ass, my fingers doing that come-hither wave till he shouts, "Yes, coming now."

I suck him harder, my bones humming with a fresh round of pleasure as I swallow his salty, musky orgasm, drinking him down like he's my new favorite thing.

Because he is.

I give him one good final lick as I ease out my fingers. Then I kiss the tip of his dick and lift my face.

Once he comes down from his high, he pulls me to him, dragging me close, my chest against his.

Declan's hands slide into my hair, and he kisses me in that tender, sloppy way he has of kissing after sex.

The way he likes it.

I know that already, and that knowledge makes my pulse surge.

Turns out I'm not only learning about myself, but I'm discovering him too. What he likes. What he needs.

It's thrilling to understand another person's desire. It's a gift when a man shows you what he wants.

Declan is fearless in bed. He's unafraid to let go. To talk. To ask for things. To tell me what he likes.

My life has been the opposite. I haven't asked for things. I haven't put myself out there in anything but baseball. It doesn't take a genius to figure out why. Growing up, I saw two people who were supposed to love me fight over everything. I saw two people who were supposed to want me act like they didn't.

No wonder I only ever went after hookups. They were easier.

This is so much harder.

This isn't a hookup.

And Declan is showing me how to take new chances. I think I can be fearless too, like him.

Starting in simple ways. Like talking about sex, about how we are together in bed. So, when we break the kiss, I say something that's been on my mind, something that drives me crazy with him. "You're noisy."

He smiles, all dopey and sexy. "I know. I'm not quiet."

"You sure aren't," I say, with a grin, letting him know I like his sounds.

"Because I love sex," he says, all low and smoky. "But not all sex." He looks me in the eyes. "When I'm into the guy, that's when I'm the loudest." He lifts his face and kisses my smile with a sexy murmur, a flick of his tongue, a whisper. "And I'm really into you, rookie."

A brand-new jolt of pleasure zips down my back.

But it's not from the thrill of contact. It's from something else entirely.

The things he says. The way he talks to me. And the way I want to talk to him.

He pulls back, flops onto the pillow, but keeps his gaze locked with mine.

My stomach flips.

That's new too, and so is the next thing I say. "Yeah, I'm pretty into you too."

A little later, we're cleaned up, lazing around in bed and talking about a TV show we both like, a how-to documentary about strange things in New York.

His phone buzzes.

When Declan grabs it from the nightstand, I turn away. Don't want him to think I'm prying as he reads a message.

"You like hockey?"

"Duh," I answer.

"Smart aleck. Tomorrow's our off day. Want to go to a hockey game tomorrow night?"

"With you?" I ask, surprised.

"No, with Lady Gaga." Then, Declan strips any flirting or sarcasm from his tone as he glides his hand down my arm. "Yes, with me. My friend Emma and me. Her brother, Fitz, is playing."

I beam, sunshine flooding my body. "Dude. James Fitzgerald is a badass defenseman. Hell yeah. I'm in."

"Good. They have an extra ticket so it can be you and me and Emma."

The sound of that makes my chest warm up, maybe even do a happy dance. Perhaps it's the endorphins talking, but I wiggle a brow, feeling bold with him, taking another chance. "Is she our cover?"

A grin spreads slow and easy as he runs a hand down my chest possessively. "Yes. But I'm probably going to have to tell her we have a thing. Easier that way. Plus, she'll probably figure it out. I tend to let down my guard with my good friends, and all it'll take is me looking at you the way I like to and she'll know. You cool with that?"

I hear the subtext—*we agreed to tell no one*. So, this breaks that rule.

But I like the subtext.

I like his hand on my chest.

I like how we are together.

"How do you like to look at me?" I ask, since I'm a glutton for compliments.

One searing-hot stare is his answer. "Like that, rookie. Like that," he growls, his hand spreading across my pecs, curling over them.

"I'm cool with that," I answer.

He drops a kiss to my jawline, rubbing his chin across my stubble. "It'll kind of be like a date."

And that's another first for me too. "I'm looking forward to it," I say in the understatement of my lifetime.

I'm looking so damn forward to it I wish it were tomorrow night now so I could go out with Declan Steele.

Then he pushes up on his elbow. "You want to talk about tomorrow?"

My brow creases. "About hockey? Pretty sure I know how hockey works. You hit the puck into a net, and it's awesome, but baseball is better."

"You're all good there. But no. I meant sex, Grant. Your list. Our plans."

My skin tingles. I love talking about sex with him. It's freeing, but kind of terrifying too. "Sure," I say on a rough swallow, waiting for him to go next.

He sets a hand on my hip, then slides it down to my ass, absently curving his palm over my skin. "Sex is better if you talk about it. Communication and all," he begins.

"Right. Sure. At least, that's what I've read online. I'm a master at reading articles on sex," I say, pushing out a laugh, maybe to cover up my inexperience.

"Good. That's all part of communication. But

listen, it might not be perfect. It might hurt," he says, gently squeezing my butt. "We can stop at any point."

"I don't want to stop," I say, at the speed of light. Is he calling this off? Panic kicks in, swirling in my chest. "Do you want to?"

Please say no.

His brown eyes flash with affection. "Did you not hear me when I said I'm into you? Did you not feel me thirty minutes ago when I was playing with your ass? When I wanted so desperately to be inside you?"

Inside me.

He's doing it again. Turning me on, breaking me down, making me ache for him.

I ache everywhere.

As the memories roar back, my hands skim over his hard body. "I was definitely there."

"You know I want you, Grant," he says in a firm voice that's like a line in the sand. It says *don't question my desire.*

"Yeah, I know that, Deck. It's just . . ." I can't finish because the words are so foreign. *I just like you so much I don't want to screw up. You fascinate me and I can't fucking believe you're into me too. I can't believe you're the first guy I'm going to sleep with, and that makes me feel like I won a World Series. Which is a crazy thing to think, but there it is.*

"You're nervous?" he asks.

But maybe that's it too. Simple, pedestrian nerves. The basic human fear of not wanting to make a mistake. I grit my teeth, breathe through my nostrils, then admit it. "Yeah," I say, and my chest lightens instantly. My jaw unclenches.

Maybe this is some of what's winding me up. The will-it-live-up-to-the-hype uncertainty. Since he's talking so openly with me, I dip my toe in those waters. "You know I told you I watched porn?"

"A very normal thing to do," he says.

"And the guys, at least the kind I watch, are just all so..."

"Perfect? With perfect bodies? Perfect cocks? Perfect loads?"

I laugh. "Yeah, all that." But quickly, I stop laughing. "Only, it's not about the bodies. It's more that they all have... perfect moves."

"I hear ya, rookie. Keep talking."

"It all goes so perfectly. When they switch positions and stuff. When one dude flips the other to his back or his side, or all fours. They're all like *boom. Back at it.* And the second the bottom has a dick in his ass, he's all like *yes, so good.* And I kinda feel like... what if I just don't know what to do? What if it's not like that? What if I don't feel that way or make you feel that way?"

"What if?" He tosses out at me. "What if, Grant?"

"I don't know," I say, raising my voice. "That's my point. *What if?*"

"You think I'm gonna smack you on the ass, pull out my dick, and walk off?"

I suppose a part of me did. Isn't that what people do sometimes? Just leave you in the lurch?

"I hope not," I admit.

Declan runs his hand down my chest. "I don't need it to be perfect. You and me, we're not making porn. We're not trying to turn everyone else on. You're the only one I want to make feel good."

Now I am hot all over. But this heat rushing through me is so much more than physical. "I want it to be good for you, Declan."

"It will be. It's already better than it's been before. Want to know why?"

"Tell me," I say, heart skittering.

"Since we're talking about it."

"You do like to talk," I tease.

"Talking is hot," he says.

"And you said you weren't chatty," I say, getting my confidence back. "You are *so* chatty."

"What can I say? I'm different with you," Declan says, and my chest glows from those last four words. Four perfect words. *I'm different with you.*

"Are you?" I ask, hoping it's not patently obvious how much I like what he's saying.

"Seems I am. And that's why I want you to know that it's just you and me in bed," he says, tapping my chest, then his. "We set the pace. We don't have to please an audience. We can just make it good for each other."

"It's gonna be good," I say, the corner of my lips curving into a grin. "I just know it. Gut feeling. I won't be wrong."

"Cocky, and I like it. But it might hurt. Just tell me if it does, okay? We can adjust."

It's cool that Declan is so caring, but I've got this.

"I will, but you know I'm a catcher, right? I'm bruised all over. Every game, I catch more than a hundred baseballs flying at me like rockets. Sometimes I catch them with my knees. I play and live with pain," I say. "It is literally part of my job."

"Show off." Declan laughs, his head falling back into the pillow, his fingers sliding through his hair. "And you know how to crouch for hours too, rookie. So, you can just ride me all night." Then he lets the laughter fade as he reaches for me, pulls me closer so I'm looking down at him. "All I'm saying is, for all your rough-and-tumble, badass baseball-is-life attitude, sex might be awkward. It might be . . . uncomfortable. But if you tell me how you're feeling, I'll do everything I can to make it good for you." He takes a pause as his gaze bores into mine, vulnerability flashing in his brown irises. "And you can do the same for me the next night when you top me. Deal?"

Best deal ever. "I'm good with that."

Then he hauls me in for another kiss. Proving what he said earlier. How much he loves kissing me. I can feel it in his lips on mine. In his hands sliding down my back. In the murmurs he makes.

And when we break the kiss, I serve up another piece of my insides to him. "I kinda had a crush on you before I met you."

His brow rises. "That so?"

"Yeah, you were hot and talented."

"And am I living up to it? To your crush?"

I stroke my chin, considering. Then shrug a shoulder ever so casually. "Ask me tomorrow night."

Declan laughs deeply. "Fair enough, rookie. Fair enough." He glances at the door, but he doesn't bother to get out of bed, or to check the peephole. He just shoots me a *we're-in-this-together* look. "I should stay till the middle of the night," he says.

"You should."

"Then, I will."

Here we go, doing it again, curling up together, his arm draped around me.

Only this time it feels completely intentional.

From both of us.

27

DECLAN

Emma lifts her golf club, waggles her hips, and stares down the range the next day. "Mark my words, gentlemen. I'm going to hit the one-hundred-yard sign," she declares.

"Next stop PGA tour," Fitz announces from his spot next to his sister.

"Don't bet against me," she says, then takes aim at the little white ball, whacking the hell out of it. It soars, arcing over the grass at the driving range, then flying high before it lands smack underneath the one-hundred-yard sign.

My eyes bug out. "Whoa. Have you been holding out on me? I didn't know you were a golf prodigy."

Laughing, she polishes her nails on her shirt. "I didn't either. Then I went to the driving range with a friend, and it turned out I was a natural."

"A friend?" Fitz asks, as he lifts his five-iron. "Is this friend a boy?"

She rolls her blue eyes. "And what if he is?"

I set down my club and wag a finger at her. "Emma, are you seeing someone and forgot to get him approved by your big brother?"

She smacks her forehead. "My bad. I must get all potential dates approved by James."

"Thank you for remembering the house rules." He stabs the head of the five-iron against the turf. "Now, I want all the details. Profession? Name? Any criminal arrests? Pets? And is he going to be good to you for the rest of your life?"

His sister cracks up as she drops another ball onto a tee. Since today's my off day, the three of us decided to snag some time on the range before we grab lunch.

Plus, I won't be able to catch up with Fitz after the hockey game, since I'm pretty sure my focus post-game will be singular.

Getting Grant naked and under me.

Stat.

But for now, it's friend time, and Grant is on the back burner of my mind.

Albeit on a simmer.

Or maybe a low heat.

Possibly a medium boil.

"My *friend* is definitely not going to be good to me for the rest of my life, James," Emma says, answering. "Because I'm not interested in a forever thing. I just returned from a year studying in England, and I have zero interest in anything serious. But his name is Clint, he works at the Getty, he studied art history, and he's hotter than Declan."

I straighten my spine. "How is that possible?"

Fitz cuts in. "So, not very hot, Ems?"

"More like, 'How did you meet someone at the hotter-than-Mercury level?' But hey, good on you." I hold out a fist for knocking and Emma knocks back.

She gives me a saucy wink. "Thank you. You're a hottie but he's a hottie-er. And I'm seeing him in LA tomorrow."

"Ah, so he's the *thing* in LA," I say, sketching air quotes.

"He is definitely the thing."

We chat more about Emma's date as we work through a few more rounds. When we're done, we turn in the clubs, then head to a nearby taco joint for some grub.

As we nosh on chicken tacos, I hunt for just the right spot to drop the news of my date tonight.

My stomach roils though, and it's not from the spicy salsa.

Why does it feel so strange to say that Grant's coming with me? Maybe because they're the first people I'm telling about him? Or maybe because I've enjoyed the secret of us.

But possibly, there's another reason for the churning in my gut.

Exposure.

What it means.

How it's gone for me in my life.

So far, not so well. I've learned when you yank a secret out of the dark and into the light, it dregs up drama along with hurt and shame.

But this thing with Grant is not my past, and I'm not dragging it into the limelight. I'm simply sharing guy news with two good friends who'll have my back.

Only, Grant hardly feels like other guys I've dated. He's not like Nathan with his empty promises, or Kyle with his lack of boundaries. They're sepia photographs that faded fast. Grant is vivid, high-definition color, and I can't look away from him.

And I'm not sure I'm ready to unpack what that means for the end of spring training. The end of our affair.

I lift my iced tea, take a cold drink, and gird myself. "So that extra ticket you gave me to use for the game tonight," I say in as even a tone as I can muster.

"Yes?" Emma arches a brow.

"I'm bringing a guy."

Fitz wiggles his fingers. "Serve it up. Who is your spring training hookup?"

I bristle at the term. Grant hardly feels like a hookup. I don't want to pretend he is. Not with two people I can be honest with. I hate lying to anyone, but especially to my friends. I won't do it.

"Actually, he's kind of more than a hookup," I say and it's strange to speak those words aloud for the first time, but also . . . not.

That time with Grant last night, talking about baseball, reassuring him, felt like one of the purest moments of my life. The connection between us went deeper, the understanding felt truer than it has with anyone else in the past.

It felt *real*.

Fitz sets down his fork, leaving his plate of tacos looking lonely. "Dude."

That one word contains multitudes.

So does the look in his eyes. Concern crossed

with curiosity. Maybe he can read my body language and tell this is no ordinary date.

"Who is he?" Emma asks as she squeezes my arm. "Also, you're in trouble. Why is this the first I'm learning of your new man?"

I swallow roughly. Draw a breath. As I test the words in my mind, they're so forbidden. Grant is completely off-limits. I'm going to shock them. Jaws will drop. Forks will fall.

I shrug, then go for it. "He's a teammate."

Emma gasps.

Fitz freezes.

And all I can do is gulp, shrug, and take another bite of my taco, like the food will cover up the enormity of the bomb I dropped in the middle of the table.

Complete with a countdown clock that's ticking fast to the end of this fling.

After several seconds of stunned silence, Fitz goes first. "For real?"

I give a what-can-you-do shrug. "For real."

"Wow." He drags a hand through his hair, processing the grenade.

"Is it serious?" Emma asks in a gentle voice with no judgment.

I scratch my jaw before I answer, my throat tightening. We aren't serious, Grant and me, so the answer should tumble from my lips.

A quick, fast no.

But *no* is wrong.

These nighttime trysts have all the ingredients of something serious. They're the recipe for an off-season affair. Only I'm having it now.

"Not really," I say hoarsely, but that sounds like

a vicious lie. So, I follow it up with something true. "But it feels like it could be."

Fitz sighs sympathetically. "What are you going to do?"

The next word that comes out tastes like sand. "Nothing."

That's the only answer in the whole universe.

There's nothing I can do about the way I feel for Grant.

And the way my feelings grow stronger every day.

28

GRANT

Today is the day, and I am fired all the way up.

Since Declan spent the night—he took off at five—we agreed to skip our morning workout.

Instead, I catch up with the other rookies in the gym for weights and nautilus machines. As I head into the workout facility, I'm already pumped. I'm a Labrador who's downed two espressos. I'm wired like it's the playoffs.

I sneak a glance at the clock. Eight-thirty. If the hockey game starts at seven, lasts about two and a half hours, we should be back by ten and in my bed by ten-thirty, so in a little more than twelve hours the rest of the world will disappear.

"Leg day!" Sullivan shouts like a frat guy at spring break, his exuberance palpable.

He breaks me out of my dirty daydream.

"Let's see who can squat the most," Miguel challenges as the two strut over to the weight bench. "You in, G-man?"

Is he for real? I tap my chest. "You guys want to take *me* on in squats?"

The rangy Miguel parks his hands on his hips. "Why not?"

I chuckle, shaking my head as I glance at the outfielder who easily weighs forty pounds less than I do, then the relief pitcher who's tall and long. "Have at it, bros."

"No, seriously, I want to know why I can't take you on in squats," Miguel pushes.

Sullivan lifts his chin defiantly, but the spark in his eyes says he's playing dumb. "Yeah, are you a squat guru, G?"

"Allow me to show you," I say, and I proceed to school the fuck out of my teammates, squatting more weights, more reps, more times.

When I'm done, I rub my thumb and forefinger together. "Do not bet against a catcher when it comes to squats. My entire life is squats," I say to them, though I'm sure Sullivan was putting on his naïve act.

"Dammit," Sullivan mutters, smacking the outfielder. "Why didn't we think of that?"

"Maybe because we're dipshits sometimes?" Miguel answers.

Sullivan cracks up, big and loud, pointing at Miguel. "Or maybe you are. How the hell did you think you could beat G-man in squats?"

Miguel grumbles. "Maybe because I'm a competitive bastard."

"Keep that up, especially on the field. And feel free to lay a wager down next time you want to compete with me in the weight room. You might not have noticed, but I'm kind of one of the biggest guys on the team. Catcher and all," I say as I move on to lunges.

"Yup. And we want a brick wall at the plate," Sullivan says, switching to deadlifts, then shifting conversational gears too. "Off day. Know what I have going on tonight?"

"A date with your Xbox?"

"A nice, hot bubble bath?" Miguel puts in, and I shoot him a *well-played* smile.

"Nope," Sullivan says with a wicked grin. "I've got a date with a . . . wait for it . . . thirty-year-old research scientist at the local university."

"Well done," I say, since Sullivan loves the brainy ladies. "But how did she find *you*?"

He clucks his tongue. "Smart women are on Tinder, and they like hookups too." Then he whispers, "And let me tell you, it has been too long without any action, know what I mean?"

"Do I fucking ever," Miguel seconds, then tips his chin at me. "But not you, I bet. You're probably getting it every night on Grindr."

I scoff. "You think because I'm gay I get laid all the time?"

"Dude, don't slut shame. That's not cool," Sullivan chides.

Miguel cringes. "Is that slut shaming?" The outfielder sounds devastated, and it's hilarious to watch since I know what's coming next from my former roomie.

Living with Sullivan in Bakersfield revealed there's much more to him than meets the eye.

"Actually, slut shaming is criticizing women and girls and often gay men as well for behaviors that might be considered promiscuous," Sullivan offers clinically, sounding like a Wikipedia entry.

"Did you take a gender studies class or something in college?" Miguel asks.

"My major was psych," he offers. "Also, straight men are rarely slut shamed for liking sex, or for engaging in behaviors like wearing sexy clothes, so it's not cool to slut shame women or queer people."

"I don't even think he slut shamed, Sully," I say.

"I know. But now he'll know what it is," Sullivan adds in a teacherly tone.

"I love getting more woke," Miguel says, rapping fists with Sullivan. "So, I am all good with this."

"Also, I believe everyone should have more sex," Sullivan says.

"What are you? Like the Santa of sex?" Miguel puts in.

"Maybe I am. Or Oprah. You get sex! You get sex! You get sex! Everybody gets sex!" he says, imitating the TV star handing out cars.

"I will accept that gift," Miguel adds.

"Also, for the record, I'm not on Grindr so no, I'm not hooking up," I correct, and it feels good to say that. Sure, I was into quick hookups in college, but right now I'm definitely not.

However, I'm absolutely into whatever is happening tonight with the shortstop.

"So, what are you doing tonight then, G-man? Bubble bath for you and a good book?"

Oh shit.

Heat rushes to my cheeks, and I go deeper into

the lunge, hoping the weights cover up the flare of embarrassment.

"Going to a hockey game," I say, as evenly as I can. Do I add *with Declan?*

Would that be weird? Or weirder if I don't mention him? But what if they see us leave together? Ah, hell, I've got to say it, and I've got to remember there's nothing wrong with going to a hockey game with a teammate. "Sweet! I heard New York was in town. I'm jelly. Good seats?" Miguel asks, as he drops down into another squat.

"Definitely. Center ice," I say, wincing as the half-truths roll off my tongue.

Miguel's dark eyes twinkle. "Got extra?"

Ah hell.

I can't hide this.

"Don't think so. Fitzgerald got them for us. Declan is tight with Fitz's sister, so I'm going with the two of them."

Please don't ask anything more.

"Got it," Miguel says, then launches into dead lifts. "You and Declan?"

My pulse spikes. Tension tightens my bones.

But Sullivan cuts in with a side-eye at Miguel. "They're friends. Don't make assumptions."

Miguel holds up his hands in surrender. "I'm cool with whatevs."

I clench my jaw, hating assumptions, hating when other people try to tell your story, hating it even more when they get it right.

"We're friends," I say. "Just like I'm friends with you guys."

That ought to make it clear, even though that's a bald-faced lie.

One that twists my gut.

* * *

When I'm back in my room, I need to find a way to untie the knot in my stomach, or it'll weigh me down. And I think I know how to do it. I grab my phone, and text Reese.

Grant: You around for a call?

Reese: For you? Anytime.

I ring her in a split second.

"That was fast. Are you okay?" she asks.

I sigh heavily. After lying through my teeth, I'm pretty sure I'm about to vomit up the truth. Like my insides are heaving, and I need to puke out all the words, I hurl them up at my best friend. "I'm having a thing with Declan. He's incredible, and we've been getting together every night, and I'm out of my mind for him."

Silence comes first, then it's chased by a long, intrigued *ohhh*.

"Really?" She sounds excited, and her tone buoys me. "How did this happen?"

"We started working out together and talking." As I flop onto the couch, I tell her nearly everything.

"Wow. That kind of sounds . . . amazing," she

says, but there's a hitch in her voice, like she knows this can't end well.

Dropping my head in my hands, I sink farther into the couch, dread stalking through my veins. "He's ... just ... soooo ..."

I can barely talk. I can hardly put into words the enormity of what's happening to me all at once. My career is shooting sky-high, I'm on the cusp of a once-in-a-lifetime opportunity to catch my first Major League game in less than two weeks, if I make the roster, and I've got a massive thing for this guy.

I squeeze my eyes shut as if it'll make the next sentence easier. But it doesn't. It's still hard to say. "I can't get him out of my head," I admit. "It's kind of making me crazy."

"Oh, sweetie. It sounds amazing and awful at the same time," she says.

"Exactly."

"So, what happens next?"

I lift my face. At least this is easy to say. "Well, we're having sex tonight."

"Ooh la la. So, I guess you're ready."

I laugh. "Yeah, I'm going to shower before the game. Make sure I'm good and clean in all the ways."

"Good plan. But I meant are you ready in other ways? Emotionally? You always wanted your first time to be with the right guy. Is he the right guy?"

My heart thunders, knowing the answer before I do, trying to tap it out in the Morse code of beats. "Aside from being a ballplayer and also my teammate, he absolutely is."

There are just those two big barriers between us.

That's all.

But I don't want to think about obstacles, so I ask what she's been up to, and we shoot the breeze for a few minutes. When we end the call, I find a new text on my phone.

One that punches me in the chest.

It's from my mom.

Mom: Hey, handsome! Did my dad tell you we'll be at Opening Day??? Can't wait to see my little boy catch his FIRST MAJOR LEAGUE GAME! Frank and I are so happy for you. He says it's been too long. He can't wait to catch up. He has so much to talk to you about.

Yeah, he probably wants to apologize for the ten thousandth time. Whatever, I'm over it.

Over all of my mom's boyfriends and husbands. All my dad's wives and girlfriends. I don't need to be their show pony.

But I find it's best to just smile and wave, so I tap out a quick reply.

Grant: Let's hope I make the starting lineup. If so, see you then! Should be an awesome day.

. . .

The day I've longed for my whole entire life. But I don't want them to ruin it, so I try to shove my parents out of my mind.

I shed my workout clothes, pull on shorts and a shirt, then grab a Lyft to The Lazy Hammock, since I'm jonesing for a distraction.

As I eat a light lunch, I chat with River at the bar about growing up in Northern California, then moving here.

"What brought you to Phoenix?" I ask.

The inked bartender sighs a little wistfully and scrubs a hand across his short beard. "A man."

"Your partner?"

He shakes his head, frowning, but seeming resigned. "Nope. He's history now. Caught him cheating."

"Ouch," I say, crinkling my nose.

"Yup. But that's okay. I won't let one bad one get me down," he says, smiling quickly, like he's letting the world know he's all good.

"Words to live by."

"And you and that guy from the other night looked quite cozy. Is he someone serious?" River's eyebrows rise in question.

I shouldn't say a word. But River already saw us. River was on the receiving end of Declan's fit of jealousy when my teammate threw down a claim on me. "He's the kind you wish you could be serious with, you know?"

River pats my hand. "I do, hun. I absolutely know." He flashes a sympathetic smile, one that seems to telegraph where Declan and I are headed. "Enjoy it while it lasts, right?"

I lift my Diet Coke and drink to that.

***

Time to kick this funk to the ground. Tonight, I'm getting laid, and that's what I want.

I don't want to think about endings.

Six hours later, I'm showered, shaved, dressed in tight jeans that make my ass look great, a gray T-shirt that shows off my arms, and a ball cap. After grabbing a hoodie, I head down to the lobby to meet Declan.

When I spot him just outside the sliding doors, tossing his keys up and down in his palm, I have to fight not to stare at him the way I want.

He's so damn handsome it makes my chest hurt.

He wears jeans and a blue polo that stretches just so across his pecs, that hugs his arms deliciously, that teases at his flat stomach that I love to kiss and lick.

But it's his face that does me in. His chiseled jaw, his full lips, his strong cheekbones. Most of all, his eyes. They are my downfall. Dark brown and brimming with passion and possibility.

Once I lock eyes with him, I will go up in flames.

When he spots me walking to him, he turns in slow motion, his eyes meeting mine. He takes me in, and shoots me a hungry, needy look that says he can't look away either.

Yep, fire.

But it's so much more. I burn deeply for him.

He's not only all I can think about. He's all I want to think about.

29

DECLAN

The second we're off the hotel property and hit the first light, I jerk my gaze to Grant.

"You look fucking incredible," I tell him.

His smile lights my soul as he says with a rumble, "So do you."

I rake my gaze over the man in the passenger seat, the air-conditioning humming around us. "Correction: you look good enough to eat."

He wiggles a brow. "You should then."

"Mmm. Maybe I will," I say, and when the light changes and I hit the gas, I reach across the console for his hand. Grant clasps his fingers with mine, sending the mercury in me rising.

But the emotions too.

Holding hands with him feels so damn good.

We're quiet for several blocks as we cruise to the rink in the desert night.

Grant stretches his right hand to the screen on the dashboard, hits the music tab, and scrolls through my playlist. With a sexy smirk he throws my way, he selects a familiar tune.

Once the opening notes of "November Rain" fill the car, I chuckle.

As I drive, Grant steals glances at me, and I steal them right back at him, and when we hit a long light, I grab the back of his head, and drag him in for a hot, quick kiss that makes my skin sizzle. This man has my number.

"Mmm. I want to take you out and kiss you everywhere," I murmur.

"On my body or around town?"

"Good point. Let's make it both."

"I thought you were pretty private about PDA?" Grant asks, curiously.

"I am," I say. "But I'd have a hell of a time resisting you wherever we were."

His lips curve in the start of a grin. "You'd have your hands all over me?"

The light changes and I hit the gas. "I probably would. Do you have any idea how hard it's going to be for me not to touch you at the game?"

"How hard?"

I grab his hand and bring it to my crotch. "This hard."

He murmurs his appreciation. "That's my favorite kind of hard," Grant says, rubbing his hand along the ridge of my erection.

I growl, wanting to give in, wanting to press my hand on top of his, let him stroke me. But I can't. Moving his hand back to his thigh, I tip my forehead toward the road. "Need to focus or I'll crash, and I don't want to die without fucking you first."

"That would be a tragedy," he agrees, then leans back against the headrest and closes his eyes.

He's smiling though.

He looks happy. Absolutely content. Like there's no place else he'd rather be.

"I'd want all that too, Deck," he says softly, a quiet admission in the dark. One that tugs on my chest. "I'd want to go out with you. If we were other people. You know? If we had other jobs. If you played baseball and I played hockey or something like that."

"I do know what you mean," I say, heaviness in my tone, suiting the turn we've taken.

"I'd want to be seen with you. I wouldn't want anyone else to beat us to it." His eyes fly open, and that blue gaze is so damn serious now.

My brows knit, but I turn my gaze back to the road, my fingers curled around the steering wheel.

I flash back to the night I met him. The things he said in the elevator. About telling his own story. "This is why you told the locker room that first day. And then later you said someone beat you to it. What happened?"

Grant's jaw tightens and he nods as he blows out a long stream of air, laced with frustration. "You ever had someone else out you?"

"No." My heart screams for him. For the awfulness. "That happened to you, babe?"

"Yes." His voice is strung tight. "In front of my whole fucking high school."

I nearly crash the car. "Wow."

"End of my senior year. Right when I figured it out. Right when I knew. I told Reese. I told my grandparents. They were awesome, just like you'd expect." He swallows roughly. "Then I told my mom and her husband."

I keep my eyes on the road, but sneak glances at the man by my side. "And what happened?"

"A week later there was an assembly at school with parents and students. It was about diversity. Awareness. Important stuff about inclusion. And right in the middle of it, Frank stood up and said, 'As the stepfather of a young gay man, I applaud these efforts.'"

Grant closes his eyes, as if the memory pains him too much.

It hurts me too, for him.

I scan the street, spotting an empty parking lot at a closed coffee drive thru. Flipping on the turn signal, I pull into the lot, park the car, and cut the engine. "Grant," I say, my heart flooding with sympathy.

"Yeah, I know." He heaves a terrible sigh, then scrubs his hand down his face. "I don't want to talk about it."

I take his hand in mine again, bring his knuckles to my lips, kiss them. He shudders when I touch him, and I record that reaction in my mind, save it for a rainy day.

Then I let go and tell him something I don't like to share either. Something that still cuts deep. "When I was seventeen, I told my dad I was gay. He said there was nothing wrong with who I like, but that I should stay in the closet. He said it would be safer. He said it would be better for me."

Grant's lips twist in a scowl. "You didn't listen to him, did you?"

"I thought about it for a little bit," I admit. "He

talked about how the minors were for him playing ball. He talked about sports being the last place for a queer guy. That I was better off being"—I stop to sketch air quotes as the bitter memory rears its head—"*discreet*. Like it was better for me to live a lie."

Grant huffs, grinding his teeth. "I hate lies."

"Me too. So much."

"What happened?"

"I thought about it, but I didn't spend my teenage years trying to escape his lies to go live another one." I tap my chest. "I said, 'This is who I am. This is me. Take it or leave it.'"

"What did he say?"

I shake my head, not wanting to dwell on the man who twists my insides every time he calls or texts. "Doesn't matter. He disagreed. Vehemently. Then he apologized the next day. Vehemently too. But he still said it. I still remember. He wanted me to hide."

Grant grabs my face in his right hand, holds my jaw tight. "I'm glad you didn't. When I met you and I said I was a big fan, it wasn't just because I had a crush on you. You were kinda my hero. You have to know what it meant to guys like me in college to see a guy like you playing in the majors."

I dip my face, not sure what to say.

"Sorry. I don't want to ruin tonight," Grant says, backpedaling. Dropping his hand.

I jerk my face up. Does he not get it? He can't ruin anything.

"Don't apologize. I like getting to know you. So much more than I should," I say, putting that much on the line, telling him what's fast becoming the truth of my heart, even though I won't be able to have what I want so badly.

Him.

"Me too, Deck," he whispers. "Me too."

A quick scan of the lot tells me we're still alone.

The sky is dark.

The sun is down.

It's only us.

After I remove his ball cap, I rope a hand through his hair, tug on it, then look around the empty lot once more. "This is what I want to do at the game tonight," I say.

I kiss Grant Blackwood with everything I have, and it still doesn't feel like it'll ever be enough.

30

DECLAN

Emma is the loudest.

"I nearly forgot what it's like to go to a game with you," I say to her above the noise and the shouting in the arena as New York evens the score against Phoenix.

My friend shoots me a saucy look, her blonde ponytail whipping as she turns to me. "You forgot that I'm the biggest fan on the planet?"

"It seems I did. Maybe sometime around when you burst my eardrums," I tease.

Grant laughs, rubs his knuckle against the side of his head. "You and me both."

"You guys can handle it," she says, then swings her gaze back to the ice as Phoenix moves the puck toward the goal.

Emma claps several times. "Come on, James. Stop that puck."

I toss a glance at Grant, a seat away since Emma is in the middle.

"She's a little passionate about hockey," I deadpan.

"Welcome to the club," Grant says.

"I'm especially passionate when my brother is playing," Emma chimes in, and when Fitz blocks a Phoenix goal, she loses her mind, jumping up and down, thrusting her arms in the air. "Yes, yes, yes!"

"You're going to lose your voice," I warn.

"I already am losing it," she jokes, her pitch a little rumbly.

"Were you a cheerleader in high school, woman?" Grant asks.

She flashes a bright smile. "Don't let my cheerleader looks fool you. I was full-on nerd."

"Nerds can be cheerleaders too," I add.

"I know. But I was *only* a nerd," she says, then shouts once more at the players.

A frizzy-haired woman a few rows ahead cranes her neck around, looks up at Emma, smiles. Next, she makes eye contact with me. Recognition flashes in her features. "Go Cougars," she says with a big, bright smile.

I tip my chin toward her and grin back. "Go Cougars."

"Spotted in the wild," Emma whispers.

"So famous," Grant teases.

I roll my eyes. "You'll be next, rookie."

"From your mouth to God's ears," he says, and we return our attention to the ice.

A minute later when New York scores, Emma unleashes the most crushing cheer I've ever heard.

It's contagious.

I'm so glad I'm not sitting next to Grant or I'd

kiss him right now. Kiss him hard and celebrate. Clenching my fists, I draw a tight breath.

Resist him.

I keep my hands to myself, but it's a tough battle. I don't know what's happening to my vaunted self-control, but it leaves the building when he's around.

Must refocus.

As game play resumes, I cast about for a random question, the pool table chatter we engage in when we're out with the guys. Something, anything so Grant feels like one of the guys, and not the man I desperately want to spend the night with.

"Question for both of you. If you could do anything else, besides be a ballplayer, or an art historian for Emma, what would you do?" I ask.

Grant gestures to Emma. "Ladies first."

She adopts a wicked grin. "Hockey play-by-play commentator."

"Oh yeah, I can totally see that," Grant says.

"And you, G-man?" I ask, tossing out the nickname Sullivan and the other guys use with him. It sounds all wrong on my tongue.

He smiles my way, his blue eyes sparkling maybe with mischief as he gives a casual shrug. "We're birds of a feather, Emma and me," he says, tapping her shoulder. He's touchy-feely with her in the way I suspect he is with female friends. Maybe in the way he's fully able to be only with women. He's a physical guy, and with females he can set a hand on an arm or a shoulder without any undertones. Then he answers, "Though in my case, I'd *play* hockey."

"Sports, natch." As I do, my brain snags on something. What Grant said in the car on the way over. *If we were other people. If I played baseball and he played hockey.* Is his comment just now about us? Is it a private remark? And why do I like it so much?

"What, this surprises you? Sports is my love," he says to me, all casual and charming.

Yeah, it's not about me. It's not about us, and that's fine too. His answer is all him, all one-track-mind athlete, and I laugh. I am in knots over him.

Grant's face goes starkly serious. "Baseball is everything," he says, then shoots me a stern stare. "Don't try to pretend it's any different for you."

"No arguments here," I say. "Baseball is life."

Emma shakes her head, laughing. "You guys."

"What?" I ask.

She lowers her voice to a barren whisper. "You're so ador—"

I growl, a warning sound.

She holds up her hands in surrender.

"She's not wrong, Deck," Grant whispers.

Emma's eyes twinkle with Cupid's arrows. "*Deck*." She clasps her heart. "I die."

"*Rookie*," I rumble in an even lower voice.

Emma gasps, flaps her hands. "Stahp, stahp."

Grant clears his throat. "Okay, how about we answer what we'd do outside of sports. I'll go first. I'd be James Bond. How about you, Declan?" he asks, making a production out of sounding all professional when he says my name.

And it is adorable.

One of the guys.

He's one of the guys.

My answer is easy—same thing I'd say to anyone. "If I could do anything besides baseball, I would shred a guitar like nobody's business. I would rock out to Guns N' Roses." I pick up my air guitar. I play the opening notes to "Sweet Child O' Mine," humming along. Grant's eyes light up, twinkling. "Damn, that's good."

"Thank you. If only I could do it for real. What about you, Emma?"

She exhales deeply. "I suppose if I can't call a game, I'd be a ski jumper or a fighter pilot."

Grant offers her a fist for knocking and then dives into a conversation with her about jets. The fact that he gets along so easily, so smoothly with everyone, but especially my friends, makes my brain scramble a little more.

I don't know what the hell I'm going to do when this fling ends in another day, another night.

This man is gorgeous inside and out.

He's the heart-stopping kind. It's frying my sense of reason.

When intermission comes and Grant excuses himself for the restroom, Emma grabs my arm, drops her voice, and murmurs in my ear, "Holy Rembrandt. Holy Vermeer."

I crack up. "Explain."

"Those are some of my favorite Dutch painters," she says, wildly animated as she whispers, "Seventeenth Century Dutch art is my favorite time period."

"And?"

"He's like a painting," she says.

I laugh. "Didn't Rembrandt paint dudes with fancy collars?"

She rolls her eyes. "Rembrandt painted gorgeous works of art. Vermeer painted the most incredible images that move my very soul."

"Fine. I hear ya. Though that's not the comparison I'd use."

"How's this? He's like a Bugatti. Is that better?"

That makes my engine purr. Grant is top-of-the-line everything. I grin, wide and honestly proud. "I know, right? He's a ten."

"More like a fifteen."

I stroke my chin. "If he's a Rembrandt, and he is, then he's a one in a million," I say, a little in awe because how the hell did someone like Grant fall into my lucky lap? But mostly I'm damn grateful that he's with me.

At least for now.

And for now, he feels like mine.

She keeps her voice low, understanding the importance of discretion. "He's funny and sweet. I bet he's as besotted with you as you are with him."

"No way. I'm not besotted."

She narrows her eyes. "Don't lie to me."

"Emma," I chide.

"I know, I know. It's impossible. Still."

"It is. We *are* impossible." I underline the cold, hard truth with a Sharpie.

"I get it," she says sadly and pats my shoulder, rubs it sympathetically. "I do get it. It's just that after college and poetry class, and the things you shared and knowing your heart . . ." Her voice hitches. This woman knows the truth about some of the toughest times in my life. She knows more about me than almost anyone.

That's not because she could never be a lover.

At least, I don't believe the absence of physical attraction is a requirement for a man and a woman to be friends. Maybe it's that Emma's friendship was exactly the safe landing I needed at that point in my life after the tumultuous end to high school, and the stupid mistakes I made.

But mostly, I think we glommed onto each other because that's who she is. A warm, wonderful person who didn't judge my past. Who just wants to love me for me.

She's a pure, true friend.

Maybe the first one I've had in my life.

My chest tightens but I keep the emotions reined in. I keep it all under control, recalling more T.S. Eliot.

I have seen the moment of my greatness flicker,
And I have seen the eternal Footman hold my coat, and snicker,
And in short, I was afraid.
And would it have been worth it, after all . . .

I think of college. The reasons I needed that class. Memories swirl past me of my father, moments upon moments I wanted to undo. All those times he showed up to my games clutching a beer, shouting my name, waving drunkenly as I stepped up to the plate in middle school, in high school.

Wincing, I try to shake away the images of teammates. Parents. Umps. Their *feeling sorry for me* faces. Ones I saw over and over again.

Then, those memories tunnel down to me. To what I did. How I nearly tanked my own career when I was seventeen.

But I didn't, thanks to my mom, to Emma, to T.S. Eliot. But my God, I don't like anyone to know how I nearly lost the best thing I ever had.

I reroute to the present, to Emma, to what she said about Grant. "Do you think anyone can tell?"

"Nah, you've got me as your buffer. Use me," she says playfully.

I don't want her to think that's why she's here. She might play a necessary part tonight, but I need her now and always. "Please say you know that's not the reason you're in my life?"

"I know, Declan. I know. But if I can help you, I will."

"So, you don't feel used? I'd hate it if you felt that way."

She shakes her head adamantly. "I feel essential to your life. And I love it, my friend. Don't forget. I'm here for you." She sets her head on my shoulder and I pet her hair gently.

"Means a lot to me."

She lifts her head, and a few seconds later, Grant returns, flashing me a smile that latches into my soul. That lights me up. That makes my fingertips tingle. My God, the desire to touch him, to slide a hand along his thigh, to wrap an arm around him—it's so fucking powerful.

He's one in a million, all right.

It's not even the way he looks. It's everything about him.

I have got to get it under control or I'm going

to be staring at him like a starving cartoon character lusting after a turkey leg.

"Bond, James Bond," Grant says in his terrible English accent.

"Slash."

Emma lifts her head, laughing. "And I'm Maverick from *Top Gun*. Also, for the record, we just attained major dork status right now."

"We so did," Grant says. And as the third period begins, she drapes one arm around me, the other around Grant, and squeezes us.

Right then, the Cougars fan in front whips her head around again, asks, "Can I take a pic of all of you? I am such a huge Cougars fan."

"Of course," I say. Emma tucks the three of us a little closer and we smile for the camera. The seats in front of us are empty, giving the woman a clean shot. She snaps the pic.

Then she nibbles on the corner of her lips, points to me then to Grant. "Do you mind if I just get a picture of the two of you? The guys on the team?"

I pause for a second.

Pictures of the two of us. These are going to go online. These are going to be posted.

"Why don't we take a picture with you in it?" I ask.

Her gray eyes widen. "Oh my God. That'd be amazing." She climbs over the seat, switches with Emma, and Emma takes a picture of the three of us.

Just two pals.

Two baseball players. Flanking a fan. That's all this is.

That's all this can ever be, and I'd do well to remember that.

* * *

When the game ends, we find Fitz and hang out with him for a little bit at the arena. He and Grant chat about the game and when we leave, I offer to take Emma to her hotel.

She says yes.

In the car, Grant opens his phone, says he's going to check Instagram, and finds the picture the woman snapped. He shows it to Emma and me at a light. "It's no big deal. It's just you and me and a fan."

"It's no big deal," Emma says in a reassuring voice.

I cast my eyes to the screen. It's nothing. It's just two ballplayers. That is all.

But my heart is beating faster, and my mind is swirling.

What if she'd just taken a picture of me and Grant. Would everyone know? Would everyone be able to tell?

I grit my teeth.

"Hey! Idea. Instead of dropping me off first, do you want me to go in with you? To your hotel?" Emma asks. "So, we can hang out for a little bit before . . . you know."

"Yes," Grant jumps in, sounding relieved. I reach a hand to the backseat, set it on his knee. He covers my hand with his, and for that split second, everything feels right in the world.

"I'll wait for you in the room," he says in a quiet

voice that's just for me, even though she can hear our private plans.

But that's okay. She's helping with them.

That's both a good thing and a bad thing. Because it's part of the problem. The *big* problem.

I'm silent the rest of the ride.

I'm not even sure what to say. Maybe I'm afraid if I open my mouth, I'll say too much.

To Grant.

To Emma.

Most of all, to myself.

At the hotel, Grant takes off for his room, giving a quick goodbye, then bumping into Crosby and Chance as he heads to the elevator.

Relief floods me when they say hi to him, then swing their gaze to us. Waving hellos.

She's the perfect cover.

Emma and I go to the lobby bar, where I order an iced tea and we make a show of being seen for twenty minutes.

Twenty minutes that last forever.

"You doing okay?" she asks.

"Yeah."

"How long will you keep doing this?"

"We set a time limit."

"And what is that time limit?"

I wince, not wanting to think about it. It's not even really a time. It's an action. It's the end-of-our-sex plans, even though we still have another week or so of spring training. But we agreed to finish this fling well before then. The longer we hold on, the harder it'll be to keep to the ground rules anyway, so it's best that we stick to Grant's dirty list. And we'll have worked our way through it in twenty-four more hours. "Tomorrow night," I say heavily.

She gives me a sympathetic smile, pats me on the knee, and then gestures to the door. "I really should go then. I'll grab a Lyft."

My stomach dips and plummets at the same time.

This thing with Grant is ending.

But not tonight.

"Thank you. For everything," I say.

"Don't mention it," she says with a smile, and soon she gets into her car.

I shut the door, wave her off, and head straight for the stairwell.

Blinders on, I hope and I pray I run into no one.

Up the stairs I go.

One floor, two, three.

I'm all alone.

Until footsteps echo in the stairwell, heading down.

Someone's singing a tune in another language. Portuguese, I think.

It's Miguel. Seconds later, I come face-to-face with the other rookie on the landing.

"Hey man, what's up?" he asks with a bright smile.

"Not much," I say, cursing privately, smiling publicly.

"Saw New York killed Phoenix on the ice," he says.

My brow furrows. Did he see the picture? Does he know we're . . . together?

"Yeah, good game," I remark, tension winding through my veins.

He lifts his chin, shooting me a reassuring grin. "G-man told us he was going with you."

"Right. Sure," I say, keeping my tone even.

"And your friend," he adds, eyes locked on mine.

"Yeah." I don't say anything more. I don't have anything else to say.

"All right. I'm gonna hit the pool. Want to join?"

I shake my head. I don't even bother to fake a yawn. I don't want to sell it to the jury. I just want to go. "Nah, I'm going to hit the hay."

"Catch ya tomorrow."

I dart out on the fourth floor, drag both hands through my hair, and breathe deeply.

I consider finding a fire escape or climbing a drainpipe up to Grant's room. All this sneaking around is driving me insane.

But I won't let *him* be the one caught.

Grant's too young. Too new. Don't want my guy to be running into teammates. Better for me to handle the run-ins.

I wait in the hallway, listening to the stairwell, texting Grant that I'm on my way. When it's quiet again, I duck back into the stairwell, race up the steps to his floor, scan left, right, then just go.

I march down the hall, imagining a scorched earth of nerves behind me.

With every step, I burn off the worries.

I shed them.

I leave them behind.

. . .

And would it have been worth it, after all . . .

Yes, T.S. Eliot. The Rembrandt is worth it.

When I reach my guy's room, I almost stop in my tracks as the realization hits me hard.

After only a few nights, I think of him as *my* guy.

And I'm motherfucking fine with that.

So damn fine with it.

I push open the door, find *my* guy on the other side, and kick it closed behind me. Grant rises from the couch, heads straight to me, and grabs my face. The rookie claims my mouth in a searing, passionate kiss that makes every stairwell encounter in the world worth it.

I see stars.

My whole body hums with pleasure as the universe goes out of focus. As need grips me.

From this sweet, desperate ache of a kiss.

I want to drown in his kisses.

I want to be smothered in them.

Want his mouth on me everywhere, unraveling me, taking me apart.

Like he's doing to me right now.

But first, I'll do all that to him.

When he breaks the kiss, he whispers hotly, "It's just you and me now, Deck."

"Me and you, rookie," I say, and nothing beyond those doors matters for the next several hours.

He is mine.

31

GRANT

I am determined to kiss him senseless. To *give* him pleasure.

I want Declan to feel incredible, and that's how I kiss him. With everything I have. And with every sweep of my lips across his, he trembles.

I kiss his mouth, his chin, his jaw. Each time, he shudders under my touch.

It's heady—his reaction to me. It's addictive and I need another hit.

Sucking on his lower lip, I draw out a wild moan from the man I want. His hands race up and down my chest, over my shoulders, into my hair. I push him against the wall, slam my crotch to his, grind against him. My hands dive into his hair and I kiss him recklessly.

Deeply.

I can't get enough of him, his taste, his scent, *him*. His groans turn to whimpers as I devour his lips, just like I want to devour his body. The need to touch him everywhere, kiss him all over, is staggering—it's like a force pulsing inside me.

Touch him.

Taste him.

Have him.

I travel along his neck, marking him with more deep, hungry kisses. Then even more.

I can't stop.

As his hands rope into my hair, he lets out a desperate sigh. "God," he pants. "You're just . . . my undoing."

And he's mine.

I run my nose along his neck, inhaling him as pride surges in me from his words. Pride mixed with white-hot desire.

I've never wanted to turn a man on as much as I want to do that to Declan. The way he melts under my touch is intoxicating.

Powerful too.

I feel strong with him.

Last night I wanted to bottom, and I still want that for my first time. But right this second, I want to feel as if I'm topping him in the way we kiss.

Maybe this is what it means to be vers. Wanting both. Sliding in and out of both roles. Wanting different things at different times.

Maybe wanting the same thing at the same time.

Whenever we're together, I discover something new about myself. I unlock a part of who I am.

But as I flick my tongue across his jaw, and Declan unleashes a frenzied pant, I learn *this*—I love figuring out *him*.

What turns him on.

What makes him vibrate under my touch.

What electrifies him.

I want him to feel wild for me, because I feel wild for him.

Completely crazy for him.

That's a terrifying but thrilling realization. Maybe *this* is why I waited.

To have everything at once.

My chest floods with emotions, sensations, desires. It's so staggering, everything hitting me at once.

I don't know what to do, where to go, how to be.

Except . . . closer to him.

I run my hands over his pecs, then raise my face, meet his gaze. "I want to get you out of these clothes, get my mouth all over you. Can I do that first?"

"You can do anything to me, with me." He grabs my hair harder, tugs it at the roots. "I can't say no to you."

"Do you want to say no to me?"

He shakes his head, his dark eyes glimmering with lust. He looks lost in the moment. Lost in me. "I want to say yes. To everything, Grant."

Say yes to me.

Say yes to all of this. You and me. Me and you.

I don't even know what the question would be. Except maybe . . . *do you feel this too?*

But now's not the time nor the place. I've got to focus on the physical, not on my runaway feelings.

This is just sex.

Just contact.

I try to zone in on that.

My skin buzzes with excitement as we separate. I'm about to rip off my shirt. Strip off my jeans.

But I slow down. Breathe. Rake my eyes over him from head to toe, drinking in the stunning sight of this man in my room.

Broad shoulders, dark brooding eyes, lips I could obsess over.

I want to remember every second of tonight.

Want to imprint it on my mind so I can use it for fodder.

Yes, this is *just sex*.

It has to be.

That's all we are, and that's fine. It's fantastic.

I tease at the hem of his polo shirt, the pads of my fingers sliding under the cotton, across the ladder of his abs. His breath hitches as I explore his skin.

I take my time, building anticipation, winding him up. "You feel so good," I murmur as I lift up his shirt, slowly at first, inch by inch, bending, so I can kiss my way up his abs as I go.

My mouth roams across his stomach, and his fingers coil around my head. "Yes, do that," he urges.

I do as asked, licking and tasting and groaning.

He groans too with every flick of my tongue.

When I reach his pecs, I speed up, yanking his shirt over his head.

Declan lets it fall to the floor. I stare at his chest, breathless.

I've gazed at him countless times. But this is the first time I've stared at him when our bodies are about to join.

Our eyes lock.

Screw taking it slow.

Faster now, I unsnap his jeans, push them down, then his boxer briefs. He helps me along, kicking off his shoes and the rest of his clothes.

My skin scorches when his cock says hello.

I curl a fist around his dick, unleashing a carnal groan as I feel his hot, hard length, then as I slide my thumb over that first, delicious drop of liquid arousal. I bring it to my lips, smear it over them, and lick it off.

"Need you now," he says on a rough shudder, then his hands fly, and he's grabbing at my shirt, tugging it over my head, yanking at my jeans.

In mere seconds, we're both down to nothing, and he backs me up to the bed, pushes me down.

I scoot up, eyes on him the whole time. He's like a tiger hunting his prey.

Hunt me, Declan.

Please.

Have me.

He climbs over me, covers me, and fucks my mouth with his tongue.

Hungry, greedy kisses.

Consuming kisses.

I am sparking everywhere.

My dick is leaking, and my body is aching for him.

I wanted to tease him, toy with him, but holy hell, the feel of his weight on me is extraordinary. I love his strength, I need his strength, and he gives it to me as he moves down my body.

Kissing my tattoos.

Licking the arrow, the mountains, the compass.

Teasing my nipples.

Biting.

Flicking.

Most of all, *savoring*.

He kisses me like he's never enjoyed kissing this much. Maybe that's crazy, but I feel all sorts of crazy tonight. "I have to have you, Grant. I can't get enough of you. Your skin, your scent, your body," he says, raising his face as he nears my cock, then buries his nose between my thighs, inhaling me.

I arch up, moaning as his nose travels across my skin, his stubble grazing my dick.

Then, with a wicked arch of his brow, and a naughty flicker in his eyes, he takes my shaft in his mouth.

"Yes," I grunt, bucking up instantly, pleasure searing my blood. He drags me in deep, sucking hard, then drawing back as he licks a stripe up the underside. I shudder out a breath. "I'm pretty sure you want me to come while you're inside me, right?"

He moans against my cock, then lets the head fall from his lush lips. "Feisty, aren't you? And yes, I really fucking do," he says darkly.

"Then don't suck me so good right now," I warn.

He hums around my length, licking the crown. "So hard to stop. You taste so good," he murmurs as lust tears through me.

I grab his head, my body trembling. "Bet I feel

good too. Bet my ass feels great. How about trying that?"

Declan lets go, lifts his face, pushes up on his arms, and prowls, just fucking prowls over me, like an animal. "You are so sexy it's killing me."

His arms pin me.

His gaze torches me.

And I don't want this to end.

I want him to take me like this.

But even though I want to be taken, I also want to show him I can drive him insane with pleasure too.

I slide my hands up his strong arms, curving over his muscles, gripping his biceps. And I flip him to his back.

As I climb over him, he arches an appreciative brow. "Nice move, rookie."

Then I kiss my way down his body, making him writhe and groan, curse and shudder.

And I memorize each sound, each sigh. I save it for later—for when this ends, for when I need to get off.

Since this is just sex.

Just sex.

Only, that's a lie, and I know it.

This isn't just sex.

At least not for me.

It's so much more.

And I kiss him that way, so he knows in my touch what's happening in my heart. I want him to feel consumed in every way, like I do.

"Grant," he rasps out, and my name has never sounded more frantic, more fevered than in his sexy, throaty rumble.

I settle between his thighs, sliding my hands under his legs, yanking him toward my face. Then I draw his cock into my throat. I moan against his shaft, loving the taste of him.

"Yes, you're so fucking good at that," he says as I lick and suck and show him how much I want him. After a hot, heady minute, he grabs my face. "Stop. We need to fuck. Now."

Best. Words. Ever.

I let him go with a loud, wet pop, then I move up his body, kiss his lips, and give him a command. "Then get me ready."

Declan blows out a long stream of air and reaches for the lube as we shift positions.

I raise my knees, setting my feet on the bed. He drizzles lube on his fingers, strokes me slowly, presses a finger against my hole.

My body twitches with pleasure.

His lips twist into a wicked grin. "Love watching you. Love your reactions," he says as he pushes in more, playing with my balls with his other hand.

I push down on his hand, asking for more. "Yeah? How do I look?"

"Turned all the fuck on," he says, as he lets go to add more lube to his fingers.

Then he adds more fingers in me.

And holy hell, it's intense.

Mind-bending too, as Declan finger fucks me for a long time, opening me up.

After several delirious minutes, I'm panting and moaning.

Ready, so damn ready. Hell, I've been ready for him for a long time.

I push up on my elbows, my mouth dry, my body on fire, then I say, "Can I sit on your dick now?"

A slow, wicked grin spreads on his face as he eases out his fingers, grabs my face and hauls me in for a wild kiss that ends quickly as he reaches for a condom.

We shift positions, so I can be on top. "This should be easier for your first time," he says. "You're in total control. You set the pace."

I nod, barely able to respond with words because the sight in front of me is too sexy.

Too erotic.

Too carnal.

Declan Steele covers his long, thick cock with protection, then coats himself in lube, and holds the base of his dick for me.

Holy fuck.

This is happening.

Him and me.

I straddle him, rising up on my knees, gazing down at the filthy sight before me. His gorgeous dick, thick and hard and hungry for me.

I angle forward slightly, press my hands to his abs, and close the distance between our bodies.

"Yessssss," he grunts as I lower myself just the slightest bit, pressing against his shaft.

He's hardly in me. And he already looks enrapt in pleasure. It's a good fucking look, so damn good it helps me breathe.

Helps me relax.

Helps me lower myself onto the tip.

I grunt as he breaches me, pushing past the first ring of muscles.

And it's tight. Really fucking tight.

And completely strange.

And I don't know how he's going to fit in me.

Don't know at all.

I grit my teeth. Suck in a harsh breath.

"How you doing?" he asks, his voice all gravelly.

I love that he's looking at me.

Love that he cares.

But I don't love how I feel.

Not yet.

"I'm good," I bite out, as I breathe in, out. Then as I drop down more, my breath hitches.

In pain.

Carefully, he sits up, one hand on my face. "I can stop. We can stop," he says, so damn concerned that it makes my heart thump harder for him.

Wilder for him.

"Just kiss me," I beg.

"Anytime," he says, bringing me closer, kissing my mouth gently.

I barely move. I just sort of hover there in this in-between space where he's an inch or two in me.

I kind of want to stop because it's uncomfortably tight, and it hurts, and this isn't a baseball hurt. This isn't someone slamming into me at home plate. This isn't an *I can take it because I'm tough* hurt.

This is letting a man into my body.

But it's not just any man.

It's *this* man.

The man who looks at me the way I look at him.

Like it's not just sex for him either.

Not at all.

He lets go of my face and travels his hand down my arm, his touch surprisingly erotic for how soft it is.

A light brush of his fingers—that's all. But the way he touches me sends a rush of warmth through my body. As I wait to move, his fingertips travel over my stomach, making me feel so damn good. It's almost that sensation of getting a massage, when you first let go under someone else's hands, when your body relaxes and sinks into the feel-good moment.

"Say the word, rookie," he whispers against my lips. "I'll stop anytime for you." Then, a few seconds later, he adds in an even softer voice, "I'll do whatever you want."

I release a breath, relaxing, picturing what I want this to be. "Don't stop."

I laser in on the stretch, on the burn.

Then what I want it to become—the white-hot desire that's just out of reach. That's right over the cliff. It's almost there and I want it so badly because I want to be close to him.

I go for it.

I sit on his dick, taking him all the way. "Oh fuck," I grunt.

"God yes," he says at the same time.

Time does stand still. It's intense as he stretches my ass, filling my whole damn body, it seems.

I feel him everywhere.

It's *this* close to good. Not quite yet though, and I want it all. I want all the feelings.

His hands wrap around my hips, and I rise, wincing at the burn, then lower myself once more.

I lift up again. His eyes swing to where we connect, and he trembles, his breath stuttering. "So fucking sexy," he says, his hands curling tighter around my hips, like he owns me.

And as I drop down, he does.

Oh hell, does he ever own me.

Heart, mind, body.

That's when the switch flips, when the sensations turn from pain to pleasure. When the too-tight feeling ebbs away and becomes something else entirely—his cock feeling just right inside my body.

Electricity crackles in my veins. My chest heats. Jolts of pleasure shoot through me as I slide my hands up his chest.

He lowers himself onto the mattress, holding my hips, watching my face, and looking like he's losing his mind. "You got me now," he says, so husky, so smoky.

I groan, since I can't form words. I work my hips, find a tempo. I am shaking with pleasure. Overcome by the pinball machine of sensations whipping through me—sparks, and jolts, and so much heat.

He keeps talking, murmuring words of encouragement, *so good, yes, fuck yes,* and I flash back to last night. To his other words. To why he talks so much. *I'm really into you, rookie.*

That drives me on. The recall. Makes me hotter, wilder as I fuck his cock, and he fucks me.

Hands slide up chests.

Breaths shudder out.

Eyes go glassy.

Grunts fill the room. The sound of flesh slapping against flesh is the background to our noises.

His sounds.

His gasps. His moans. The curses that fall from his lips.

The feral grunts.

The way he never stops looking at me.

He never takes his eyes off me.

As I ride him, I get to know his body, get to know what makes him tick.

The answer?

Me.

I wind him up.

I drive him crazy.

That is all I want. For him to feel the same way I do.

In every single way.

Declan's hands slide along my arms, up into my hair. He rises up as he tugs me closer, kissing me desperately as we fuck.

A sharp charge rushes down my spine, and it hits me.

I *can* come soon.

But I *don't* want to come like this.

I want something else.

"Deck," I breathe.

"Yeah?"

"Can you do something?"

"Anything. I'll do anything for you," he rasps out, and I believe his *anything*.

We lock eyes, and I tell him my fantasy. "I want you to put me on all fours. That's how I want it. I really want to feel you fucking me."

His eyes glimmer with shameless lust. "I'll fuck you so good, rookie."

I ease off, scramble to my hands and knees, get in position. He moves behind me. "Raise that beautiful ass," he instructs, all smoky and impossibly sexy.

I lift higher, giving myself to him, trusting he wants everything I have.

For a split second, I tense, but I breathe through it as he sinks into me.

"*You*," he rumbles.

I crane my neck to watch him fuck.

Declan's staring at me savagely. "So fucking hot. You taking me," he says, and *take* is exactly what I do.

I take him all the way.

Then, he eases out, almost all the way, before he sinks back in. "You like this? This what you want?"

"Love it," I answer.

"Me too," he says on a long, lingering groan, his hand sliding up my back, over my shoulder. "Love it too."

That word rushes along my skin, sets up camp in my chest, makes the moment so much more intense. I stare at Declan as he finds his pace again.

As pleasure annihilates my body.

I barely know if it's from the fucking or the watching or the man.

Or *the everything*.

All of it.

Don't know. Don't care.

All I know is I'm being fucked by a guy I'm crazy for.

A man I'm unequivocally falling for.

And that right there is why sex feels out of this world. "Gimme your mouth. Kiss me while you fuck me," I demand, needing this madly.

Declan does, covering me with his body, grabbing my jaw. I drown in his hot kisses, his tongue plundering my mouth as he drives deep into my body.

I bring my hand to my shaft, but he swats it away.

"You're mine, rookie," he snarls in my ear, and I tremble as his hand wraps tight around my dick. "I'll get you there."

Relief. At last, some fucking relief.

"Jack me. Please, Deck. I'm begging you," I say.

"God, you make me so fucking hard. I've never been this aroused," he says.

Every grasp of his fist, every thrust of his cock, every brush of his lips ignites another fire inside me, and I am nothing but flames, nothing but lava as Declan shows me all my fantasies, as he acts them out with me, as he gives me everything I've longed for.

Passionate sex.

I close my eyes, sinking into the otherworldly sensations, into the full-body ecstasy of this moment.

The intimacy too.

Wave after wave of lust crashes over me. My hold on reality spirals away and I'm on the verge of coming. "Yes . . ."

"Give it to me," he moans, sounding lost in me once again, but somehow found too.

The exquisite agony coils into a vibrating knot of ecstasy, one he undoes in one more stroke.

I am devastated by an orgasm that rockets through me.

"Yes, fucking yes," he groans as I come and come and come into his hand, while Declan fucks me into the mattress, then stills, tenses and groans for days. "You feel so good."

And I do feel good.

I feel spectacular as a man comes inside me for the first time in my life.

Not just any man though.

The man I'm pretty sure I've inconveniently, stupidly fallen in love with.

The man I desperately want to sleep with again, be with again, see over and over.

But you can't always get what you want.

32

DECLAN

I had no idea sex could be like that.

That good. That close. That connected.

After I pull out, I wrap an arm around Grant, nuzzle my face against him. His skin is shiny, a post-sex sheen that I want to savor, selfish bastard that I am right now. "You smell well fucked," I murmur against his neck, inhaling the sweaty smell of him, the musky scent of our bodies having come together.

"I *feel* well fucked," he says, all hoarse and gravelly.

"Good. You should." I draw another lungful of him, loving his scent. But while I want to stay here, my nose buried in his neck, I'm not *that* selfish. I need to ditch the condom, and we both should shower. "Let's clean up," I tell him.

"Yes, boss," he deadpans.

We're in and out in less than four minutes, then we return to bed. I strip the messy cover, grab a new one, and flop down next to my lover.

My guy.

I'm still basking in endorphins, bathing in the afterglow, and I just want to lie here and fall asleep, drift off into dreams.

But I don't want to end this night too soon.

Plus, there's the matter of this man who probably can't walk straight for a couple hours.

"So, how do you feel?"

"Besides well fucked?"

"Yes. Are you sore?"

Grant shakes his head. "Just a little. A good sore, like after a workout." His brow knits. "But tomorrow? Will it be worse?"

"Probably just sore," I say, honestly. "Don't worry—you can still catch the game."

"Damn well better be able to," he says, then his expression goes thoughtful again. "Will I always feel like this?"

"Practice makes perfect," I tease.

"I like the sound of practice. And hey, I'm a competitive athlete, so I'm willing to train and train hard," he says, showing me that playful side I dig.

"So, I take it that means you like sex?" I crook a grin. I mean, I am pretty sure he had a fan-fucking-tastic time. But I don't want to assume.

He sighs contentedly, his voice tired. "Just a little."

God, he looks good like this. All stretched out and satisfied, his features relaxed, his smile soft. But when he turns his gaze to me again, his blue eyes flicker with a hint of concern.

Oh, hell.

I know why.

I'm in my own head, but I need to be thinking of him.

He's got to be wondering how it stacked up for me.

I run my hand over his pecs, my fingers playing with the fine dusting of chest hair, remembering how I felt a few nights ago after The Lazy Hammock when we stopped on the side of the road. I use those same words. "Wow. You are just wow," I say.

"Yeah?" His voice pitches up, like he needs confirmation. "Was I? Okay?"

His words are breathy, nervous.

But I'll have none of his worry.

I can't let him think he was anything but everything I wanted.

"You're out of this world," I say, running a finger down his chest. "You're a moonshot. You're a grand slam over the fences. That's *you*, rookie. You're my walk-off home run."

His smile grows wider, more relaxed. "You sure?"

I tilt my head, trying to figure him out, to understand why he would doubt me. "You didn't think I enjoyed it? Did you not like fucking me?"

"I loved it. It was amazing. I just want to know . . . if . . . I mean . . . you're so much more experienced than I am. I have no idea if I'm . . ." He nibbles on the corner of his lips.

"Any good?" I supply.

"Yeah," he says on a harsh swallow.

My hand glides down his stomach, over his abs. "Grant, there is no man I want more than you. No one I want to fuck so thoroughly. No one who turns me on like you." I kiss his smile, wanting to add *and there's a reason for that*. But I don't know how to venture into those shark-infested *feelings* waters now, or whether I should. Clean and simple is my MO, so I keep it that way. "You do it for me. You just do."

"You really do it for me. In kind of every way," he says, putting himself out there once again.

Like he always has.

Since the morning he said he wanted to sleep with me. Since the night he told me he was a virgin.

Does he realize what's happening here? Does he feel all the same things I do?

My chest tightens with need. With desire. But none of it is sexual. All of it is *real*.

I am . . .

My God . . . Emma nailed it.

I am besotted with Grant Blackwood.

And that's all new. Entirely virgin terrain. Words stick in my throat. My mouth goes desert dry. A wrecking ball slams into me.

It's so obvious it's embarrassing.

It's so patently apparent what's happening to me.

I've spent my adult life with neat, compartmentalized off-season affairs. I meet men, I date them, I romance them. We do it up right. Fly to exotic locales, drive fast cars, play hard, fuck harder.

And I say goodbye at the end.

With barely a second thought. Never a look back. When endings grow complicated, I work even harder to keep the men in the past.

I control everything, and I need that control to keep my life together. To keep baseball in the center of it all. Baseball—the thing that saved me from my father, that saved me from me.

And now, I'm tempting fate.

Gambling with my most prized possession. The game I love.

And for what?

My chest clutches, my heart hammering viciously against my rib cage since it knows the answer, has for some time now.

For *this*.

This soul-deep connection.

Grant Blackwood is my undoing because he gets me. He understands me. He gives more of himself to me than anyone ever has.

I want him beyond these walls, beyond this room, beyond tonight.

Only, I can't have him for keeps.

There is no way for us to work.

But at least there's tonight. I reach for his gorgeous face, slide a thumb along his jaw, and lock eyes with him. His blue orbs flicker with vulnerability and something new too.

Hope.

Just raw hope.

"I'm glad you waited. I'm glad it was me," I say, starting with that bare truth.

Grant's lips curve in the start of a smile. "Me too."

"Being your first was incredible. Sex with you was incredible," I add.

A light shrug comes my way. "I have nothing to compare it to, but I'd have to agree." He stops and corrects, "Wait. Hold on. I can compare it to my fantasies, and it was better. Worlds better." He's found his confidence again, but he doesn't have to be all swagger and charm with me. I love seeing all his sides—his insecurities and his fears. I love, too, helping him through some.

And having him here to help me through mine.

Like this one—offering a real and true piece of my heart.

But he deserves it.

"Do you know why it was so good between us? So good for me?" I ask, digging down deep to find the guts to say something truly daring, something incomparably risky.

"Tell me." His tone latches onto mine, hangs on my every word.

"I'm not more experienced than you in some things. Because with you, I feel like I'm experiencing *everything* for the first time too," I say, trying that on as I start into a topic that's terribly new. It's like stepping off a cliff. I've no idea what's down below—if I'll land on soft grass or jagged rock.

His voice is quiet in the night. "How so?"

My heart climbs into my throat, and I wince. This is so fucking uncomfortable. This out-of-control feeling wrenches my guts.

Grant and I, *we're* out of control. We're spilling past all my boundaries. Scrambling over all my walls.

But I don't want to stop. I want more, and more, and more.

I swallow roughly and pour out as much of my heart as I can possibly spare. "I am so crazy for you, Grant. I don't know what happened in the last few days, but that's how I feel. *Out-of-my-mind crazy.* I know this has to end, but I don't want it to end. I want you to be mine," I say in a rush of words and emotions, and horribly messy feelings —feelings I wish I didn't have. But they're here. Lodging into my chest, wedging into my brain as I add, "All mine. *Only* mine."

Grant's blue eyes sparkle with wild hope, and his lips hook into a grin. "I'm falling so fucking hard for you," he says, and that's it.

I'm just done.

I'm too far gone.

I grab him, kiss him, and give him everything I can.

For now.

Because that's all we have.

When we break the kiss, he gives a helpless shrug. "Sorry, not sorry."

"No apologies. I'm in this too. I'm so far in this, and I wish we could last."

The catcher on my team lets out a sharp breath, his eyes brimming with sadness, resignation. "But we can't."

There is no question mark.

Since there's no question.

We are impossible.

"But at least we have one more day," I whisper.

Too bad I wish tomorrow wouldn't come.

33

GRANT

Newsflash: I am not sore the next day.

Nope.

I'm not sore as I crouch behind home plate, catching a scrappy inter-squad game before our afternoon one against the Bandits.

I am not sore what-so-fucking ever as one of our starters throws to me and the team goes through a split-squad scrimmage.

Okay, maybe I *am* sore.

But I don't care.

I know how to put pain out of my mind to focus on my job.

That's what I do because as amazing as last night was, I still have a goddamn job to do, and the memory of my shitty game against the Sharks isn't far from my head.

How could it be?

I'm not stupid. I know why I'm catching this scrimmage.

The same reason we're having one.

Our last game sucked.

My last game sucked.

This is the hierarchy. This is how it works. Show that you have the mettle for the starting job.

The bullpen catchers aren't here today behind the plate. It's me against Rodriquez. Rodriguez against me.

Can you say *metaphor for my entire spring training?*

Right now, he's at the plate. He's on the squad with the stars—Crosby, Declan, Chance.

Which probably means he's starting today's game against the Bandits.

That's not good for me.

But it's also an opportunity.

If he starts it maybe I can finish it. Maybe I can show the skipper why I deserve the starting catcher slot on Opening Day. Rodriguez is good but I need to be better.

There's no room for pain.

Plus, I know the man's weakness. Dude swings at sinkers every time. Misses most of the time. I call for one, and he shifts his hips, then slices the bat through the air as the ball drops.

Yes!

That beautiful white orb finds a home in my glove with a welcome *thunk*.

A few more like that, and Rodriguez whiffs.

Better luck next time.

Not.

Crosby ambles over to the plate, adjusting his helmet, chewing gum, then blowing a bubble and cracking it so damn loud I swear it splits my eardrums.

"Is that your new distraction strategy?" I ask.

He wiggles a brow. "Yeah. Is it working?"

"Considering I figured it out in a second I'd say no," I say, then laugh. He snaps his fingers in an aw-shucks gesture as he adjusts his batting glove, hoists the bat, and then gets into the stance, taking a few practice swings.

"Big game today," he says, since he's always been a chatty mofo at the plate. He does it to drive catchers crazy. To distract them.

"Why is that? Do you have a tee time that you don't want to miss?" I tease as I settle into the crouch. If I'm not distracted by the lingering ache of a big cock up my ass last night, I'm not gonna be distracted by Crosby's yammering.

"Touché." He laughs, and I'm firing on all cylinders at being a part of the team today. Giving the guys a hard time and talking smack.

I guess sex is good for me.

Maybe I'll go on a streak thanks to great sex.

Maybe I could convince Declan to keep this up throughout spring training.

But I shake that notion from my head as the pitcher nods at me and I give him a sign. A few pitches later we send Crosby packing to the dugout with a checked strike.

Two outs and it's Declan's turn.

Lowering my mask, I crouch back down, wishing *this* could be our norm. Opposing teams.

That would come with its own set of challenges, but it'd be worlds better than being on the same team.

Opposing teams would be workable, not insurmountable. We'd be competitors, but on a path to *more* rather than a road to nowhere.

Me behind the plate, him at the plate—we'd be doable.

I let that new fantasy play out for a few seconds as he takes a couple practice swings.

A baseball fantasy.

Striking out my lover.

Oh, fuck yes.

I want to watch him go down swinging, and my gut tells me how to do it. It shows me a flash of the game where he hit the grand slam off the slider last season. As I replay it, the memory sharpens.

Did the pitcher hesitate?

I don't know, so I shelve it, but leave a mental Post-it to look it up on YouTube later. For now, I stick to a solid plan.

Velocity.

I call for a fastball, and he connects with a sharp line drive to second that turns into an easy out at first.

Not a strikeout, but I'll take it, thank you very much.

I grin, since, damn, it is so satisfying to send my lover back to the dugout. As Declan walks away, I pretend he's on the other team.

But even though he's not, maybe we can pull this off for a little bit longer. Would that be so crazy? Another few nights? Another few days?

That idea takes hold of me the rest of the morning, and on into the afternoon when the Bandits arrive.

Hell, if I pulled off that excellent scrimmage, I can pull off a terrific game.

Especially since Fisher has me start.

Yup. I've got this. I've *so* got this.

* * *

Except in the second inning, a pitch skitters past me and I *don't* fucking have it. I race after the passed ball, hustling to the backstop to field, but the runner on third scores and I curse.

That was one hundred percent my fault.

I return to the plate. As the pitcher goes into the windup, the runner on first makes a move to steal. Once the ball hits my glove, I throw to second. It should be an easy out—the runner lumbers like a bear—but I'm too late.

He's in safely.

Fuck me.

I grit my teeth, huff, and finish out the inning.

When I reach the dugout, I park my sore ass on the bench and drop my head. Crosby claps me on the shoulder. "Focus, rookie. Get your head in the game. Is it someplace else?"

I wince. Can he see right through me? My head is in the same stupid place as my stupid fucking heart. It's fantasizing. It's galloped off to tra-la-la land after the scrimmage. It's picturing things it doesn't have any right to picture.

Declan's not on another team.

We can't keep on doing this.

We're done at the end of tonight, and that is all. Baseball is what matters.

I laser in on that when I'm at bat. But a pop fly to center ends my chance.

Fisher pulls me aside and says Rodriguez will finish the game.

"Hit the shower, rookie," he says.

Kiss of fucking death.

"Yes, sir."

"We'll talk later."

Dread crawls over me as I go into the locker room, shower and dress, and wait for Fisher.

But all he says when the game ends is a crisp, "We need you to pick it up soon."

"I will, sir," I say tightly, then I take off before the rest of the team pours in.

I call my grandfather when I leave, walking along the road by the complex so I can burn off these fumes. "I had the worst game ever, Pops," I say, my head hanging low.

"But that happens. You have bad games," he says.

I blow out a long stream of air as I stalk down the street. "I can't have bad games. Rodriguez has been playing better. I went into spring training thinking I had this locked. That he'd be my backup catcher. But he might get the starting spot, and I don't even know if I'll be the backup or if the team will call on someone else," I tell him, my voice as strained as my heart. "I don't know what's going to happen."

"All you can do is focus on the fundamentals, kid. Focus on the game. You know how to play. You've always known how to play. And the only times you've been frazzled is when personal stuff has gotten in the way," he says in that calm, paternal voice he has. "Remember all that stuff with Frank in high school and what a tough couple of games you had at the end of the season?"

I stop near a bus stop as I listen, lean on the signpost as I drop my head and grit my teeth. "Yeah, I remember."

"And what did you do?" he asks.

I swallow roughly. "I went to you. I talked to you, and you helped settle my state of mind."

"By reminding you that you're a great ballplayer. The game is mental as much as it is physical. Your physical game is great. If you're out of sorts, it's usually because your mind is elsewhere."

He says it gently, but firmly. It's a message from someone who knows me. Knows me like he can see inside my soul.

God, I want to tell him.

I want him to know what happened.

I fell in love with this guy, and he's all I can think about. I want to find a way to be with him, but I can't. Do you have any idea what I should do, Pops?

I know what he'd say, though.

Tough break, kid. But you need to let him go.

"You're right, Pops. I'll keep my head in the game. Crosby said the same thing too," I say heavily as I walk to the bus stop.

That's what I vow to do tomorrow. Tonight is my one last time with the man I'm falling in love with.

Tonight, we end.

Tomorrow, I reignite my love affair with baseball.

"Grant," he says, his tone thoughtful. "Is there anything else going on?"

A breath shudders out of me. I pinch the bridge of my nose. Emotion clogs my throat. And the truth comes pouring out. "I met this guy. He's kind of amazing. But nothing will happen, so I just need to end it."

End it.

It's like a knife serrating my heart.

My grandpa sighs, a supportive, loving sound. "That's hard. Love is hard when it comes at the wrong time."

I close my eyes, the desert sun beating down on me as I sink onto the bus stop bench. "Yeah, it is."

"You want to talk about it?"

I shake my head. "No. I just need to do what I have to do."

"I'm here if you need me," he says.

"I know. I love you."

"Love you too" he says, and when I end the call, I let my head fall back against the concrete of the bus shelter.

Banging it once. Twice. Three times. Then the squeal of brakes makes me look up.

A bus has stopped.

I'm the only one here.

I wave it off.

It feels like my life passing me by.

* * *

On the walk back to the hotel, I put my finger in the fire and do something I rarely do.

I google myself.

Wincing, I find a sports blog covering spring training. The subtitle of *It Ain't Over Till It's Over* reads: *Who'll be behind the dish for the Cougars? It's a toss-up.*

The report mentions the Scoundrels game where the pitcher and I disagreed on the calls, then the hitless Sharks game, then today's passed ball.

Embarrassment churns through me.

I close it and call Haven. She answers right away. "Talk to me. What's on your mind?"

I tell her what happened at the game.

"It's spring training. It's one game," she says, reassuring me.

"No. My game the other day was terrible. The one before wasn't great." My stomach twists with nerves. "Can you please try to get some info on where I stand? My role with the team?"

"You know they're not likely to tell me who's going to be their starting catcher. Do I think it's going to be you? Yes. Do all signs point to it being you? Yes. But teams make their own decisions."

"Can you try?" I ask, wracked with desperation. "Make some calls? Don't you have sources or something?"

She takes a beat. "I'll make some calls. I'll see what people are saying. I'm heading to Arizona, anyway, for some meetings. But I can't promise I'll have any information."

"Thank you. I appreciate it."

When I return to the hotel, the game is over. I run into Sullivan and he motions for me to come to his room.

I bet he wants to dish on his date last night. I know I need to be a better friend, so I should listen.

Inside his room I sit on the edge of the couch. "What's up, man? Did you have a good night with that research scientist?"

"I did, but that's not what I wanted to talk to you about." He parks himself in the desk chair, pulling it closer to me.

I sit up straight. "This sounds serious."

"I want to ask you something because we're friends, and I know you. And this might be awkward. I know you and Declan went to the game together, and I could be wrong, but . . ." Inside my head, the sirens wail like when the hero in the thriller breaches security in the government building, and all the guards come charging after him. Sullivan goes on in the same even tone. "But if he's the reason you're not playing well the last couple games, I just want you to know I'm here to talk to you about anything."

A secret agent would escape by any means, avoid the guards by rappelling down a telephone wire with his own belt.

I heave a sigh, shoot him a sharp look, and twist my gut with my own lie. "Are you really going there, man? Assuming something's happening between the two of us?"

Everything is happening. Everything is ending.

He raises his hands in surrender. "No. Just seems like there's a connection between the two of you, that's all. I'm not telling you what to do or not to do." He holds my gaze, nothing but support in his eyes. "I'm telling you that I'm your friend, no matter what."

Half of me appreciates the sentiment.

The other half says I need to man the hell up and fix this mess I'm making. "Thanks. But I've got this. I would never get involved with a teammate. I'm not stupid."

"I didn't think so, but I had to put it out there," he says, and my feet touch ground, a secret agent escaping by the hair of my neck. Now, all I have to do is walk away. "I want you to be catching for me for a long time. And I know relationship stuff can mess you up. Hell, any relationship your rookie year can be difficult. That's why my date was only a date. I'm avoiding entanglements like the plague, and you should too."

He believes me.

I pulled off a clean getaway.

Reaching across the table, I knock fists with him in agreement. This is no ruse—I am determined to follow his advice. Declan's advice too.

Avoid relationships.

Avoid love.

"I promise, bro. I am not getting involved with a soul," I say, renewing my vow.

But after I leave, Declan texts me that he has good news and he can't wait to tell me.

And I can't wait to hear what it is.

I need some good news.

Need it badly.

34

DECLAN

A few hours earlier

After the morning scrimmage, I steal away for thirty minutes to grab an iced tea at Dr. Insomnia's, a coffee shop around the corner from the complex. Fitz meets me there—he has another game tonight, and he's coming to mine this afternoon.

He grabs a protein pack with a hard-boiled egg, some carrots, and nuts, waggling it my way. "Want one?"

I shake my head. "I'm all good. I had a big breakfast."

"And I'm going to have a big lunch. I like to eat."

I laugh. "No shit. Me too."

"And I like to eat often. And at *your* game too. Speaking of, I haven't been to a baseball game since you lost in the first round of playoffs."

I stare sharply at him. "Thanks for the reminder, asshole."

He pays for his food, then smacks my shoulder. "I'm psyched to come today. Glad I could fit it in before I have to get out of town."

I take the iced tea and we walk out of the shop, heading back toward the complex. "Same here. I vastly prefer friends at games over . . ."

Him.

My father.

"Over . . .?" Fitz prompts.

I shake my head. "Nothing."

"Dad stuff?" he asks, straightforward as he's ever been. He knows the basics, but that's all.

My shoulders tighten into thousands of knots. "He texted me this morning about the picture of me and Grant at your game last night," I say, gritting my teeth when I'm done.

Fitz whistles. "Jesus. What did he say?"

I adopt an older man's voice. "*Is that guy your type? He seems cute. You look good together.*" I cringe. "I'm guessing he knows Grant is gay, but what's up with the awkward '*Are you dating, son?*' convo? We're not buds who talk about that."

"The picture isn't even date-ish," Fitz says with a *what gives* tone.

"Exactly. The fan is in between us," I say, taking a drink of my tea as we walk. "But you know how it goes. People see him and me together, and they make assumptions."

He nods sagely. "I hear ya. Do you think they've been making assumptions about you guys all along?"

"I'm sure if people saw us together"—I point to Fitz then me—"they'd make assumptions too."

Fitz gives me an appraising once-over, humming. "You're not my type."

I flip him the bird. "You're not *my* type."

When we reach the park, my father's name flashes across the screen of my phone, and my stomach corkscrews. I wish I could learn to avoid his calls.

But I don't know how. Avoiding his calls only makes me feel worse. Makes me worry that I'll miss something vital. That I'll be blindsided. That he'll show up someplace unannounced.

I hate surprises. I hate them so damn much. But I can't have the specter of my father hanging over me during the game, not knowing if he might be asking for money, asking for help, asking to talk.

Nothing is worse than not knowing.

"I better deal with this."

Fitz waves and ambles down toward the park as I hang back, pacing the parking lot as I call my dad back. "What's going on, Dad?"

"Just wanted to know—if I come to a game, can I meet your boyfriend?"

I pull a face. Is he for real? "No. Because he's not."

"Are you sure? Seemed like it," he says in an easygoing tone, like this is a normal question when it's not at all.

I breathe heavily through my nostrils, like a dragon. "Shockingly, I'm not involved with every gay guy in sports."

"Of course, I know that," he says with a buddy-

buddy laugh. Right. Like we're a couple of pals. "But you two just look like you're together."

The sun blazes overhead, pelting me with its unforgiving rays. I grab my shades from the neck of my shirt and shove them on as if they can shield me. "It's not like I've gone on a date with every single queer guy in the game. It's not like we have Zoom meetings every Thursday. That's not how it works."

"Fine, fine. I hear ya. I'm just trying to do a better job at being . . . a dad."

My chest tightens and caves in. It expands and it falls at the same time. "Thanks," I bite out, since it's easier than continuing this conversation.

"And I'm happy for you that you're living your best life."

A storm brews inside me, picking up speed and strength. "Now? Are we doing this now?"

"Are you still upset about what I said when you came out? I don't want you to be upset."

Gale-force winds swirl, ripping past me.

I try to breathe. Just breathe. I turn to the sky. Searching for a bird. A sparrow, a falcon, a woodpecker. Anything. I'll take anything. Any form of escape.

I breathe out hard as metal. "No."

"Then why can't I meet him?"

I grit my teeth and explode. "He's not my boyfriend."

"Sheesh. I just thought so. He's cute, okay? You can't blame me for thinking he's cute for you."

I shift gears. "What's going on, Dad?"

He sighs heavily. "Things have just been kind of rough around here. Kara isn't happy with me."

It's coming, I can feel it. *The ask. The favor.*

"Did she kick you out, Dad?"

"Eh, women. Am I right? Wait. Nope. That was not cool of me to say." He clears his throat. "I'll find another place. Honestly, it's not a big deal. I'm working some angles. Listen, I'm sorry I called and laid this all on you," he says, then shifts to contrition mode. "This was total bullshit of me. I'm trying not to do it. I told the guys at the meeting that I would do a better job. I wouldn't lay this at your feet."

With the word *meeting*, I let go of a smidge of tension. All I ever wanted was for him to recover. "I'm glad you're going to meetings."

"In fact, I've got to get to one soon. And honestly, I was just calling to make amends. There's a lot of shit I want to make amends for, son. And I want to make amends for how I handled it when you came out."

Now? He wants to do it motherfucking now?

"Dad, I think that's great, but I just can't do it this second. I have a game soon. Can we talk about it another time?"

"Yes, of course. You go knock in some homers," he says, sounding as awkwardly uncomfortable as a duck wearing a three-piece suit.

I turn off my phone, breathe fumes of fire, then march into the complex. In the locker room I stuff the device into my locker, avoiding Grant, avoiding everyone, needing to get into the zone.

I put on my uniform, head out to the field, and stretch as I recite The Love Song of J. Alfred Prufrock.

And would it have been worth it after all.

I look at Grant once.

And I know the answer.

I know the answer because it hurts so much to see him struggle in the game.

But I have to put my blinders on. I know how to wear them. I know how to use them. My blinders are my special skill. Better than hitting a fastball over the fences. Stronger than fielding a hot rocket up the center of the diamond.

With my tunnel vision, I have an excellent game, clobbering in a two-run homer.

When the game ends with a win, the guys clap me on the back. After I take a shower and get dressed, I grab my phone and turn it back on. There's a text from my father.

Dad: I watched your game online. Tell your boyfriend his weight is too far back on his knees. I doubt he's even aware of it, but he needs to shift his weight a millimeter forward and he'll be golden.

I leave in a trail of fire, walking through the complex staring daggers at my phone. "Fuck you. Fuck you. Fuck you."

I am not passing that on to Grant. I'm not giving hitting tips to Grant from my father.

Even though it skewers my heart that my guy didn't play well two games in a row. I flash back to Kyle, my rookie year. To how that relationship messed me up. To how close I came to being sent down.

Love is dangerous. So dangerous.

So are fastballs.

When I reach the corridor, my phone rings.

It's my agent. I answer right away. "What's up, Vaughn?"

"Dude, are you sitting down?"

I duck into an empty weight room, sink onto a bench.

Vaughn talks quickly. But precisely. "You've heard of this team called the New York Comets?"

"No, I was too busy to watch the World Series last year," I play dumb and Vaughn laughs.

"If you'd had your eyes on the prize, you'd have seen they were lacking a slugger." He pauses, takes a breath. "And have you heard of something called fuck-off money?"

I crack up. "Who hasn't?"

"The Comets just traded for you, and they threw in some fuck-off money too."

I blink. My body hums, alive with possibility. A strange, wild sensation rushes through my body.

Surprise.

But for the first time in my life, I don't hate the unknown.

I think . . . I like it.

"The New York Comets just traded for me?" I make sure I'm hearing him right. That I'm not imagining my wishes coming true.

"They did. And they want you in their next spring training game in Florida tomorrow. They're going for another World Series run, and they're shoring up on players. They think you're the missing piece."

Tingles race down my spine.

The missing piece.

I've had a good run in San Francisco over four years. A great run. But this is . . . next level.

This is the most storied franchise of all time, with more World Series crowns than any other team by a mile.

I pinch the bridge of my nose, a million thoughts tearing through my head. I've always known this could happen. Trades are de rigueur in baseball. Especially at my level. With four years' service, I don't have a no-trade clause.

For a fraction of a second, a dark fear wedges under my skin. "Is San Francisco trying to get rid of me?"

Vaughn scoffs. "Dude. Nooooo. Don't think that. Not for a second. New York came calling and San Francisco would be stupid *not* to trade you with what New York offered. Cougars need pitchers, and New York has them. New York is ten-feet deep in firepower on the mound thanks to its farm system—but they desperately need an anchor for the lineup. They're picking up your contract extension, and wait till you hear the amount they're offering."

He dives into specifics about the extension and the dollars, and I swear my jaw comes unhinged. I'm already making good money—Vaughn scored me a hell of a deal in arbitration. But the money New York is dangling is insane.

Plus, it's New York.

It has one fantastic priceless feature that San Francisco doesn't: It's far, far away from my father.

Then again, it's not as if I have a choice—I've

been traded. All I have to do is pack my bags. "So, when am I leaving?"

"You can either take the red-eye tonight, or you can get on a flight at six a.m. tomorrow morning."

Grant. One more night with Grant.

My answer is instant. "Put me on the six a.m. flight."

We talk about details for a few more minutes. My uniform will be waiting in my locker, the guys usually stay in rental homes, designated hitter, Brady, has an extra room, and will be happy to put me up for the final week.

When the call ends, I just sit there, alone in the weight room, absolutely floored. I stare at the mirror, processing the fact that I've been traded away. I'm no longer on the same team as the man I'm falling in love with.

And that is the *best damn part* of this news.

It's so fucking good I want to kiss the sky.

I open my texts and send him a message, then count the seconds.

C'mon. Write back.

Like he can read my mind, he replies in just ten Mississippis.

I tell him to wait in his room and I go straight there, not giving a flying fuck if I run into anyone on the way.

But I don't see a soul, and that's fine too.

Grant opens the door, and once it falls closed behind us, I park my hands on his shoulders, look into his eyes, and smile like crazy. "Guess who's not your teammate anymore?"

35

DECLAN

Here's the thing about getting traded.

Your bros want to send you off in style.

You can't really say *sorry, I need to go hole up in a hotel room and spend the night with the hot-as-sin catcher.*

So, I can't say no to this last night with the guys. I still don't want them to know what we've been up to. Protecting Grant doesn't end when I get to the other side of the country and put on the other team's uniform.

Our spring fling is our secret, and always will be.

When Crosby and Chance hustle me to the Cactus Club, I go along with it. Grant and I have a plan, after all.

We shoot pool, toast with iced tea for me, Diet Coke for him, and beer for some of the others.

"Man, I cannot wait to pitch against you when we go to New York," Chance says as he leans against the pool table. "I am going to strike you out so damn hard, and I'm going to love every second of it." He hisses like he's on the mound—because I'm sure this dude does hiss on the mound.

"We're going to demolish you," Crosby says, then swings his gaze to Chance. "But no sliders, K? Don't forget that hanging slider this guy hit against the Aces. That grand slam was insane."

I laugh privately. If they only knew the truth about that hanging slider. "Guess word got out around the league," I say, keeping my response light. I don't mind at all that I'm the Loch Ness Monster with sliders. No one's seen me hit one well, but my reputation for going long with them precedes me.

"Guess I know what pitch *not* to call when Declan is at the plate," Grant drawls as he sets down his Diet Coke, then lifts his cue and takes aim at the red-striped ball on the table.

After Grant misses and loses the game, he makes a show of checking out his phone, arching a brow, then licking his lips. "I'm outta here, guys," he says.

"You gotta go so early? It's only nine," Crosby says.

"As you may have noticed, I've been playing like shit, so I'm going to get laid tonight and see if that breaks my streak." He waggles the phone, flashing the Grindr app before he puts it in his pocket.

"Ooh, get it, bro," Crosby calls out.

Chance pumps his hips. "Break the streak."

Sullivan whistles. "Guess you got on Grindr

after all. And I'm sure your hookup appreciates your commitment to baseball."

Grant laughs, then high-fives everyone.

Myself included. "It was fun playing with you for, what, four weeks? See you in September when we pummel you."

My guy leaves.

Fifteen minutes later, I yawn. "I've got a six a.m. flight, and I want to impress my new team, so I need some shut-eye."

I say my goodbyes to the folks who have been like my brothers, then I get into my car, suitcase already packed, and I head for the hotel near The Lazy Hammock.

I park, grab my overnight bag and walk to a suite in the corner with an outside entrance. It's private. No hallways. No one here we know. No one to see us go into a room together or leave together.

My pulse spikes as I near the door, slide my card key across it, then head inside.

I drop my bag by the bathroom, turn the corner, and groan.

Grant is stretched out on the bed, naked as a jaybird, lazily stroking his cock. The card key I gave him to get in the room is on the nightstand. The ends of his dark blond hair are wet.

"Merry Christmas to me," I say, as I kick off my shoes, tug off my shirt, and climb over him. Dropping my lips to his, I kiss the fuck out of him. His hands slide into my hair, curling around my head, and he yanks me closer.

The only place I want to be.

His legs wrap around me. "Yes, gimme this

banging body," Grant murmurs as his arms hook around me while I bury my face in his neck, kissing him there, inhaling that sexy clean scent, the just-showered smell I dig.

But I love him dirty too.

Love him sweaty.

Love him smelling like a sexy beast of a man who needs me the same way I need him.

We kiss for ages, all over.

Necks, jaws, earlobes.

Pecs, stomachs, throats.

The difference this time is we aren't frenzied. We aren't kissing like the world is ending.

Even though we've barely had a chance to figure shit out, we've figured out this much—tonight feels like it could be the start of something rather than the end of everything.

I slow our kissing. Raising my face, I take a second to admire his swollen lips, his kiss-drunk smile, the twinkle in his eyes.

Grant shoots me a dirty grin. "Are you just going to tease me all night, or are you going to let me fuck you?"

Pleasure jolts down my spine in a hot rush, but as much as I want to get naked with him, I want something else too.

I want him in November.

And I don't want to leave this up in the air. We didn't have time to talk about the details earlier. Now we do, and I want to lock this in.

So, I push up on my arms, brace myself on my palms, and stare down at the rookie. "What are you doing in November?"

"Umm . . . napping. Taking a long-ass vacation

somewhere warm. Am I supposed to say golf? I don't think I like golf, but maybe reading on a beach. I've always wanted to go to Miami. Relax on the sand, get lost in some books," he says, then his tone wavers, worry flickering in his beautiful eyes. "That is, if I make the roster."

My heart squeezes for him. I bend closer, brush a soft kiss to his cheek. "You'll make it. You just need to focus, babe. OK? Trust me on this. Just focus on baseball. You've got it."

"I hope so," he says, his voice thin. Then he draws a deep breath, exhales. "I remember what you said though. When we started working out. Relationships are distracting. Especially your rookie year. You cut yours off."

"I did." But Kyle wasn't Grant. Grant is a galaxy away from Kyle. Grant is the guy I'd move mountains for. Grant is the best thing I've ever had. But I don't want to be the worst thing for him, so I nod, firmly. "Best decision I ever made. I had a great rookie year. I want *you* to have a great rookie year."

"I just want to make the team."

"You will. Keep your eye on the prize," I say, then I nuzzle his neck, whispering against his skin, "But come November, all that stuff you're doing, like reading on the beach?" I lift my face, meet his eyes. "Do it with me."

Grant arches a brow, his lips curving in a grin. "Are you asking me to be your sidepiece in the off-season?" He's sarcastic, feisty Grant again.

I shake my head. "I'm asking you a real question. And it's important."

My chest clutches. My nerves spiral. But I'm in this. I'm so in this.

Grant scoots up, his expression turning serious. "You want me to be your boyfriend? Like, when the season is over? When you do your fling thing?" His questions come out analytically, like he's taking stock, writing a pros and cons list.

I can't read him. Can't tell if he's about to turn me down or stake his claim on my time. My heart gallops to my throat. Have I read him wrong? Does he not want this? Worry trips through my questions, but I ask them anyway. "Yes. What do you think? Want to meet me in Miami?"

My guy's blue eyes twinkle as he nibbles on the corner of his lips. "I'm going to ignore you so hard till then. Then when November rolls around, I am going to find you on the beach and kiss the fuck out of you." He sighs happily. "But nothing during the season, right? We've got to focus on baseball during the season."

I smile, glad he's on the same page I am. "One hundred percent."

"I waited years for a guy *like* you. I can wait all season for *you*," he says, his voice stitched with a vulnerability that cracks my heart wide open.

"I'll wait for you, rookie."

I press a quick kiss to his lips, and he smiles, like he's as happy as I am. Like he's as lovestruck as me. "Guess we broke our ground rules," I murmur.

"Pretty sure we just smashed through every single one of them," Grant says with a grin.

"And I have no regrets."

"Me neither. I told you I wouldn't regret you."

"I could never regret you, Grant Blackwood," I say then shuffle off the bed, popping open the button on my jeans, enjoying the way he rakes his gaze over me as I get naked for him.

I give him a show, pushing my jeans down over my hips, my boxer briefs following, my cock springing free. I give my shaft a tug.

The second he sees how much I want him, he's panting and moaning, gripping his dick, stroking it nice and hard for me.

I push my jeans and briefs to the ground, step out of them.

Then I grab the lube from my bag, toss it to my guy, and get in bed, landing on my back.

"Are you ready to fuck a man for the first time?" I ask with a groan.

He runs his fingers along my jaw. "I'm ready to fuck the man I'm crazy for."

"Mmm. Me too, babe. Me too." I draw him in for one more kiss, hoping he feels everything. Hoping he knows I'm falling madly in love with him.

But that word—*love*. It's so hard to say. Too hard to voice. Too out of control. All I can do is come close. Dangerously close. "I'm falling for you. And I want to fuck and fall tonight."

"Fucking and falling sounds perfect." My lover moves down the bed, between my legs, and gets to work on prepping me.

"Such a fast learner," I praise as he slides his fingers in me, opening me up.

"I have a really good teacher," he murmurs as he crooks a finger, making me arch into his talented hand.

Making me moan.

Gasp.

Hiss.

Then, when he drops his lush lips to my dick, I thrust up into the warm paradise of his mouth.

Mmm. The things I want to do with his mouth. But he takes his mouth away, lets go of my cock, and licks the head, his eyes like blue flames.

"I want to watch you jerk off some time, Deck. I want to shoot all over you. I want to do everything with you," Grant says, then brings the head of my dick back into his mouth as I touch myself, trailing my hands up and down my body as he scissors his fingers in me, lighting me up.

"I want to feel all the things you can do with that wicked tongue," I moan, and he lets go again, eases out his fingers, climbs up me. He plants his hands on each side of my face and stares at me like he wants to eat me for breakfast.

"You want me to taste you everywhere, Deck? Lick you all over? Fuck your ass with my tongue?"

This man and his filthy mouth. His dirty mind. "You've come so far," I say as my cock twitches, throbbing as a drop of pre-come leaks from the tip. "And yes, I want that. Save it for me, rookie. Save that wicked mouth for me. I want that so badly."

Grant dips his face to me. "I'd do it now," he says, sounding so aroused. "Lick you everywhere. *Eat* you."

His cock slides along my stomach, leaving a trail of arousal, and that's what I want. Him in me. "Mmm. I want that with you. Giving and getting. But I'm gonna want to come that way if you get that wicked tongue near me," I say, my voice all smoky. I lift my face closer to his, haul him against me, paint his lips with mine. Then I break the kiss. "Right now, I want to be close to you. I need you inside me."

Grant shudders, his skin flushing, his body vibrating, his desire rolling off him in waves.

He reaches for a condom, opens it, and slides it down his shaft. "First time I've ever worn one of these," he says, kind of in awe, reaching for the lube and adding more to the protection.

My God, it's so sexy to watch him do that. Safe sex is the hottest thing ever.

Except that's not true. Safe sex with Grant is the hottest thing I've ever experienced.

When he's covered, I lie down, reach for the back of my thighs and lift my legs in the air.

He settles between my thighs, and I help him along, guiding his cock against me, my knees up, my body open.

Ready for him.

And my God, does he look a sight.

Turned on, aroused, and ready to have the man he's falling for too.

"Fuck me, rookie. I'm yours."

36

GRANT

I'm shaking with lust.

Trembling with desire.

He's so gorgeous, so sexy, and he's here. Giving his body to me. I don't want to let him down. I want to make it so good for him. Want him to feel as incredible as I do.

With my weight on my knees, and one hand on the bed by his shoulder, I rub the head of my cock against his ass.

"Yeah, that's it," he murmurs.

For a second, the fear of hurting him needles my mind. "Will you tell me if you don't like it?"

"I promise, but I'm gonna love it." Declan's dark eyes are fevered, frantic with desire as he urges me inside.

I believe him completely.

And I push in, the crown of my cock breaching his body.

His reaction is all my fantasies. All my wet dreams.

"More, give me more," he commands, his voice thick with lust.

The feeling is nearly indescribable. I'm made only of sensations. Of heat, of electricity, of white-hot magic.

Then I sink deeper and deeper still, and holy fuck.

I'm there.

I'm inside my man.

This is where I belong.

My muscles quake from how staggeringly intense this is, him gripping me, me filling him. "This is insane," I whisper.

"You feel so good," he groans as he widens his legs more, opens himself up, lifts his ass higher.

And holy fuck. Holy hell. Holy bliss.

My balls are singing hallelujah. My dick is conducting an erotic symphony. And I am dying, just dying, from the utter perfection of this moment.

I'm fucking the man I'm in love with.

And he's fucking me right back.

He lifts and rocks.

I pump and thrust.

Rolling my hips, I go deeper, pressing my hands against the mattress. "Yes," I grunt since once again, words escape me.

But not him. The man is a champion talker in bed, and he ropes his arms around my back and tugs me closer. "You feel incredible," he moans, all soft and desperate. "I love the way you're fucking me."

I tremble everywhere, up and down my body, from his words of praise.

"You like this?" Declan asks on a ragged groan.

"Oh God, I love it," I say, recovering speech, because how can I not tell him?

This is everything.

A shudder rolls through me as I indulge in several long, slow strokes, and my man just moans and groans.

Then, he shoots me a daring look, parts his lips and says, "You like . . . *this?*"

And he clenches his ass around my cock. I grunt, sounding like an animal as pleasure spins wickedly in me, hitting me full throttle. "You cocktease. I'm gonna come if you do that," I rasp.

Declan reaches for me, hands grabbing my face, staring hard at me, lust in his eyes. Passion laces his dark gaze. "I want you to come, rookie. Want to watch you lose control."

"You first," I beg. "Please."

He drags me close, spears my mouth with his tongue, and rolls his hips, working me with that sexy body, and sending me toward the edge.

I'm aching to come as I plunge in deep.

Sweat slicks down his chest. "You want me to jack myself?" he asks. "Are you close?"

I give a few deep thrusts. "You have no idea."

He lets go of my face, reaches for his cock, and grips it hard, stroking fast.

In a blur.

I nearly blackout from how lethally sexy this is.

I just . . . I never . . .

I'm on another planet, in another solar system, as pleasure throbs through me while Declan jerks himself under me, groaning, tossing his head back, losing his mind to the sensations he's bringing himself, to the sensations I'm bringing him.

To everything.

To us.

"Yes, fucking yes, coming now." He shudders, hot jets of come spilling all over his hand.

Need overcomes me. I've got to have his release.

"Gimme," I say, mouth open, waiting.

Declan lifts his hand, and I suck off his orgasm, getting high on the taste as he urges me on. "Come in me, babe."

My orgasm wracks my body, hammering its way through me as I curse and shout incoherent cries of bliss as I climax even higher than I did last night.

Then, he's right here with me, his mouth soft and tender, his lips seeking mine, somehow sealing all this impossibly hard, rough, passionate sex with a kiss that reminds me this is not the end.

It's a whole new beginning.

37

DECLAN

Sex makes me hungry. Especially when I haven't eaten in hours. After we shower, we walk across the street to The Lazy Hammock.

It's like a safe house.

Plus, if someone sees us here, I can live with it, but I doubt it'll be a teammate.

Once inside, River looks up from the bar, his brown eyes welcoming. He pushes his floppy hair off his forehead, then hustles over. "Good to see you two again. Table on the deck? In the far corner?"

"Yeah, same as last time, thanks," I say since that spot felt the most out of the way.

The owner pats my arm, then winks at Grant. "Absolutely. Did you guys enjoy the day? I went hiking up Camelback Mountain, and if you haven't done that yet, it's a must. We have the best hiking here and fantastic views."

"No. But I'll give it a try next time I'm in Phoenix," I say.

"And don't you dare forget the Grand Canyon. Sunset there is sooo romantic," he says with a wink as he guides us to the deck.

River doesn't mention baseball at all. And I love it. I love that he's simply an ambassador for the state of Arizona. When we reach the table in the corner, away from prying eyes, he shoots us both a grin as we sit. "By the way, it makes me so happy to see you two together again." He clasps his hand to his chest. "Can I take the credit? I kind of feel like Cupid."

Grant laughs. "Maybe you can."

I reach for Grant's hand across the table, taking it in public view.

Fine. This isn't like kissing him at a ballpark.

But that's not the point. I'm just making my intentions known in as public a way as I can.

River *awws* happily. "Let me know when you two want to order."

"Actually, I'm ready," I say, and I order a chicken salad and Grant opts for chicken and veggies.

"Athlete food," I say, once River leaves.

Grant pats his belly. "Gotta keep the abs tight both for baseball and for this guy I'm seeing in November."

"This guy you're seeing likes you for more than your abs," I say, feeling a little like an infatuated fool.

"But the abs help," Grant says in a conspiratorial whisper, then he sends me a shy smile. "Is this our official first date? Kind of out in public and everything?"

"Seems it is." I squeeze his hand harder. He squeezes back.

"Do you think any of the guys figured it out? That I was leaving to see you?"

I shake my head. "No, but you better play well tomorrow. So I'll know I broke your streak."

His grin is magnetic. "You broke my never-been-laid streak."

I crack up. "So, what's the verdict? You like topping me?"

"I love it. I love it all. I love sex. I want to have sex every night, every day. I want to do it again and again and again with you. I think you made me addicted to it."

I growl. "Good. I want to service your addiction."

"Service me all you want, Deck," he says, letting my nickname roll around on his tongue.

"Still turns me on the way you say it," I murmur.

"Good. Everything about you turns me on." His brow knits. "But I have a question. That whole thing with you and sliders?"

"That's a one-eighty."

"Yeah, but I still want to know. It's not true, is it?"

I grin, slow and easy. "Why ever would you say that?"

Grant hums, like he's deep in thought, then taps his temple. "See, I replayed that pitch in my head. And I remembered the pitcher hesitated, that maybe, just maybe, he didn't throw you his best slider. So, I found the clip on YouTube while I was waiting for you in the room." I keep a straight face as Grant continues assembling the clues. "He threw you a cement mixer slider. That ball was begging you to hit it. And it became legend. But it wasn't because you're an evil genius with sliders. It was a bad pitch that you went yard on."

Letting go of his hand, I slow clap. "Well, aren't you just a regular Sherlock Holmes. Figuring me out."

"And now the whole damn league thinks you're Hank Aaron at the plate and you eat sliders for breakfast."

I blow on my fingernails. "Yeah, they do. But guess what?" I say, leaning closer to him, lowering my voice.

"Tell me," he says, curiosity dripping in his tone.

"I will but you can't tell a soul."

"Oh. Do you want me to sign an NDA?"

"You are my NDA."

Grant wiggles his finger for me to serve up the goods. "What's the deal?"

"I mean it. Don't share this, okay?"

He rolls his eyes. "Who the hell am I going to share it with?"

I give him a look like the answer is obvious. "Your team."

Grant raises a palm like he's taking an oath. "I won't tell anybody."

"They're my weakness," I whisper. "Can't hit 'em for shit."

He whistles in appreciation. "What do you know? The great Declan Steele has a weakness."

I level him with a stare, then speak from the bottom of my heart. "You're my weakness, rookie."

A tingle rushes down my chest as I say those words, then along my whole body when he whispers back, "You're mine."

I take his hand again, rubbing the pad of my thumb over his knuckles. "It's going to be hard waiting till November."

"I know," Grant says heavily, then perks himself up. "But hey, I have a long list of things I want to do with you in bed. We only got through *four*. Four. I want so much more than four."

A zip of pleasure slides down my spine. "Tell me."

"Well, rim jobs. Giving and getting. As you know," he adds.

"And I can't wait."

"Sixty-nine. I definitely want to do that. Because what's better than one blow job? Simultaneous blow jobs."

"I'm down for it."

"And," he says, taking a beat, letting a rumble slide past his lips, "I really want to flip fuck. I'm kind of obsessed with it. Always have been."

Images flicker past my eyes, him and me, taking turns. I have him first, he takes me next. We trade off in the same night. After I linger on those pictures, I tell him something I think he's really going to like. "I've never flip-fucked with anyone."

His eyes widen. "Yeah? You're serious?"

"Never have."

Grant's tone borders on desperate. He stretches his hand across the table and holds my face. His thumb strokes my jaw. "Save it for me."

"I will. I want to with you," I say, then I let out a heavy breath as he lowers his hand. "Grant, it's going to be hard not talking to you. Not seeing you."

"But we need to," he says, eyes locked with mine, gaze serious.

He's right. I know he's right. But still. I want what I want. "Do we, though?"

He crooks his lips at the question. "Do we what?"

"Do we really have to go cold turkey?" I ask, reaching for something, anything. My desperate heart doesn't want to go without him. "What if we talked? What if we FaceTimed? What if we Skyped? Maybe not during spring training. Maybe you need to figure out what's going on over the next few days. But I don't know that I can go six months without you. Why can't we Skype and FaceTime?"

Grant doesn't answer because River arrives with the food. "Bon appétit," he says.

"Thanks, River," I say, but I don't pick up my fork. Neither does Grant.

"You really want to do that?" the man across from me asks. "Long distance?"

"Better than nothing." But I don't want to make things worse. I don't want to get in his head. I wave my hand, like I can lighten the mood. "Think about it. I don't want to put any pressure on you. But the truth is, I'm going to miss you so fucking much. And a little bit of Grant is better than none."

"Deck, you know I've never been able to say no to you. You know I've never been able to resist you," he says, laying out his truth.

"I'm glad, because you're irresistible," I say, then I pick up my fork and we eat.

When we're done, I pay the bill, and then we tell River goodbye and return to the room to spend our last night together for six long months.

* * *

He rises at four in the morning, kisses me hard, then says he's catching a Lyft. "I should get back to the team hotel."

I drag him close—one more kiss for the road—then I gird myself to say something I'd rather not say. But I know my dad's right. And it'd be wrong not to tell Grant.

"In the last couple games," I say, "your weight was too far back on your knees. Shift forward maybe a millimeter. Like you usually do."

Grant's smile is easy and carefree as a bird soaring across the bright blue sky. "You're right. I'll do that today."

He leaves.

A little later, I head to the airport, but I stop in my tracks when I spot a TV playing a report on the Cougars on The Sports Network. Grant's passed ball yesterday blazes across the screen.

38

DECLAN

I adjust the bill of my Hawks ball cap as I watch the report. My stomach curls, but it's like an accident on the side of the freeway and I can't look elsewhere.

A woman's crisp voice blares from the overhead screen at my gate.

"The San Francisco Cougars are shaking things up at spring training. Yesterday evening, we broke the news of star shortstop Declan Steele's trade to New York, and now our sources are saying it's no longer a neck-and-neck race between rookie Grant Blackwood and league veteran Jorge Rodriguez for the starting catcher slot. The veteran backup just might be pulling away from the new guy. A couple of wobbly games both at the plate and behind it will do that to you. Now it's looking like Rodriguez just might come out of spring training on top." She takes a long pause, stares at the camera. "And that the rookie might be sent back to Triple-A for some more time in the minors. Back to you, John."

Gritting my teeth, I tear my gaze away from the screen of doom, my chest knotted, my muscles tenser than a courtroom waiting for a verdict.

I head to the jetway as the gate agent calls for my group, then make my way onto the plane.

Sinking down in the cushy leather seat, I grab my phone, and google Grant.

The first hit is a sports blog, *It Ain't Over Till It's Over.*

A headline from yesterday says it's a toss-up between Grant and Rodriguez. But today's post says the slot is the veterans to lose.

"What the hell?" I mutter.

I've had bad games in spring training. Hell, I had bad games my first time there. I still made it.

But...

I wasn't up against a solid vet who'd put in the time as a backup. Dragging a hand down my face, I read on.

With every word, regret swirls in my gut.

I promised myself I wouldn't get involved.

I told Grant not to get involved.

I said *make sure you have no distractions.*

And what did I do? Broke all the rules. I put myself in his path. I let my attraction get the better of my reason. I let my desire overrule my logic. I knew this could happen especially to him.

Me? I've been wearing blinders since I was a kid.

But Grant is all new. I should have kept my distance. Resisted temptation.

I curse under my breath, bang my head against the headrest, and close my eyes.

Should have, would have, could have.

I fucking did it.

Rubbing my temples, I open my eyes, click on my messages, and scroll to his name.

All my instincts tell me to send him a text. Tell him he'll do great. All he has to do is keep his eye on the ball.

But I'd just be distracting him then, wouldn't I?

I don't write to him about the news report. As much as I want to reassure him, it won't do him an ounce of good. I power down my phone as my gut twists and my heart tears in half.

39

DECLAN

The flight from Phoenix to Tampa is four hours. I spend them all worrying.

That's four hours contemplating Grant's future.

I should be sleeping. Resting up after last night when I didn't get much slumber. But I have no regrets. Unlike Grant, I'm not on the chopping block.

I wish there were something I could do for him. Some way to help him, to protect him.

But when the plane lands, I have to do what I came here to do.

Play ball. We have an afternoon game, and I need to be One-Track Steele.

That mentality has gotten me through the majors, brought me to where I am today—safe and sound from my past, and far away from the men who belong in the rearview mirror.

Far away from the damage.

Including the damage I've done.

I get off the plane, sling my carry-on over my shoulder, walk to baggage, and wait for my suitcase.

As the carousel goes 'round, my phone pings with a text.

My heart skips a beat with the wish that it's from Grant. But when I open the messages, it's my group chat with Crosby and Chance.

Crosby: Going on record now. I'm going to finish the season with more homers and RBIs than you, and when I do, you're gonna buy me a beer in New York at the Sports Network Awards.

Declan: And you can buy me an iced tea when I school you.

I'm about to put the phone away when I sense an opportunity. The guys are my friends. They'll hopefully be Grant's friends for a long time to come. No reason they can't look out for him now, especially with the news reports circulating. Hell, I looked out for him as a friend. It's time to pass the mantle.

I write back.

Declan: In all seriousness though, can you guys look out for Grant for the next week? I know he's nervous AF about the starting catcher job and maybe getting sent down. Take him out tonight, or grab a bite with him or something, okay? I'd appreciate that.

Crosby: We'll have his back.

Chance: Um . . . Declan . . .

I wince at those two words. That can't be good.

Declan: Spill.

Chance: You know we have the same agent, Grant and me?

Declan: I didn't know that, but okay. What does that mean?

Chance: Crosby and I just ran into her after we finished our workout.

My pulse skyrockets. My nerves tighten as I write back.

Declan: And what does that mean?

As the dots wiggle on the screen, I glance at the luggage belt. I spot my bag coming around.

. . .

Chance: She's here at the complex. But she didn't come to see me. She's here to see someone else and she wouldn't say who. The thing is . . . she usually only shows up in person like this, unannounced, if she needs to let someone down.

My heart sinks—a hard, heavy weight. No way. No way can this be happening.

Declan: Look, if he gets sent down, just remind him it's not the end of the world. It's happened to plenty of others, and he'll have another shot.

Crosby: Of course, man. We'd do that anyway.

Chance: We'll look out for the rookie. He's a good one.

Declan: He is.

I thank them, close the thread, and curse under my breath. I march over to grab my bag, and a few minutes later, I'm in the black limo the New York Comets sent for me.

The driver's chatty, wanting to talk shop, discuss predictions for the season. I don't have many, but I offer any tidbits I know about this team, mostly to take my mind off Grant. I finish with, "I hope to take them all the way back to the World Series and to bring the trophy home."

When I reach the ballpark, I ask the driver to drop my bag at Brady's house where I'll be staying, not far from the Tampa complex.

The driver says he will, then I get out, head into the vaunted home of the New York Comets, and breathe in the history of this epic team. I reach the locker room, say hello to some of the guys who I know from playing against them, then button up the blue and white uniform they have waiting for me.

Number eighteen, just like I had in San Francisco.

It's good to be treated like baseball royalty. Once more, my heart thumps painfully as I think of Grant.

He deserves to be baseball royalty. He deserves to be treated well. He's so damn talented.

But what's the best path for that?

What can I do to help him?

A dark thought flickers through my head, but I shove it away.

I trot out to the field, ready to join my team for batting practice before the game, when my eyes laser in on a familiar set of shoulders.

Is that . . .?

No. It can't be. Not here. Not now.

I peer over, narrowing my eyes at the back of a man.

He's in the first-base seats, leaning over the side, chatting with the players.

My chest craters, my heart slamming to the

ground as my skin prickles cold and clammy when he turns around.

His eyes find mine.

A man from my past.

In one cruel second, everything I tried to put behind me breaks away. My past lurches viciously forward, spilling into my present, landing smack-dab in the middle of my new life.

40

GRANT

The next day

Haven calls.

I hit ignore.

I'm not in the mood to talk.

Not one bit.

I need zero distractions. Need to get in the zone. This is it—do or die. The job is on the line. Coach is giving me one last chance and it's time to go balls to the wall.

I'm not in the mood to talk. Not to anyone. Not after the text I got late last night.

Sullivan walks behind me, stops to clap me on the back. "You've got this," he says.

"Thanks," I mutter, powering down my phone, stuffing it in the back of my locker, as if that'll erase the sting of the message.

I shove it far, far away.

I need to get away from the text. Must erase it from my mind.

With a clenched jaw and a rapid heartbeat, I make my way out of the locker room and head straight to the diamond.

Keep your head in the game.

My grandfather's words play on a loop in my mind.

I have to play my heart out and my ass off.

Baseball is mental and I will laser in on the pitcher, the plays, the ball.

When stray thoughts try to enter my mind, I will swat them away like flies. Kill them dead. I picture the arrow on my chest. My reminder to focus on my goals.

But I don't need the talisman for that today. I need protection from the people who let you down. The arrow is my armor today.

I take batting practice, and once it's time for the matchup, I crouch behind the plate, pull down my mask, and call the first pitch.

The Las Vegas Coyotes batter swings and misses.

Like that, I set the tempo and give the signs. My pitcher retires the side for a flawless first inning.

In the dugout, I stare straight ahead the whole time, seeing nothing, thinking nothing. No one talks to me. No one says a word. I refuse to let my mind meander to what's in my locker.

When it's my turn at the plate, I shift my weight back the slightest bit like I usually do, like I've done my whole life, and *thwack*—I knock in a runner.

Take that.

I know how to fucking play.

Soon, we return to the field, shutting the Coyotes out until the fifth inning, when our pitcher gives up a walk, then a single.

They've got a runner on first and second when the cleanup hitter comes to the plate, takes a few swings, then gets in the box.

I call for a curveball, and it drops at the corner. The batter takes a massive swing at it, connecting with a loud crack, sending a line drive out to left field. It's a double, for sure, and the runner on second goes full throttle to third, the base coach waving him home.

Oh, no you don't.

Not on my watch.

Not today.

The left fielder throws to Crosby at third. I rip off my mask as Crosby relays it my way. The ball is coming in hard, careening near the plate. I step into the base path to field it. The runner barrels toward home, mere feet away, but I scoop up the ball into my glove, ready to lay a tag on the runner when—

Boom!

The runner steamrolls into me.

And as the air rushes from my lungs, all the pain, all the hurt, all the anger comes roaring back while my brain replays Declan's text to me from late last night.

Declan: This is killing me, Grant. You have to know. But making plans was a mistake. We can't do this. Any of this, including November. Miami is a bad idea.

I grit my teeth, try to soften the blow, but I hit the dirt with a deafening *thunk*.

The pain radiates everywhere and my world starts to dim…

Grant and Declan's epic love story continues in WINNING WITH HIM, the next book in the Men of Summer series, available everywhere.

Be sure to sign up for my mailing list to be the first to know when swoony, sexy new romances are available or on sale!

ALSO BY LAUREN BLAKELY

FULL PACKAGE, the #1 New York Times Bestselling romantic comedy!

BIG ROCK, the hit New York Times Bestselling standalone romantic comedy!

THE SEXY ONE, a New York Times Bestselling standalone romance!

THE KNOCKED UP PLAN, a multi-week USA Today and Amazon Charts Bestselling standalone romance!

MOST VALUABLE PLAYBOY, a sexy multi-week USA Today Bestselling sports romance! And its companion sports romance, MOST LIKELY TO SCORE!

WANDERLUST, a USA Today Bestselling contemporary romance!

COME AS YOU ARE, a Wall Street Journal and multi-week USA Today Bestselling contemporary romance!

PART-TIME LOVER, a multi-week USA Today Bestselling contemporary romance!

UNBREAK MY HEART, an emotional second chance USA Today Bestselling contemporary romance!

BEST LAID PLANS, a sexy friends-to-lovers USA Today Bestselling romance!

The Heartbreakers! The USA Today and WSJ Bestselling rock star series of standalone!

P.S. IT'S ALWAYS BEEN YOU, a sweeping, second chance romance!

MY ONE WEEK HUSBAND, a sexy standalone romance!

CONTACT

I love hearing from readers! You can find me on Twitter at LaurenBlakely3, Instagram at LaurenBlakelyBooks, Facebook at LaurenBlakelyBooks, or online at LaurenBlakely.com. You can also email me at laurenblakelybooks@gmail.com

Made in United States
North Haven, CT
16 May 2022